Midnight Falls

John Evans

ROWAN PROSE
PUBLISHING

To you, Dear Reader,
For in this literary dance there are only two people that matter,
the one who writes and the one who reads.
Everything in between is just meaningless fluff.

"He who makes a beast of himself gets rid of the pain of being a man."
~ Dr. Samuel Johnson

PROLOGUE

Fifty miles north of Fairbanks, Alaska
February 5, 1992

The cold seeps into my bones, but it's nothing compared to the icy grip of fear that clutches my heart. I write this as a sort of last will and testament.

To all those who come after me, be warned. What I did in Midnight Falls was necessary. It had to be done. That godforsaken nightmare and the fiendish creatures who called it home had to be stopped. They, who had for centuries, feasted upon humanity, had to be purged from this world.

They weren't human, not really. Oh, they walked and talked like us, wore the masks of normalcy with ease, but beneath the surface, they were monsters. Twisted and evil. They were demons, and Midnight Falls was the place the Devil had set them loose.

I did what I had to do six years ago, and I don't regret it.

And yet, as I sit here in this frozen wasteland, I can't shake the feeling there are more of them out there. Small towns, tucked away in the forgotten corners of the world, where the monsters can run free and unchecked. Maybe they're lurking in the dark forests of Maine or the rugged mountains of Oregon and Washington. Maybe they're waiting, watching, hungering for their next victim.

The more I think about it, the more I believe Midnight Falls was a trapped community, soon to be discovered, had it not been for what I did that night. It's the reason why I'm writing this. What I'm hoping to pass on to others, so that my deeds are not forgotten and what evil the world was spared. The horror of that night still haunts my sleep, and there hasn't been a single night since then where I haven't awakened screaming in a cold sweat. Even on the nights I drink myself into a stupor, the nightmares still come to me and play out their horrors on the inside of my eyelids.

Their voices ring in my ears, the screams and cries of those who were being torn apart, and howls echoing through the long, lonely nights as the creatures burned. I hear them even when the moon doesn't shine. Those howls, those damned howls, are why I sit here now in this old hunting cabin in the middle of this wintry hellscape writing this. Here, where it's colder than a witch's tit and inhospitable to anyone, and yet I can feel their hot breath on the back of my neck.

They're coming for me, the survivors of Midnight Falls.

I know I can't run forever.

I've seen them, the paw prints in the snow. They were there last night. They have come for me. They're out there in that white hell, hungry and waiting. Baring their fangs, knowing soon they'd have their revenge.

It started last week when I spotted the tracks for the first time. They were getting closer, bolder, more determined. I knew then I couldn't hide anymore. I had to face them, had to stand my ground and fight. But as the darkness closes in around me, I wonder if I made a mistake. Should I have left well enough alone and fled when I had the chance? Or had I done the world a favor by ridding it of those monsters?

This isn't the first time they've caught up to me. It's been nearly six years since I've been on the run, hiding. At first, I thought I had gotten away, but it wasn't nine months later, and I noticed the footprints. When I saw those tracks, I knew not all of them had perished, and the survivors would be coming for me.

The prints had appeared in the field behind my cousin's house. He'd mentioned them one day after coming in from an early morning hunting for turkeys. Turkeys are early risers and had themselves a regular Butterball gala out in his field. In fact, those birds were the only reason he owned the field. Brent was no great shakes at farming and could never grow anything more than weeds.

"The oddest tracks I've ever seen," Brent had said, wiping his brow. Worry was etched in the deep lines and furrows of his ruddy face. "I've seen coyote and dog tracks, but those are way too big. They looked for all the world like wolf tracks, but that dang sucker would have been the size of a bear to make those."

I'd waited until the sun had come up and made sure I had my trusty Remington in my hands before venturing out into the field. As I'd crouched in the tall grass, examining the tracks, I couldn't shake the feeling something was watching me. It was as if the trees and scrub that made up the rolling hills and mountains were alive and examining my every move.

Sure enough, there had been at least three deep prints in the drying mud. Whatever had made them had been big, but there was something else I noticed that Brent had overlooked. To make those prints, the creature would've weighed a great deal to leave them so deep. Something massive and heavily muscled had come into the field and stood right there to watch the house.

I'd remained there for what seemed like hours, alternating from looking at the tracks to scanning the woods. I knew as I watched the trees, they were watching me.

I tried to dismiss it, to play it off as some large dog or maybe a lame bear, but the next day, there were more tracks. There had not been just one set, this time, but at least three. The creatures had come again and sat together, facing the house, looking for something or someone. Looking for me. They had crept closer in their daring efforts, sniffing out their prey.

The third night they'd been closer still. They had halted just at the edge of the field. The tracks were only in the tall grass, as if they were not brave enough yet to step out on the neatly cut grass of the backyard. They didn't dare venture into the open. Not yet, but I knew they would be soon.

And so, I waited.

I'd sat up that night, waiting and watching for what I knew was coming. I wasn't disappointed.

In the dead of night, there they were. Dark shapes skulking through the field. Slinking towards the house, towards the window, towards me, but I was ready. I had set rifle ammo on the dresser in front of the window, waiting for them. There was at least half a dozen of the things.

I waited for them, crouched on the floor with my shoulder to the stock and my eye to the scope. I waited until I could see their glowing eyes burning like hot coals in the inky blackness.

They paused at the line that divided the yard from the field, surveying for potential threats or witnesses for the carnage they had planned. One of them slowly stepped out of the field and into the yard. It put out one leg and set it gently down on the freshly mowed lawn as if it were a swimmer testing the temperature of a body of water.

In my frenzied haste, my finger pulled the trigger instead of squeezing it. The blast exploded into the stillness, echoing through the air, utterly decimating the silence. The shot dropped, hitting the ground in front of the animal, and sent a plume of dirt and debris into the air. The beast's leg jerked back in a flash of movement that vanished like a ghostly apparition. I slammed a fresh round into the chamber and took aim, firing blindly into the field. If the creature had still been within my sights, the bullet would have found its mark, a fatal blow between its unseeing eyes.

They had fled at the first shot, their massive bodies thundering through the high grass as they disappeared into the night. I fired at their masses as they moved through the high grass. For creatures of such bulk, their speed was almost supernatural, gliding through the shadows as though they were made of fog.

I didn't have time to reload, my heart pounding in my chest as I realized my mistake. I was vulnerable, and exposed, and they were coming for me. When they returned, I planned to not be here.

I'd had to answer to Brent for waking him and his wife at one in the morning with the gunfire. I was easily forgiven when we found the fresh prints in the morning and a pool of blood. I must have gotten lucky with at least one of my shots, and one of them was bleeding badly. Not that it would be enough to kill it. They were tough sons of bitches.

By noon, I was packed and headed out. The Charger's engine roared to life, a beast in its own right, as I peeled out onto the highway, heedless of the speed limit or the law. I was a man on the run, with nothing left to lose but my own life. The Remington sat loaded and ready beside me, a grim reminder of the danger that lurked in the shadows, waiting for its chance to strike.

I was headed north, but not before making a detour south to New Orleans. There, I'd gotten news that was a knife in my gut, a cold shock which threatened to consume me whole.

I had put in a call to my cousin, to no avail. At the Post Office, I managed to order a local paper. The headline made me puke. I couldn't believe it.

I had gotten my cousin and his wife killed.

It had happened the night after I left. They were found the next day. All the windows had been smashed in, and both of them had been torn apart by an unknown predator with jaws like steel traps and teeth like razors. The authorities had no answers, no leads, and no suspects. All they knew was the bite marks were too large, too savage, too inhuman to have been made by any creature known to man.

I had to keep running. Fighting wasn't an option. I had fought and lost. I was alone and without a plan. There was nothing I could do. They would come for me, and nothing would stop them.

So, I ran. Again.

This time, I'd headed north, and I didn't stop until I reached Alberta, Canada, where I rented a small house in a little town that reminded me of home.

The snow had a romantic beauty to it. It was melancholy, yet playful at the same time. I would sit up at night writing, the rifle always within reach. I would bang away at my typewriter and watch the snow fall while drinking hot chocolate or tea.

It was a little over two years before they'd found me again.

During that time, I'd grown a beard and cut my hair. I wore it shorter than I had in my younger "hippie" days, and it gave me a more professional appearance. I'd gotten a job writing for the local paper and had sold the Charger. Yes, I'd loved that car the way any young man loves his first sports or muscle car. I needed the money and a more practical vehicle that could handle ice and snow. I'd bought a Bronco with snow tires so big, I hardly ever had to put the chains on.

I'd heard it one night, and I recognized the sound. My blood turned to ice in my veins. The sound of death coming for me.

It was the second full moon in October, a blue moon, I believe it's called. It was beautiful as it shone its silvery light over the world. It had just snowed some nights before, which was piled deep. The generator roared in its shed as it chugged gasoline to power the house. Every time it snowed, it knocked out the power. The snow would build up on the lines and weigh them down until they broke. One year, one of the poles had frozen, and then, as it thawed too quickly, it had caused the wood to explode with a sound like a gunshot. I'd nearly driven off the road when I heard it.

That was nothing compared to how *this* sound froze my blood. It felt like all the air inside the house had turned to ice, and I expected to see my own breath. I sat and listened for it again. Far off in the distance, but it was unmistakable.

A howl.

It could have been a wolf, I'd told myself, but then came the answering calls. It seemed as if it were a rather large pack now.

After several sleepless nights, I'd awoken to horror. Footprints everywhere. They circled the house as if to draw a ring around me, warning others I was theirs and theirs alone. Dead carcasses had been left at both my doorsteps like an omen of my forthcoming doom.

Each door had a large bloody paw print. What scared me more were the footprints I found outside my bedroom window. They had come right up to the pane and looked in on me as I'd slept. One of the beasts had been mere inches away on the other side of the glass. Watching, waiting, and planning.

Why hadn't they just smashed through the window as they had at Brent's and killed me in my sleep? Maybe they were waiting for something, maybe just trying to scare me.

I have not slept soundly since that night.

I left Camrose and fled to Ibex Valley in the Yukon. It was a year and a half before they'd found me again. I had rented a cabin from some old-timer who had retired to Florida and didn't have the time or energy to get back up to the cabin anymore. It was a small place with only two rooms. One kitchen combination with a living room, and one bedroom with its own bathroom. Not bad for the price. The bathroom didn't work and had been one of the first things I had to fix. The generator had to be replaced, as well. The first time it snowed, I'd found myself without power. Thankfully, the cabin had been equipped with a wood stove, so I didn't freeze to death.

That time I'd gotten lucky. I actually saw one of the beasts on the first night I believed they'd arrived. I had been fetching more firewood for the stove. I'd become accustomed to sitting by the warm woodstove during the night. Something about its warm glow comforted me. I hadn't had a TV or a phone since Midnight Falls, and I had taken to making my coffee the old-fashioned way with a boiling kettle.

I was too young to be getting so old, but fear and life on the run ages a man something terrible. Night terrors and paranoia were taking their toll, and when I looked in the mirror, a man at least twenty years older than he should've been stared back at me. My hair had even begun to gray at the temples. Not normal for a man in his early thirties.

When I'd opened the door to visit the woodpile, I saw it. The driving snow had piled up against the door as it tends to do in the north, pinning it shut. I had to put my shoulder to the wood and shove with all my strength. My calf and thigh muscles bunched and tightened with the effort. Having to force doors open against ice and snow had built up my legs quite a bit over the past couple of years. Life on the lam tends to make a man's body hard with tightly wound muscles. Tripwires in a minefield, ready to go off at a moment's notice.

As I finally got the door propped open so I could bring in wood, I looked up, noticing night had already fallen. Snowflakes danced in the moonlight, taunting me with their playful beauty as my breath expelled in frost clouds. A snippet of that old song 'Twilight Time' by the Platters went through my head as I gazed into the darkening woods. I stood there in my own little world, the cold wind on my chapped and tired face, and my brain finally realized what I was looking at.

I stood frozen in my tracks, my heart pounding like a jackhammer in my chest. It lurked there, just beyond the tree line. Its massive form was a thing of nightmares, standing tall and proud, a primal force, covered with a matted coat of thick, bristly fur, snarled with sticks and leaves. Eyes, piercing and cold, glimmered like diamonds in the pale moonlight. Snow piled on its wide, powerful shoulders as I watched, mesmerized by its raw power. The creature's breath came out in short, ragged snorts of hot steam, curling in the frigid air like smoke from a dragon's nostrils. Its tongue, long and black, slipped out to lick its muzzle, revealing rows of long, white fangs that gleamed.

The forest had fallen silent, even the trees knew to be afraid of the monster who watched me with unblinking eyes. The snow barely came up to its knees, as if the earth itself feared to touch the beast. I could feel its hunger, its thirst for blood and flesh, emanating from the monstrosity.

Its eyes blazed with a fierce, unyielding hatred, as though they could burn through my very being. We locked gazes, two predators sizing each other up. Time stretched out, each passing moment feeling like an eternity. I wanted to reach for my rifle to defend myself, but my limbs refused to obey. Fear paralyzed me, leaving me helpless before the monster's wrath. It raised its shaggy head to the sky, releasing a mournful howl that sent shivers down my spine. It was a sound of pure sorrow and rage, a warning to any who dared cross its path.

In that moment, I knew I was in the presence of a creature beyond my understanding, a force of nature beyond human comprehension.

As quickly as it had appeared, the creature vanished into the darkness of the forest like a mist dissipating into the night. I stood there, shaken and trembling as if waking from a nightmare. But the jagged scar on my side, the burns on my chest and hands, were painful reminders that what had happened was all too real. I couldn't simply brush it off as a figment of my imagination. The wounds on my body were proof of the monster's existence, and the memory of its hateful eyes scorched into my mind like a brand.

No, it wasn't a nightmare. It was a warning, a reminder that a debt was owed, and it was owed in blood.

I left that cursed place that night, carrying nothing but my typewriter and my gun. I didn't stop until I hit the Pacific Ocean, and then I turned north, as far away from that nightmare as I could get.

But even as I fled, the monsters would never stop pursuing me. That's what they do. They run their prey to the ground, chasing them down until they're exhausted and helpless. When the moment is right, when the victim is at their mercy, they go in for the kill.

Eventually, I found myself in a small town called Northern Lights. It was time for me to stop running. I was too tired, too broken to keep going. So, I settled in, hoping to find some measure of peace. But I knew, deep down, the creatures would always be out there, lurking in the shadows. As much as I wanted to believe I was safe, that I had escaped its grasp, it would never truly be over.

I decided it was time to stop running and end the nightmare.

I'd rented a cabin in the woods just north of town, hoping the dense trees and isolation would keep me safe. But as the days turned to weeks, and the weeks turned to months, I began to realize I was never truly alone. The woods were alive with sounds I couldn't explain, with shadows that moved in ways which defied explanation.

Until I saw the tracks again. The same tracks that had haunted my dreams for years. They had found me once more, and this time, there would be no escape.

I pulled out my old Underwood typewriter and began to write. I had to tell my story, to warn others of the danger that lurked in the shadows.

You might wonder why I didn't run to a congested city, where I could lose myself in the anonymity of the crowd. If they could track me this far, through two countries and countless miles of wilderness, they would find me anywhere. And in the city, there would be no warning, no signs to alert me to their presence. I'd learned that lesson the hard way, at the cost of another person's life.

So, here I sit, typing away as the sun sets on my final day. I know they will come for me soon, but I refuse to go down without a fight. My story may not save my life, but it may save someone else's. And in the end, that's all that matters.

I have a carton of cigarettes and a bottle of whiskey to get me through. There's some solace in the knowledge this will be the last time I have to face the nightmare. My eyes keep wandering over to my desk drawer where there is a loaded .38.

As I said before, this ends tonight.

One way or another.

CHAPTER 1

Midnight Falls, Kentucky
May 28th, 1986

In the spring of '86, I was a naive twenty-five-year-old, convinced I had the world by the balls. Little did I know, the world had its own plans for me.

Growing up just over in Flemingsburg, I thought I knew everything there was to know about small town living, but Midnight Falls was a different beast altogether. A mere speck on the map with a measly population of two hundred or so, the place was like something out of a Steinbeck novel. The streets were named haphazardly and laid in nothing resembling order. Towns like this just grew up around themselves like weeds in a garden, crowding one another until they choked everything else out.

Don't even get me started on the school. Midnight Falls Elementary was a relic of a defunct era, its walls practically oozing with decades of wear and tear. The older kids were luckier, as they got to go to school in Flemingsburg, like I had.

In the heart of Midnight Falls, there was only one store to speak of, the In and Out, a shoddy joint peddling gas and sundries at the crossroads of Main and Mount Olive Road. That's where I set up camp, so to speak, although I didn't have much to my name, save for a car my mother had given me when I'd left for college, and a big dumb husky named Nimrod.

Nimrod, a shaggy golden-maned Siberian husky, had been my faithful companion since my college days. I'd picked him up as a pup during my sophomore year, and named him after a god of Norse mythology, though in hindsight, the Americanized definition of "nimrod" might have been more fitting. Like most stereotypical blondes, he wasn't the sharpest tool in the shed, but he made up for it with his goofy attitude.

He needed a patch of grass to call his own, having spent his early days cooped up in studio apartments and crammed into the backseat of my car. City life didn't quite agree with him, and fresh air was a rare treat. That's why he loved my car so much as it was one of the few ways he could catch a whiff of the great outdoors in the midst of New York City's hustle and bustle. If you can even call the polluted air of New York City fresh, that was.

During those sweltering summer months, Nimrod and I would make our way down to the local Irish pub where the kindly bartender, a burly man with a thick brogue, would ply my pooch with free beers. The sight of the hulking dog perched on a barstool, lapping up his suds from a battered old mug, never failed to amuse the patrons, who declared Nimrod the only Russian they'd ever let inside their establishment.

Of course, it was up to me to haul the sodden hound back home after the bartender had gotten him good and drunk. If you've never had the pleasure of dragging a tipsy dog through the streets of New York City, you're missing out on a real treat. You'd be surprised at how unfazed the jaded New Yorkers were by such bizarre occurrences. They hardly bat an eye at the sight of a man wrestling a liquored-up canine down the sidewalk.

It was nice to finally have a proper garage to house my beloved Charger. A sleek black 1970 model, the very same one the Duke boys used to tear up the screen, complete with gleaming chrome grill and bumpers. The mighty engine rumbled and growled like some kind of ferocious beast, especially when it was in full flight.

Nimrod adored the car's spacious white leather seats, and he'd poke his head out the window, tongue lolling in the wind as we careened down the roads at breakneck speeds. The thrill of the ride seemed to bring out the best in him as he basked in the heady scent of the countryside whipping past us, and the tires bit into the pavement with a satisfying crunch.

In the crisp autumn months, we'd often take the Charger up to Maine to see the turning of the leaves. There's nothing quite like the sight of the trees ablaze in a riot of oranges, yellows, and reds, and the cool fall air whipping past us as we cruised through those sleepy towns and picturesque villages.

Nimrod's life was full of simple pleasures, but the long drive from the city to our humble abode was undoubtedly one of his favorites. Perhaps it was the rush of the wind in his fur, or the thrill of seeing new sights and sounds whipping past us at dizzying speeds. Or maybe it was just the simple pleasure of being in the company of his faithful companion.

He'd plant his big paws up on the armrest as we roared through Pennsylvania, Maryland, West Virginia, and finally, back to our humble roots in Kentucky. For all I know, it was the highlight of his life, the one thing he'd never forget, though he might not have understood why.

As we left the city in our wake, his eyes would light up with unbridled joy, the sheer thrill of being alive and free filling every fiber of his being. And as we pulled into our little slice of heaven, Nimrod's tail would wag furiously as if to say, "We made it, partner. We made it."

I cruised the long stretches of interstate, the miles disappearing behind us, and passed the time listening to the sounds of classic rock and roll tunes from the 50s and 60s on my cassette tapes. I belted out the lyrics with all the enthusiasm of a teenage boy on a Friday night, my voice cracking and breaking as I hit the high notes. Nimrod occasionally chimed in with a bark or a howl, his own rendition of the classic hits. I couldn't help but smile at the silly sight of the two of us, rocking out like a pair of fools on the open road.

The sunshine was beautiful and made everything seem to have much more life to it than I'd ever witnessed in the city.

As I drove the winding country road, my senses were overwhelmed by smells I had long forgotten. The fragrance of freshly cut hay mingled with the sweet aroma of wildflowers and the warm, comforting scent of the sun on my skin. But it wasn't just the pleasant smells that greeted me. No, there was the unmistakable odor of horse manure and cow dung wafting from the nearby fields. It was a smell that might have made others gag, but to me, it was the sweet perfume of home. I took a deep breath and felt a sense of belonging wash over me, as if I had finally come home after a long, difficult journey.

I could only imagine what it must be like with a dog's nose. I remember reading about how powerful their sense of smell was. Police dogs were supposed to be able to pick out the tiniest particle from even the most well-hidden drugs. Not that I ever wanted to test that, having seen those old films from the 70s where the police set the dogs on crowds of hippies.

One that stood out vividly in my memory was a particular anti-war protester whose crotch was grabbed by a German Shepard. The kids laughed and joked at the film while the poor guy was shaken vigorously by his balls, as the dog bit and tore at the hippie's pants. Several students hooted and hollered, and one wiseass stood up and danced around in exaggerated mockery of the protester's struggle. *Oh, his balls were being torn off by a mean ol' doggie and he wouldn't have to worry about all that damage the pot had done to his sperm.*

All I could think about were those long fangs sinking deep into human flesh.

It had given me nightmares that still plagued me on occasion. While asleep, I was that protester, the hot breath of the police dog on my skin as a huge Shepard, more wolf than dog, opened its long snout, filled with rows of spike-like fangs. The rows of railroad spikes moved back and forth like a chainsaw as they bit into my crotch. Blood sprayed like a Grindhouse horror movie as the sickening crunch of bone and the fangs tore through my jeans, ripping into my flesh. My hand flew to my bleeding crotch, and two things fell into my hand. As I looked down, my own testicles were in my hands, still warm and slick with blood. And all around me, the ignorant fools in the classroom danced and hollered, mocking my agony as if it was nothing more than a cheap sideshow.

So, we ended up returning to Flemingsburg, a town that reeked of desperation and dead dreams, greeted by empty smiles. The place was a living embodiment of the phrase "better to be from than to go back to," but there was no escaping it.

My parents welcomed me home with open arms, blissfully unaware of the real reason for my return. They still saw me as the golden boy, the brilliant young writer who was destined to make it big in the Big Apple. If only they knew the truth, that my tenure at NYU had been cut short, my visions of success shattered like glass on concrete. And now, here I was, a failure returning to the bosom of my family, with nothing to show for my time away except a few poorly written short stories and a mountain of debt.

My parents didn't understand why, a couple weeks later, I chose to live in Midnight Falls. They thought it was madness to leave the comfort of Flemingsburg and move just a few miles away to a place that looked like it belonged in one of Stephen King's novels. Truth was, after living in a concrete jungle like New York City, I needed to be surrounded by nature, even if it was a bit eerie. Besides, the town had a certain charm to it, buried very, very deep, something that spoke to me on a profound level. Maybe it was the way the mist curled around the trees or the lonesome sound of crickets in the stillness of the night. Whatever it was, I felt at home in Midnight Falls, even if it was a home that came with its own brand of darkness.

I think that's what initially drew me. The darkness. Perhaps I thought I didn't deserve better after failing in New York or no one would notice me licking my wounds.

The silence was spooky, and I couldn't shake the feeling that something was missing. Something that should have been there. Something that was *supposed* to be there. The world had gone quiet, and all that was left was an empty, dead space where nature's symphony should have been playing.

I'd tried sleeping with the windows open, hoping to catch a breeze or hear the rustling of leaves, but it was no use. The stillness was deafening, and it made my skin crawl. It was like the town itself was holding its breath, waiting for something to happen. Something ominous, something dreadful.

In the country, time seemed to crawl at a snail's pace. The people here had a secret deal with Old Father Time, agreeing to give up their late nights in exchange for endless years of repetitive routine. It was a deal I couldn't bring myself to make. I didn't fit in with the early-to-bed types, and I sure as hell didn't care to. So, I spent my nights reading, letting the pages lull me into a trance, or popping in a book on tape from the library, letting someone else's voice fill the silent room. In between, I smoked cigarettes, one after another, until the embers burned to ash and I was left with nothing but the soft glow of the moon outside to keep me company.

Stupid and dangerous, but luckily, I didn't fall asleep with a lit coffin nail and burn the place down. Smoking kills, they say. How right they are. My parents told me too many stories about sloppy smokers who fell asleep and set the couch on fire. I swear, I am smarter than that. Honestly, I am. I had been battling insomnia ever since what had happened in college. It cost me not only my academic career, but many a night's sleep.

When I'd first rolled into town, I had put my nose to the grindstone to find a job as soon as I could. I hadn't had much money saved up when I'd decided to return home. Salmon probably put more planning into returning upstream to spawn than I had when I'd packed up the car and lit out for my old stomping grounds. Like in that old Robert Frost poem: *"Home is the place where, when you go, they have to let you in,"* or however it goes.

The first thing my father had started in on me about was a job. He didn't want me to come back home thinking I could just bum off them. I assured them that was not my intention, and that I had a bit of money in my savings to draw on until I found employment. Flemingsburg was a one-horse town with only two factories to its name. One was a car parts joint that churned out seatbelts and seats for the likes of Toyota and whatnot. The other was some shoe company, and it was on its way out. Sure, there were a handful of mom-and-pop shops and gas stations, and even though the rest of the country had started to pull itself out of the tailspin of the 70s, Flemingsburg wasn't so lucky.

My mother, bless her heart, gave me the one thing that saved my ass. Our county was dirt poor with tobacco and moonshine being our main exports since the Great Depression. But we did have a newspaper, The Flemingsburg Gazette. This little rag printed all the local news fit to print, along with church bulletins and coupons for the local grocery. It was run by an old-timer named Jerry Baker, who had started the paper back in the 1950s.

Jerry's staff was about as big as a gnat's ass. Just three folks, including himself, when I came around looking for work. It was so small, they couldn't even afford to print it on site. They had to send their stories and page formats off to another county just to get it on the damn page. But beggars can't be choosers, and I was damn grateful for the opportunity.

He granted me a short interview, purely as a favor to my parents. He said he couldn't pay me much, and what work he could give me would purely be freelance. It was made clear to me that if my work slacked off or became too much of a bother for his editors, I would be down the road looking for work elsewhere. I thought it was tough, but fair, and I could work from home.

So, I did my articles and worked from home, writing everything from advice columns to horoscopes and obituaries. Not that I minded. Sure, it wasn't a great use of the writing skills I had honed through school and practice, but it was a job I could handle, and it paid just enough to keep the wolf from the door, so to speak.

Two weeks after I moved to Midnight Falls was the day I met *her*. Elizabeth Clayton.

I was just coming out of the Post Office, a building that was practically attached at the hip to the Community Center. I couldn't afford a phone in my shabby little home, so whenever I needed to make a call, I headed over to the Post Office, or to the gas station if it was closed. It was a small town, and there wasn't even a postman, so everyone just went to pick up their mail. The women who hung around there chatted and gossiped, and I guess it gave them a sense of community.

But my attention was caught by something else entirely.

The first thing I noticed about Elizabeth was her firm ass. It sounds crude and vulgar, but she was on her hands and knees, tending to a flower bed in front of a pretty old country house that sat in the middle of Old Convict Road across from the Midnight Falls Community Center. The way her butt stuck up was kind of cute with her cropped-off work shorts perfectly framing it. The seat of those shorts was stained with a light dusting of garden dirt and mulch.

That day, as most days during the week, I would stop in the office to pick up my mail, or send in my finished articles, and place a call to the newspaper to check in on new assignments, verifying they got the last ones. I could drive to the Gazette office, it was only a ten-minutes from Midnight Falls, but I think I still had too much of the city in my system, which forced me to use my legs more than my wheels, plus it gave me a chance to put Nimrod on his leash and take him for some exercise.

I couldn't bring the big mutt inside the damn office, so I did the next best thing. I tied him up out front to a rickety wooden bench bolted to the sidewalk. He sat there, panting like a son of a bitch with his tongue lolling out, letting any passing kid give him a good ear scratch or belly rub. Dogs are better company than half the people out there. They don't judge, they don't hold grudges, and they'll give anyone the benefit of the doubt. And, as long as you feed them their weight in kibble and give them a place to poop, they pretty much are the picture of contentment.

As I stumbled out of the Post Office, my arms full of mail, that big shaggy idiot was bouncing around like he'd just won the damn lottery. And, let me tell you, seeing one hundred and seventy-five pounds of blonde fur bounce, wag, and slobber in a dozen different directions at once is a sight to behold. I have no earthly idea how an animal can have that much energy coursing through his veins all damn day long.

I tugged at the leash, trying to unhitch that hulking blonde monster from the bench out front. It was less like untying a dog and more like trying to unhook a horse from a rail. He was massive, and it was a hot May afternoon. The sun was beating down so fiercely, it felt more like mid-summer than late spring. I was sweating like a pig, my hands slick with dampness, and before I knew it, the leash had slipped from my grasp.

And that's when things got really interesting. When a husky that size decides he's had enough of being tethered, there ain't much anyone can do about it. They lower their big old heads, set their broad, muscular shoulders, and dig in with their back legs. The leash was just a suggestion at that point, a flimsy thread of restraint that might as well not even exist.

Like a furry missile, the shaggy beast zoomed across the asphalt, narrowly avoiding a tan Lincoln careening down the street. The right fender grazed the dog's tail. Not that he noticed. The driver leaned on his horn and stuck his hand out the window with one finger extended in the universal sign that didn't mean 'have a nice day'.

I grinned sheepishly, waved back, and then flipped up my own one-finger salute at the car's vanishing taillights.

Chapter 2

Elizabeth had been oblivious to the chaos around her—the deafening roar of car horns, the crude hand gestures of asshole pedestrians, and even the chaos of the rampaging dog. Her focus was unwavering as she tended to her gardening duties.

That's why she didn't even realize Nimrod was there until that big, slobbering brute of a dog sauntered up and pushed his snout right into the crevice of her behind.

Elizabeth's reaction was instantaneous. When a woman's personal space is violated, they react, and with good reason. As she whirled around, flustered, and red-faced, all I could think was how lucky that dog was. To be able to touch that perfect, unblemished skin with his snout, even for just a fleeting moment.

Christ, sometimes I envy that damn dog.

Her body contorted in a sudden, explosive movement that defied all laws of gravity. Her straw hat flew off her head as she launched herself nearly a foot and a half off the ground, her body suspended in mid-air like a marionette. And then, with the agility of a trained acrobat, she twisted and landed gracefully on her knees, without even bothering to get back on her feet.

It was a spectacle to behold, and I couldn't help but watch in awe. But what really caught my attention was the sound that followed. A resounding thwack, like the crack of a whip, echoed through the garden as she brought down her little plastic hand trowel on top of Nimrod's head.

Elizabeth was obviously not one to be messed with.

If it hurt the big dog, it didn't show. He wore a grin that stretched from ear-to-ear, panting loudly, his tongue lolling out like a wet pink carpet. I think it took her by surprise. Whoever she'd expected, the big dumb husky had not been it. She dropped the trowel when she realized what she'd done and grabbed him around the shoulders, hugging him to her chest and apologizing profusely for hitting him.

I watched in amusement as I crossed the street and approached the pair. She looked up at me as I got closer. Her dirty blonde hair was disheveled, falling across her forehead in a way that was both cute and alluring. Her emerald-colored eyes glistened in the sunlight, peering up at me with a coy, mischievous look that made my heart skip a beat. Even her nose, wrinkling as she squinted against the bright light, was endearing in its own way. I felt the urge to reach out and brush the strands out of her eyes, to feel the softness of her hair and the warmth of her skin.

"Hey, is this your dog?" Her voice was tinged with a hint of amusement.

"Uh, yeah, but you wouldn't know it from the way he acts."

She let out a laugh that lit her whole face, causing little lines to appear around her eyes that only served to make her more beautiful. For a moment, I forgot about everything else in the world and was lost in the sheer joy of her laughter.

As it finally subsided, she looked up at me, her eyes flashing with a mix of amusement and contrition. "Sorry, I didn't mean to hit him." Her voice was laden with regret. "I was just caught off guard and thought maybe it was that Earlywine boy again. He and his friends are a menace, you know."

There was a twinge of bitterness as I spoke about the Sheriff's son. "Yeah, I am a little too familiar with Jarrod." My voice was laced with resentment. "His dad is the Sheriff, so there isn't much you can do about it."

"He and his shithead friends roar around in that truck of theirs, jeering and carrying on. About had my Gran on them the other day when they were out here catcallin'."

I noticed as she got more worked up, her accent became more pronounced with that familiar Appalachian twang. I sunk deeper into a sense of comfort and familiarity in her presence. It was a dialect I had missed during my years up north, surrounded by the exotic accents of New York City.

But now, here in this small town, I felt like I was home again. The old holler was like a warm blanket, wrapping me in its soft embrace. It was a reminder of simpler times when life moved at a slower pace and people still had a sense of community.

Who says you can't go home again? I thought to myself as I listened to her talk. Maybe this was where I belonged all along, in this small town nestled in the heart of the mountains.

"Your grandma is Mrs. Sexton?" I looked at the house whose yard we stood in.

It wasn't anything special, a typical two-story conventional farmhouse that had been built before all the others around it had sprung up. Maybe a little rougher around the edges than its neighbors, but nothing a little maintenance couldn't fix. There was a loose shingle or two and a bit of peeling white paint, but it was all just the kind of entropy that creeps in when the man of the house has passed away, leaving his wife to rely on neighborhood boys needing summer jobs for a bit of cash on date night.

"Yeah. It's just me and Gran. Though, she isn't really my grandma. She's like my grandmother's second cousin or something. You know how it is."

"I believe it was Einstein who said, *Kentucky is where everyone is relatives.*"

She laughed again at my dumb joke as she rubbed Nimrod's belly. He sprawled on the sidewalk, his massive body spread out like a furry island in the middle of a sea of concrete. His legs jutted out like palm trees, and his tail whipped back and forth like a hurricane wind, tossing up clods of dirt and broken flowers from the nearby bed. His head dangled over the curb, vulnerable to the passing cars that zoomed by without a second glance. It was a miracle no one had taken it off yet. The world was a strange place, and sometimes fate intervened to spare even the dumbest of creatures.

"So, you moved in down the street?" Elizabeth asked when she had regained her composure.

"Uh yeah, just one up from the store." I jerked my head in that direction, as most folks do when talking about places just 'over yonder'.

"Bit of a fixer-upper, isn't it?"

"That's why the rent is cheap. The landlord is giving me a break on it so long as I do a bit of maintenance."

"Isn't that Don Field's place?" She took a break from petting my dog.

Nimrod's head shot up, a confused look on his face, wondering why the belly rubs had stopped. His blue eyes darted between Elizabeth and me, searching for the source of the interruption. But before he could bark or growl in protest, the belly scratches resumed, and his tail went back to wagging with the force of a propeller. He threw back his head, and let his tongue loll out of his mouth again, revealing a set of impressive teeth. He seemed to radiate contentment, and I was envious. Life would be simpler if all it took to be happy was a good belly rub.

"Yeah, but to be fair, I think he owns about all the rentals in the Falls." I shifted my weight from one foot to the other. The sun beat down on us, a relentless hammer, pounding away at our skin until we were slick with sweat. My inner voice, always eager to cut any conversation short, promising a cold beer and a recliner if I just ended the chit-chat to head home, but I fought it off, determined to savor every minute of our conversation.

"I don't envy you, then. I hear he can be a bit unscrupulous."

I laughed at her use of the word. It was unusual to hear someone use what my father had called 'five dollar words'. Not saying people in this area were uneducated or dim, it's just not seen as fashionable to sound intelligent. In some cases, it was discouraged with a passion.

She frowned in confusion at my laughter. "What?"

Even her frown was cute.

"It's nothing, just still getting used to being back home. I'm not used to people using words with more than one or two syllables."

"What's that mean?" she asked in a warning tone.

I just shook my head. "Nothing, just acclimating. Spent the last several years in New York. It's nice to be back, you know. I'm not making fun."

"Oh, by the way, my name is Elizabeth. Elizabeth Clayton, but call me Lizzie. Everyone does." She stuck out one hand towards me.

"Josh Blevins." I took her hand. Even though it was still dirty from digging in the flower bed, it was soft.

The handshake lingered a bit too long. It broke when the screen door on the house banged open and a wizened old lady shuffled out. She didn't seem to notice either of us until she had made her way to a wooden rocker the porch.

Once perched on its seat, she turned her eyes on the two of us. Her wrinkled old face still managed to focus on us with hawk-like attention. Not exactly disproving, but definitely with a strong opinion on how young women and men should interact with one another. Old-world customs that kids today just thumbed their noses at.

I yanked my hand back like it had been burned. The old woman's gaze was intense, like she could see into my soul. I felt naked and exposed under her scrutiny.

Lizzie seemed to be feeling it, too. She shifted uneasily from one foot to the other.

It was clear this was the end of our conversation. We muttered our goodbyes, and I made a hasty retreat, but Nimrod was reluctant to budge from his spot on the sidewalk. It took a good deal of coaxing before I finally got him to follow me home.

I made my way with the dog padding alongside me. Just a man and his dog, like that old short story by Harlan Ellison, only without the depressing post-apocalyptic world. I paused to poke a fresh cigarette between my lips and lit it with a flick of my zippo.

The summer heat was starting to get to me as I sat on my porch step, lazily smoking. That beer was starting to sound really good, but I'd be damn if I was going to drink before five o'clock. You do that, and you have bigger problems than the heat.

Nimrod lay beside me, panting heavily. I scratched his head absentmindedly, lost in thought. It was strange, but since I'd met Lizzie, I felt like something had shifted in me. Like I was seeing the world through a different set of eyes. It was hard to explain, but I felt like things were finally starting to turn in my favor.

Nimrod loped over to his doghouse, his tongue lolling out of his mouth and his tail wagging lazily behind him. I used the opportunity to clip a tether to his collar. The big dog could be stubborn when he didn't want to do something. He hated being chained to his doghouse, yearning for the freedom to run and roam the neighborhood, but when he dug in his heels and set his shoulders, he became immovable, like a rock in a riverbed. It took all my strength to drag him away from whatever he was fixated on. Once, he even dragged me down the busy streets of Manhattan, ignoring my desperate pleas to slow down.

Nimrod's ears perked up at the sound of the lawnmower.

Brad Jefferson, the only black man in Midnight Falls, was taking advantage of the afternoon to cut his grass. His house was wedged between mine and the In and Out. He had been a master electrician up in Maysville before retiring late last year. Once he had gotten his affairs in order, the first thing he did was haul up stakes and move to the Falls. Something to do with the lower cost of living, or so he'd said.

Brad had just finished moving in a few weeks before I had, and he'd introduced himself over the fence that divided our yards. We shared a beer as he talked about his life, but there was something restless about him. Retirement had left him with too much free time, and he seemed to fill every moment with work around the house. He was constantly painting, mowing, fixing, and repaving. I couldn't help but wonder if there was something else driving him, some deep-seated need to stay busy he couldn't quite articulate.

Nevertheless, he was a nice enough guy, and we passed the time chatting over the fence often.

I watched as he trudged back and forth with the little red push-mower. He was heavily set, and without a shirt, his big brown belly bounced with every step. Sweat shone from his bald pate in the afternoon sun. He wore red shorts with white piping, stretched tight across his wide ass, and he did another lap. Back and forth, back and forth. Like one of those maddening executive toys that never tired or slowed down. It was almost hypnotizing.

My attention was diverted from Brad's yard work as Joey Ackerman came chugging down the sidewalk, sweat pouring off him like rain. He was a teacher at the elementary school and had taken up jogging in a desperate attempt to shed some pounds. He was a hefty man, and his exertions made him look like a walking heart attack. His light blue sweatband had long since given up the fight against the deluge of sweat that streamed down his face. With every step, he panted and wheezed like an old steam engine, struggling to keep going despite his obvious discomfort.

I watched him until he turned the corner at the end of the street and was out of sight. Leaning back, I propped myself up with my elbows and closed my eyes. The sounds of the town floated on the warm air. Youngsters whooping and frolicking on the school playground, an amateur mechanic wresting with an obstinate engine, the discordant clang of screen doors slamming shut, and mothers shrieking after their offspring. All the maddening hubbub of small-town existence.

Then, out of nowhere, the most unsettling feeling of apprehension and dread dropped over me. Goosebumps erupted on my arms as shivers ran up my spine. It was so powerful that it was almost like precognition and, for a moment, my mind's eye could nearly make out the events to come. Just as one knows a word or name, and it's on the tip of their tongue, but couldn't quite grasp it. It was jarring, icy, and profound, causing every muscle in my body to tense.

A psychic shiver.

As quickly as it had come, it was gone. Like a dream with every passing second, it rapidly faded, and I dismissed it as what the old timers called 'a goose stepping on my grave'.

Chapter 3

It was a sweltering day in July a few weeks later when I was atop my roof, sweat dripping down my back like tears of regret. During a previous heavy rainstorm, I discovered a leak in my kitchen ceiling. It was just the latest in a long line of problems. I had patched walls, replaced carpet, and rehung cabinets, but shingling the roof was the first big undertaking, though not beyond the scope of my skills.

Thankfully, I wasn't alone. With the promise of a couple days' work and free beer, I managed to get Brad to help me out. That found us sweaty and miserable, but at least we had each other to bellyache to about it. The heat was only made worse once we had gotten the old shingles off and began spreading tar. The hot black goop only served to magnify the sun's scorching rays and then bounce them back at us. Heat waves shimmered just above the surface of the tar, making it look as though the black liquid was flowing like water. This illusion made me a bit dizzy and wary of my footing. The last thing I needed was to slip and fall off the roof. From there, it was a two-story fall resulting in, at best, a broken limb and, at worst, a broken neck.

The work was a kind of hell we could scarcely have imagined. We took breaks whenever we could, gasping for breath and struggling to wipe the sweat from our brows. But the heat was an unrelenting demon, bearing down on us with a weight that seemed to grow with each passing moment.

In a desperate concession to the relentless sun, we had long since abandoned our shirts, our bare chests glistening with sweat and streaked with grime. The tar seemed to cling to us like a living thing, coating our skin in a thick, sticky film that made every movement seem as if we were swimming through molasses.

As people walked past or drove, I couldn't help but feel their eyes on me as though they were watching us, paying a little more attention than was warranted for a couple guys on the roof. I tried to tell myself it was just in my head, but the feeling had been persistent for some time now. It had started around the time I'd met Lizzie a few weeks before, and only seemed to get stronger. Sitting on the porch, walking the dog, going to the Post Office to get my mail, or whatever I was doing at the time, I would get this sudden hair-raising sensation. Often, I'd look up, feeling as if several pairs of eyes were on me. Watching. Waiting, maybe, but for what I don't know. Sometimes, it seemed like just a touch of paranoia, yet at others it was something darker.

A hunger. A warning or omen. I just couldn't shake the feeling of always being watched.

Instead of heeding these psychic shivers, I tried to push them out of my mind when they happened.

As the day wore on, my skin was burning bright red, a searing reminder of the torment we were enduring. And yet, every cool breeze that came our way was a gift from Heaven, a fleeting moment of relief in a landscape of unending agony.

Brad straightened with a series of loud pops as his spine decompressed. It sounded like a small volley of miniature gunfire. He put his hands on his wide hips as he leaned back a bit further, causing me to worry he might tumble off the roof. His big belly gave a halfhearted effort to rise above where it sagged past his belt line. It had seen too many years and good meals, and its prime was long since passed. Even with his constant projects and mowing, no amount of exercise would slow the entropy of aging. He was still strong. He hadn't lived a life of softness and easy work. Brad Jefferson was a big man, and had the strength of a lifetime of hard labor to go with it. He'd barely shown any effort when it had come to lugging stacks of shingles up the ladder. Each one had probably weighed as much as I did.

"Well, looks like we can have the front half-finished today, but we'll have to pick it up there tomorrow to finish off the back side." Brad nodded.

A large yellow school bus rolled by. The shrieks of children pierced the hot summer air, high-pitched cries echoing through the open windows and reverberating down the street like a siren call.

We had been so absorbed in our work that we hardly noticed the time slipping away until, suddenly, it was three o'clock, and the world around us had transformed. The kids poured out of the school in a flood, a chattering, giggling mass of energy and excitement as they made their way home.

"How's the damage on the inside? Are you gonna need to replace the kitchen ceiling?" Brad asked.

I was tired and hot, with a river of sweat running down the crack of my ass, and here he was looking for more work to do. Or maybe he was just curious. I didn't know. I didn't even want to think about it. All I wanted was to shower, then crawl into bed and pass out with the AC turned up as high as it would go until the room was an icebox.

"Nah, just a little patch and paint, if that." I ran my hands through my unruly mop of hair where it stuck to my neck and forehead from all the sweat.

It had been hot all summer, but this year, it seemed worse. The weather reports were calling it a record-breaking heatwave, a relentless assault that had pushed temperatures into the high nineties for weeks on end.

Today was different. The mercury had climbed to a hundred degrees, a scorching milestone that seemed to herald the arrival of an apocalyptic inferno. As far as the eye could see, the world was a blur of shimmering heatwaves and dancing mirages, a desert landscape that seemed more suited to a fever dream than to reality.

Even the ground itself had begun to yield, its once-green grass reduced to a brittle, yellow-brown husk that crunched underfoot like dry kindling. And in places, the earth had cracked open like the mouth of a vast, insatiable beast, its gaping maw devouring everything in its path.

I breathed a sigh of relief I was no longer tied to the land, no longer subject to the whims of the harsh summer sun and the brutal demands of a life spent tending crops or livestock. It was going to be a rough year for the farmers, that much was clear. The heat was going to take its toll, withering the crops and scorching the earth.

I knew all too well the backbreaking work that went into keeping a farm going in times like these, the endless toil and sweat which seemed to never end. And with more and more agriculture businesses moving in, looking to buy up farms and buy out families, the future looked bleak, indeed. But the people around here were a tough lot, hard-nosed and bull-headed, resistant to change and fiercely protective of their routine way of life. They weren't about to go down without a fight, and I couldn't help but admire their tenacity and grit in the face of such overwhelming odds.

Their days ahead would be long and hard, fraught with danger and uncertainty, but as I looked out over the endless fields, I couldn't help but feel a sense of awe and reverence for the land that had sustained us for so long, and the people who were willing to fight tooth and nail to keep it theirs. No self-respecting farmer worth his salt around here would ever dream of selling off his family farm, no matter how dire the circumstances. These farms had been passed down for generations, dating back to the bloody days of the Civil War, and even before.

The tight-knit community of farmers in this area could be downright hostile to outsiders, especially those who dared to try their hand at something different. Rumors would spread like wildfire, especially when it came to the crops grown. Soybeans? The very notion was a disgrace, a sacrilege to the memory of those who had tilled and toiled on tobacco farms for generations. In the midst of such close-mindedness, the slightest deviation from the norm was seen as a threat to their very way of life.

It wasn't just crops, either. Outsiders were viewed with suspicion, their very presence a potential danger. The word "liberal" was thrown around like a curse, a label that could ruin a person's reputation in a heartbeat. Even worse was the accusation of being "gay," a word that carried with it all manner of dark implications in this deeply conservative corner of the world. In such a place, it was easier to conform than to stand out, to blend in than to be noticed. And woe betide the person who dared to challenge the status quo.

The small town's narrow-mindedness was like a festering wound that never fully healed. It wasn't full-blown xenophobia, but it was a close relative. The worst they would do was talk behind your back and, if you were unlucky, hurl some insults your way from a passing car. There were a few tough guys who might take it a step further, but they were the exception rather than the rule. Still, it was suffocating, like a cloud of smog you couldn't escape no matter how far you ran.

Joey Ackerman's car pulled into his driveway. Summer school was out for the day, which meant the stout little guy would soon be doing his jogging route. Though, in this heat, I couldn't imagine him getting very far before heat stroke took him down. He was a stocky man, but he had been running tirelessly every day since I'd arrived in town. Even when a torrential spring downpour had turned the streets into rivers, he was out there pounding the pavement. It was as if he was driven by some inner demon that refused to let him rest. Yet, despite his daily exercise, he remained the same shape and size, trapped in some sort of endless, sweaty purgatory.

Suddenly, a sharp voice pierced through the haze, pulling me back to reality.

Brad and I turned our heads to find Lizzie standing on my parched lawn, beckoning us with her delicate hand. Her pristine white sundress and the oversized straw hat she wore created an image that belonged in one of those idyllic paintings by Norman Rockwell, only missing the basket of goodies. However, what she held in her hand was not a basket, but a large pitcher, filled with something that I couldn't quite make out from this distance.

"Hey, you guys look hot," she called up.

"Well, thank you, young lady. I think it's nice to know that I still got it at my age," Brad joked.

She laughed, and her face lit up again in that cute way which caused her nose to wrinkle.

Once we'd made our way down the ladder and back to terra firma, I felt a little better.

"Gran said I should bring this over since you two looked like you were working so hard." She held up the pitcher filled with iced tea.

"That's mighty kind of your granny." Brad nodded. "Tell her thank you from a truly grateful man."

She smiled as she handed him the pitcher, and he pressed it against his forehead.

I went into the kitchen and fetched three glasses, and we sat on the porch drinking the cool tea. It was almost too sweet. The first swallow had drenched my parched throat, but the aftereffect was a dull aching in my teeth from the sugar. Still, it was heavenly after a hard day working on the roof.

Nimrod emerged from his refuge in the doghouse, a shaggy behemoth struggling to cope with the relentless heat. With a heavy thud, he settled himself beside Lizzie, his massive head resting on her lap. Despite the heat, he leaned into her touch, his tongue lolling from his mouth in a desperate attempt to cool himself. The husky was a creature of the cold, bred to pull sleds across frozen tundras, not to wilt in the oppressive heat of summer. But here he was, his breath ragged and labored, as Lizzie tried to soothe him with her gentle strokes.

I slouched against the porch steps, my fingers tapping a rhythm against my thigh. The gallon of tea we'd been chugging was now just an empty jug at our feet. Brad and I were lounging in the shade of the porch, catching a much-needed reprieve from the merciless sun. A slight breeze danced along the edges of the eaves, teasing us with its coolness.

Joey Ackerman jogged by, his shirt already stained a deep, sweaty gray. He didn't glance our way, his walkman headphones blocking out the world as he trudged on, his eyes fixed on some invisible prize. I couldn't help but wonder what drove him to run every day, especially while this hot. But, then again, we all had our ways of coping with the oppressive monotony of small-town life.

As we watched him go, a rusty white pickup truck with a loud muffler rumbled around the corner at the other end of the street and slowly made its way up the block. As it drew level with us, I realized it was three high school boys in the cab. All of them were giving us hard looks, their cold piercing stares tinged with thinly veiled hate. The one on the passenger side stuck his arm out the window to flip us the bird. Another one, I couldn't tell who, yelled out, "Fags!" and the truck roared down the street, where it nearly got hit by a passing car as it took the corner too sharply.

"What the devil was that about?" Brad asked, frowning after the truck.

"Jarrod Earlywine and his friends." I sighed. "They are none too happy with me and seem to be holding a grudge after Jared tried to buy my car."

"Ain't that the way of it. Boys, especially ones like that, are all about their ego, and the hormones cooking away in their brains don't help any. In fact, it's worse, more likely to make bad choices." Brad mused. "Probably lash out and let his fists do the talking, rather than thinking things through. You ought to be careful, 'cause with his daddy being the sheriff, he might not incur the same negative consequences of his actions they'd inflict on someone else, if you know what I mean."

Oh, I knew what he meant. My run in with the sheriff's son hadn't been pleasant and, no doubt, would have unforeseen consequences.

CHAPTER 4

I had already crossed paths with the Earlywine clan, both father and son. It was the day after I had settled in, and I was out in the driveway tending to my Charger. The journey from New York hadn't been too grueling, but the city pollution had piled up on my ride in a thick layer of grime. And with the luxury of time and nothing better to do, I bestowed upon it the cleansing it so desperately required.

I had just finished waxing and buffing the car to a mirror sheen, and it looked as if it had just rolled off the showroom floor, when I was approached by a boy. He was tall for his age, though I couldn't tell exactly how old. I was guessing high school since he was already over six feet tall with a build that resembled a fortress. Out here in the countryside, it was customary for farm boys to be brawny, but this kid was in a league of his own. There couldn't have been many who dwarfed him in size. His square head only added to his intimidation, and his hair was cropped so short in a buzz cut, I couldn't really make out what color it was.

There was something about his eyes, a sort of intensity I didn't like. They were dark, almost black and flinty. Chips of obsidian. He had cockiness that could've been confidence had it not been so aggressive. He wore it the way he wore his tight black t-shirt and faded jeans, all a display of his projected dominance.

And the way he moved was almost spooky. It was not exactly graceful, but showed signs of someone who knew how to be agile when they needed to. Animalistically so. It was far stealthier than a boy of his size had any right to be.

I was in the midst of perfecting the car's finish when he appeared out of nowhere, catching me off guard. I spun around to find him standing mere feet away, his eyes fixated on my car with an air of admiration.

I was accustomed to the Charger getting this kind of attention. It was a classic, a cherished possession that once belonged to my mother. She had a fondness for muscle cars, and my father had indulged her tastes. She'd treated the car with the utmost care, meticulously washing and waxing it every weekend, much to the satisfaction of some of the neighbors since she had been quite the looker in the years before she'd become a mother. She would quite often joke that I had wrecked her figure, and before I came along, she'd been partial to short shorts and tight tees. Every time, it left me red with embarrassment while my father would merely shake his head, hiding behind the safety of his newspaper.

As I looked up from my task, I was a tad taken aback to discover someone had violated my personal space. I had been so absorbed in the soothing ritual of waxing, a murder could have taken place in the street, and I wouldn't have noticed it. Growing up on the smaller side of average, I had never liked being overshadowed and postured to by bigger kids, and it brought out an almost suicidal defiance in me.

"Nice car," he said.

"Thanks." I gave the black hood another pass with the shammy. The sky was reflected darkly in it. A beautiful parody that turned day into night. As the sun shone above, its dark twin, the moon, glowed up at it in turn.

"What is she, a Mustang?"

I winced. Jesus Christ, I was never really a motorhead, but I couldn't stand when people mixed them up. I know it was a bit of a tall order to expect from people whose mothers weren't into cars or didn't grow up in that particular sect, but there was a vast difference in the vehicles, obviously notable by emblems, if nothing else.

"70's Dodge Charger." I capped the wax, the cloth slung over my shoulder.

"How's she run?" he continued as if he weren't intruding on my day.

"She runs great," I replied. "Everything is all factory, change the oil every three thousand miles, get a tune-up every fifty.

Sixteen years, and not a problem. She ain't much, but she gets me where I need to go."

"How much?"

The question didn't quite register with me for a few seconds. I don't know if it was part of still being off balance from the surprise visit or that I was offended at the sheer audacity of someone assuming they could simply buy whatever they fancied from a complete stranger, but I was stunned. After all, there was no indication the car was for sale. No 'For Sale' sign, or anything of the sort.

"I'm sorry, what?" I battled through my mottled confusion. The merciless heat was furtively impeding my thought processes, and I'm sure the handful of beers I'd while washing the car wasn't exactly helping my cause. It was almost as if my brain had been infused with honey, every thought and action sticky and unhurried.

"How much for the car? I can give you two grand in cash right now." He shifted his weight, the scuff of his boots against the concrete filled the silence that hung thick between us. His hands were stuffed deep in the back pockets of his jeans, fingers fidgeting with something unseen.

Behind him, the other two boys sat in the front seat of a battered pickup truck, eyes leering at me with a predatory intensity that made my skin crawl, hinting at something deeper, darker.

The truck itself was a pitiful sight, a rusty shell of its former self. Once, it may have been a creamy hue, but the relentless assault of time and the elements had stripped the paint of all color, leaving it a bleak and soulless shade of gray. A strip of dark brown ran along its side, though it was incomplete, chewed up by the voracious appetite of rust. It seemed to have been through a war and come out the loser. One quarter panel had been beaten back into shape, the metal stretched and pulled like a scar from a vicious wound, giving the whole thing a sort of lopsided appearance. It couldn't have been more than ten years old, from my guess, but it had clearly seen a lot of long, hard roads. No surprise really, given that it belonged to a teenager, and was easily secondhand.

"Sorry, not for sale," I said when I finally managed to collect myself. I found the thought of this punk tearing around in the car somewhat offensive to the gods of automobiles.

"Three grand," he countered, and I started to get a little annoyed.

"I said, it's not for sale, kid." A bit of that annoyance was starting to creep into my voice. I snatched the shammy from my shoulder and slung it into the suds bucket. It made an angry slapping sound and punctuated my mood like a thunderclap.

"Fine, alright. My dad can get you five grand. How about it?"

Another vain attempt to persuade me.

Christ, he couldn't take a clue, and mentioning his father helped me to realize what I was dealing with—a spoiled brat who usually got whatever he wanted. He was used to getting his way, no matter the cost, with his fists or intimidation. If not, he would run to Mommy and Daddy.

"Fuck off, kid." I was done with this shit. It was hot, and I was putting off an article deadline when all I really wanted was a nap. Yet, here was this self-entitled brat who couldn't take a hint and move on.

He leaned in close, and there came the dry sound of bone on bone as though his knuckles were popping from clenching his meaty fists. It was a God-awful sound that set my teeth on edge as he crowded me. For some reason, the grinding rang in my ears, *crack, crack, cracking*. It seemed to come from nowhere and everywhere. It felt somehow almost sinister. There was a sheer absence of other sounds. No rustle of leaves, crickets, or birds. Like the world had paused to wait for whatever outcome resulted. It became a vacuum, one in which a shiver trickled up my spine and wove into my skull.

Something about it all just felt wrong.

Besides that, his imposing frame invaded my space like a predator marking his prey. He had me by about half a foot and at least fifty pounds of lean muscle, and I was pretty sure he wasn't done growing.

I slowly came back to myself, realizing either the heat was getting to me or I'd had one too many s.

The only problem with this brute's tactic was that I was used to it. I had always been the smaller kid growing up and I'd had my fair share of bullies like him. He was going to have to do better than that to get under my skin. Though, he was so close, I could smell him. It was a sickly-sour odor, like a mouse rotting away in a forgotten gym bag.

His hazel eyes blazed under his heavy brow, burning with a fierce intensity that rivaled the heat of the day. For a brief second, I could've sworn I caught something move behind his eyes. Liquid and dangerous, a snake coiling to strike. I couldn't say for sure what I saw, if I saw anything at all.

"My dad is the sheriff," he snarled, "so you really don't want to get on my bad side, hippie."

I pulled a deep breath and shook it off.

He was really going about it the wrong way to try to get something he wanted. Of course, at that age, most guy's dicks were calling the shots. Their raging hormones take the helm and steer them toward foolish decisions. Making choices based on ego was just par for the course when you were a teenager, lost in a sea of confusion and insecurity.

Not that I was really making the best decisions at age twenty-five, but I knew better than to show any sign of weakness in front of an aggressor. It was like waving a red flag in front of a bull. It only motivated them to attack with even greater ferocity.

So, I gritted my teeth and stood my ground, glaring back at him with all the fury I could muster. I could feel the tension in the air, the calm before a storm, and I knew deep down if he decided to swing at me, I would have to take it like a man. He was the type whose fists worked faster than his brain. I could tell just by looking at him, and it wouldn't be the first time my own stubbornness had gotten me a black eye, but I refused to cower.

Not now, not ever.

"I don't give a damn who your father is, so take your boyfriends there and get the hell off my lawn."

A low growl came from somewhere around the vicinity of my knees.

Nimrod stood there with his head slung low, his normally happy, goofy demeanor gone. His ears were flattened back against his head, and his teeth were bared in a snarl that exposed his sharp canines. Another rumbling growl erupted from deep within his barrel chest.

He had evidently gotten up from the porch where he'd been napping to see what all the commotion was about. He was always excited to greet new visitors, bouncing up to them all gleeful and expecting a head pat with his tail wagging and his nose nuzzling for a scratch behind the ears. He was such a lousy guard dog, that in New York, if killers had broken into my apartment, I was convinced he would greet them with a wag and a lick, all too willing to have his belly rubbed even as they put a bullet in my head. The way he held himself now and growled deep in his throat indicated he was more than just a lazy mutt.

I was glad the dufus had my back, but it was a bit scary to see him acting so aggressively. They say dogs are keen judges of character. Not Nimrod, because he was a bit dopey and seemed to love everyone, but he clearly didn't like this kid any more than I did. Something in how we were acting, or maybe it was something in the air, had upset him, and he'd come to my side to protect me. I didn't know if he would actually attack anyone, and while good-intentioned, Nimrod biting this punk could get us both in a lot of trouble. If his dad was the sheriff, he would undoubtedly raise Cain, and my dog could be looking at getting put down.

I reached down, putting a hand on Nimrod's head to calm him, but also, at the first sign of a lunge, I could more easily grab his collar.

The snarling caused the kid to back-pedal a few feet, where he stopped and gave me a dirty leer. After a few seconds of glaring, he turned and walked back to his truck.

The driver's door closing was a gunshot, echoing through the afternoon air when he slammed it shut. The truck started and the engine bellowed. Not the sound of power, but of one struggling for air with every cough and sputter, blasting a large gout of black exhaust smelling strongly of diesel and oil. It was a wonder I didn't hear it when they'd first pulled up.

One of the other boys hanging out of the passenger window flipped me the bird and laughed, showing a gap-toothed grin. What I could hear of their mocking laughter over the sound of the truck sounded like a group of hyenas yucking it up. They peeled out, leaving a trail of black smoke the length of the street before turning left at the intersection, failing to heed a stop sign, and forcing a car coming the other way to pull up short to keep from hitting them.

The car's angry horn bleated in the afternoon air. I continued watching as the sound of the truck faded into the distance. I knew this wasn't over, petulant brats like that never just move on. They would be back at some point in one fashion or another until they finally got bored.

I was proven partially correct when the sheriff's car crawled up to the curb a few hours later.

I had been lounging on the porch with my feet kicked up on the wobbly railing. It damn well needed fixing, but that was just another item on my endless list of chores. I had been editing my article, which I hated doing because editing always gave me a headache. Staring at the page, everything had become one big blur. Five hundred words on the new little league field they had just built behind the elementary school, causing me to burn through nearly half a pack of Marlboros. Another cigarette hung from my mouth like a forgotten appendage, unlit, as I had absentmindedly forgotten to light it.

I idly spun a pencil between the first three fingers of my right hand. It was a nervous thing I did whenever I was frustrated with writing. The pencil blurred as it tumbled from one finger to the next, creating the illusion it had become liquid. I didn't pay any attention to it as I tried to force myself to focus on the page before me. A couple of empty bottles of beer sat next to one foot, and another half-empty bottle rested on the arm of my chair, slowly turning lukewarm in the sun.

My attention shifted to the cop when the door of his cruiser popped open, and the giant man heaved himself out.

Giant might have been an understatement. It was a wonder he fit in the car. He settled his wide-brimmed hat on his head as he mounted the curb and started up my walkway. He seemed to double in size as he got closer. He had to be over six and a half feet tall, probably closer to seven, and barrel-chested. Clearly, his bulk was all muscle, the kind you see on lifelong dedicated weightlifters.

His brown uniform shirt could barely contain him, and his biceps strained at the sleeves, threatening to burst the seams. The boots he wore made loud booms like thunder clapping when he climbed the steps.

I couldn't help it, and my eyes went from the shiny badge on his enormous chest to the gun on his hip. It looked like one of those oversized magnums Charles Bronson used in those action movies.

"Howdy." He stepped fully onto the porch. "I'm Sheriff Earlywine."

As if the uniform and badge didn't give it away.

He stuck out one massive paw that would have only looked small if it was on a bear. I shook his hand, mine disappearing completely in his. His shake was firm, but not bone-crushing. There was restraint in it, as if holding back some terrible power, and how he easily could have crushed my hand if he'd wanted to.

"Hello, Sheriff, can I get you a beer?" I motioned to the small cooler sitting on my other side. On top of the cooler sat my pack of cigarettes, lighter, and an ashtray overflowing with used butts.

"No thanks, son. I'm here about a little incident that happened earlier."

Ah, I thought as my brain made the connection. He was the spoiled kid's father, and apparently, Junior had tattled on me. Now, Daddy was here to make sure I knew the pecking order.

"And what incident would that be?" I turned back to my paperwork dismissively as if the world's biggest cop wasn't standing on my front stoop after I'd sent his kid packing. I was just waiting for the hammer to drop.

"Well, my boy, Jarrod, was out this way earlier. When he said he stopped to look at your car, you sicced some kind of wild animal on him and his friends."

I felt my face flush in anger. The petty little shit had gone and made up a little story in an effort to get back at me.

"Your son is lying." I put my work aside and stood. The change in height did nothing to make up for the difference in our sizes, but I felt a little better now that he wasn't looming over me. "Yeah, he stopped here and tried to get me to sell him my car. When I said no, he got ugly and tried to intimidate me. His two dumb friends never left their truck. And as for the wild animal..."

I jerked my chin behind him, and he turned to see Nimrod trotting out of the house.

I had left the door open, hoping to create a breeze to cool it off. It had been so unbearably hot and sticky inside, I had moved my work to the front porch. The husky had been asleep on the couch, but our talk must have woken him.

As Sheriff Earlywine watched, the dog made his way over to the property line between my place and Joey Ackerman's, where he squatted and pooped. When he was done doing his business, he lopped over to the center of the yard and flopped over on his side with a loud *whumpft*. He proceeded to roll onto his back and then wriggle back and forth in the freshly cut grass. With his tongue hanging out and his eyes rolling madly in his head, he hardly looked like a wild animal.

"Look, Sheriff, your kid was rude, and he upset my dog, so he growled at him. As you can see, he is about as dangerous as a biscuit."

As the Sheriff watched, Nimrod gave up on his rolling and began commando crawling across the lawn on his belly, dragging his hind legs behind him and stopping to snuffle the grass every foot or so.

"I am sure my boy probably embellished a bit, but we do things a certain way around here, and your kind of people need to respect that, or else there will be trouble." The tone of his voice dropped for that last part, and he put particular emphasis on 'your kind of people'.

I couldn't help myself, and the several beers had pretty much eighty-sixed my better judgment.

"What exactly do you mean, *your kind of people*?" I gave him my hardest stare in an attempt to show him I wouldn't be steamrolled.

"You know, out-of-towners. You just blew into town a few months ago from New York, I think it was, and we do things differently here in Midnight Falls. We give respect where respect is due, and take care of our own." His voice started to get a dangerous edge to it. Almost like there was a threat buried in there somewhere. "Son, if you aren't careful, you are likely to land yourself in a whole heap of trouble. And when that happens, I am gonna come down on you—" he clapped his huge hands together for emphasis "—like *that*."

"Mr. Earlywine, I was born and raised in Fleming County. I know how things are done here. Which is why I am not afraid of you or your son. All I want is to be left alone so I can do my job in peace." I put a little edge in my own voice to show I was just as serious. Inside, I was all but pissing my pants in anxiety.

"It's Sheriff to you, and you should be careful who you disrespect around here. I know a lot of people. Like that boss of yours over at the paper, known him a long time. It wouldn't take much, I reckon, just the right bug in the right ear, and you'll find yourself out on your ass."

"Is that a threat, Sheriff? Because I know quite a few people, too." I was bluffing. "That's the thing about small towns, everyone knows everyone and everything. There are no secrets in places like Midnight Falls." I offered him a saccharine smile to really salt the wound.

Sheriff Earlywine's face cramped into an ugly frown and his eyes blazed with hate as traces of that dry cracking sound filled the space between us, setting me on edge. There was that flicker again in his eyes, and I could swear I saw something move behind them. Truly terrifying, hinting at a darker inner madness. The kind that leaks in small doses through acts of pettiness and abuse. The type of eyes you see on a man who will beat his wife and kids for his own mistakes and failures, that lashes out blindly in anger when sufficiently poked. There was a danger there, lying in wait, just looking for a place and time to happen. Dangerous poisoned blood that was passed down from father to son in trailer parks all over the country.

"Listen here, smart mouth," he hissed, as he leaned in, making an obvious effort to control, but I could still hear what sounded like knuckles cracking, or maybe it was from his clenched jaw, as he steadied himself. "You just keep your peace and don't cause any more trouble. Because not all the secrets in Midnight Falls are known, and you don't want to be one." With that, he turned and walked back to his car.

Thankfully, I was already sweating from the heat, otherwise, the cold sweat running down my back would have been obvious. Sheriff Earlywine's last remark had been darkly sinister.

I have no naive notions of good and evil. While Kentucky is not the deep south, there is enough of that type of outlaw mentality in the rural areas that Hollywood movies based on corrupt backwoods cops have some credibility. Making someone disappear in the country is actually far easier to do than in a place like New Jersey. Lots of heavily wooded areas and farms to dispose of a body, should one happen to need to. The look in his eyes had scared me. There was clearly something behind them, something I didn't want to ever see in the full light of day. Things of nightmares. There are places, dark damp hidden places, where things like that dwell, and to look upon them would drive a person mad with fear.

I don't think my mind could handle it.

Sitting there with Brad and Lizzie on that hot afternoon remembering, I received yet another of those nearly psychic shivers, but pushed it out of my mind and returned to enjoying their company.

CHAPTER 5

The next few weeks were uneventful as July rolled into August. I continued working on the house, with the occasional help from Brad and Lizzie. She helped me redo the kitchen ceiling, which had begun developing yellow water stains. I had started to enjoy her company, and it was nice to have a hand with the work.

Nimrod seemed to like her, too. He would always greet her in his usual way of launching himself at her like a furry cannonball. He would bound up and down until he received sufficient head patting, and then he would lumber off to find a place to nap. The goofball had only made a nuisance of himself once.

We were repainting the living room when he decided to take a tumble into the paint bucket. He stumbled, tripping over his own two left feet, and went headfirst into the can. He barked and jumped around in a frenzied panic. With paint splattering everywhere, he sprinted across the room, leaving a trail of white paw prints in his wake.

This had sent Lizzie into fits of laughter, her face lit up with pure joy.

God, was she beautiful when she laughed. The sound was like a warm cozy blanket, wrapping around me and banishing all my worries. She had one of those laughs that brightened up a room.

It made me think of all the other girls I'd known, with their shrill, grating laughs that pierced eardrums. One, from Flushing, had a laugh like a donkey with a broken nose. Needless to say, that relationship didn't last long.

Lizzie was different. A sweet melody that made my heart lift.

In that moment, as we stood there covered in paint, I wished time could stand still and this would last forever. Something about the way she looked at me, or how she smiled, or even how her brow furrowed when she frowned. All of those little moments would catch me off guard, and it was like I truly saw her for the first time, every time. In these random moments, she made me wish I were a better person. I'd been so burned out and cynical for the last several years, I hadn't let myself experience sheer joy, and I was almost afraid to let it in when it came again. Once she got to know me better, she probably wouldn't like me. I didn't even like myself most days, so how could she? We were a fleeting thing that would wax and wane, two ships passing in the night.

The two of us spent the latter part of that afternoon hosing down the dog. Poor Nimrod was covered head to toe in paint, and we needed to get him cleaned up before it dried and set. It did devolve into senseless horseplay. We took turns chasing each other, the spray from the hose drenching us both. Nimrod, for his part, seemed to be having the time of his life, darting back and forth, and snapping at the water as it arced through the air. By the time we were done, all three of us were soaked to the bone.

Lizzie was a breath of fresh air in a town that had long since given up on the written word. She wasn't antagonistically illiterate. Some stereotypes persist in backwoods communities, and Midnight Falls wasn't an exception. Intelligence, education, and literature were not exactly prized virtues, with many people preferring not to read or learn unless they had to, and anyone who dared to embrace knowledge was viewed with suspicion. Beyond the morning paper, pretty much everything else was learned from TV. The only library nearby was over in Flemingsburg. It wasn't just books she loved. She was passionate about learning, expanding her mind, and exploring new ideas. It was a trait that set her apart from the rest of the town, and one that drew me to her.

It was a relief to find someone who shared my passion for literature and discuss what we called in college the "death of the great American novel." We spent long hours debating such things as the pretentiousness of Henry David Thoreau's 'Walden,' or the other works of Herman Melville. To Lizzie's surprise, yes, Melville wrote things other than 'Moby Dick.' Which, of course, led us to the works of Poe, Lovecraft, the more recent works of Stephen King, and the collection of short stories he had released the year before.

I wrote mostly for the paper articles, but there had been a few tentative starts and stops on would-be novels. I made a few attempts, but they always ended the same way—with a blank page staring back at me, mocking my inability to put words to paper. I would sit at my typewriter for hours, the page daring me to write something, anything, but the words never came. My muse had abandoned me, leaving me alone with my thoughts and my blank page. It was as if my taste for the work had soured with nothing but a bitter aftertaste.

I also drank too much. I knew it, and there wasn't much I could do about it. Most days, you could find me at the kitchen table, hunched over my typewriter like a man possessed. A yellow legal pad lay nearby, its pages covered in hastily scribbled notes and half-formed ideas. Next to that would be an ashtray overflowing with butts. I was smoking nearly as much as I was drinking, my lungs and liver in a constant state of revolt.

Beside the ashtray would be either several empty beer cans or a bottle of Jack Daniels. It would start full and be mostly empty by the time I gave up writing. Same with the cigarettes. So, I drank and smoked and wrote, each word a painful labor that only the booze and nicotine could make bearable. Then, when I was finished, I would stumble to bed, the taste of regret on my tongue and the knowledge that I would do it all again tomorrow.

Often, in the late night or early hours of the morning, still reeling with a head full of alcohol, I would have more of those near psychic moments. Anxiety-driven hallucinations where I thought I could hear a distant howling or something scratching at the door, even sudden remembrances of that sound of the dry, grating cracking. Those instances, I would think back to Jarrod and his father, and their eyes...that whatever I'd imagined I saw.

Just beyond my window, late at night, there felt like something, almost the town itself, lurking, and no one, including Lizzie, had seemed to notice.

Perhaps I was going insane. Too much booze, not enough sleep. Toxic paint fumes. Something.

Except, sometimes, Nimrod would lift his head or whine like he'd picked up on it, too. Though, he wasn't the sharpest tool in the shed.

Come sunrise, the trash can was always full of half-baked manuscripts and empty bottles, evidence of my failed attempts at writing. But the articles, those were different. They were the bread and butter of my meager existence, and I couldn't afford to send in anything less than my best. I would set them aside, knowing that, in the morning with a clear head and a fresh eye, I would have to polish those turds into something salvageable. More often than not, that's exactly what I did. I would rewrite and revise until it was serviceable, and then I would send them off to the Gazette, hoping they'd be good enough to keep me afloat for another week.

Lizzie had asked me about my writing when she found one of my abortions in the trash. She'd come over unannounced on a dreary Saturday night, finding me sprawled out on the sofa, lost in the pages of Mort Rainey's 'Everyone Drops the Dime,' but despite the dark and twisted tales within its pages, I was struggling to stay engaged.

I put the book down on the coffee table when Nimrod started doing his racehorse impersonation. He would gallop from the living room down the hall to the kitchen and then back again, his claws scrabbling against the hardwood floor as he ran at full speed. This meant someone was at the front door. The sound of his pounding paws echoed throughout the house, making him better than any doorbell or alarm system.

I got up and made my way over to the door, peeking through the window.

Lizzie stood on the porch holding a pizza box, so I unlatched the door to let her in.

As the door swung open, Nimrod lunged forward, his massive frame hurtling towards her like a missile. I snatched the pizza box from her grasp, narrowly avoiding a collision with the frenzied dog. She stumbled backward, her eyes wide with surprise as Nimrod slobbered over her, his tail wagging in excitement as he bore her to the ground.

With a flick of my wrist, I tossed a piece of pizza toward the kitchen, and Nimrod leaped after it. He caught it almost before it hit the floor and it disappeared with a single snap of his jaws, his tail wagging happily.

While he was distracted, Lizzie picked herself up from the floor, closing the door behind her with a firm thud.

I deposited the pizza box on the coffee table before fetching plates and beers from the kitchen. I kept an eye on the dog, knowing better than to leave him unsupervised with a box of pizza. He had a tendency to devour the entire thing in record time.

When I made my way back to the living room, Lizzie had made herself at home on the couch and was scrutinizing the book I'd been reading.

"Any good?" she asked, cocking an eyebrow.

"It's okay. I mean, he's no Mike Noonan." I opened the beers and passed her one as she tossed the book aside.

"I've been reading a lot of Paul Sheldon lately." She selected a slice of pizza from the box.

"Ugh, I think my opinion of you has declined now that I know you're one of those 'Misery' fan girls." I took two pieces for myself, teasing her.

Nimrod sat on the other side of the table, looking up at us, begging with big sad eyes.

"They are Gran's books, not mine. Her selection is pretty limited to Victorian novels and westerns. Mostly Zane Greys, but there are also a couple of Roberta Anderson's."

She picked pepperoni off her pizza and tossed it to the dog.

He caught it mid-air and wagged his tail.

We continued talking as we ate, discussing books and writers as well as local events. She told me about an upcoming one at the

Community Center. It was some sort of annual potluck get-together they had before the new school year would commence. Everyone was invited, she told me, and then went on about how her grandmother was trying to play matchmaker to get her to find herself a man.

We both laughed at that.

Once we'd finished eating, I took the empty box and plates, and shuffled them back to the kitchen. When I returned, she had fished one of my previous writing attempts out of the trash bin at the end of the couch. She flipped through it, clearly interested. I cracked open a beer for myself and poured a generous amount into Nimrod's dish.

She looked up at me from the crumpled pages. "This is pretty good. Why did you toss it?" She returned to what she'd been reading.

I'd been trying all afternoon to write, mostly procrastinating by finishing the porch rails. After about three hours, the whole thing had turned on me, and I'd thrown it out.

"It wasn't any good, so I chucked it." I took a swig of beer. "I'm not really that into writing anymore."

"So, what made you give up? I mean, I've read some of your articles, and they aren't bad. Better than most of the other stuff people write. But, this? This is really good." She held the pages out to me as if, somehow, I would reconsider them.

I sighed and took them from her. "It's a long story about something that happened in college. Since then, I just can't seem to get my groove back, so pretty much everything ends up in the trash." I looked at them. The ink from the typewriter had smeared a bit on the latter pages, and the top one had a wet ring from a bottle.

"Well, I have time, so tell me about it." She smiled and stretched.

The motion did amazing things for her body. She was wearing a plain white t-shirt tied at her midriff and jeans, and I realized that, up until then, I had only seen her in shorts or sundresses. Though they covered more, the jeans were form-hugging and really accentuated her long legs. Her toes wiggled through Nimrod's fur as she used her bare feet to rub his belly while he lay on the floor in front of her.

I decided to bare my soul to her about everything that had happened.

CHAPTER 6

Lizzie sat beside me on the couch, running her feet through my dog's fur. I didn't know if she'd judge me for my past, but I knew she'd call me out on my bullshit. Either way, I would have to brave the ghosts of my past.

"During my second year of college at NYU, I found I couldn't really afford my tuition. So, I joined the PA program. By working as a Professor's Assistant, I could get breaks on costs, in addition to all the grants and allowances I'd applied for." I sighed, daring a peek at her. She had her full focus on me. "I was hanging on by the skin of my teeth, grades-wise, and bussing tables in a diner at night. Somehow, I just barely managed to qualify."

At my pause, she nodded for me to continue.

And it was as if a dam inside me had burst, the words just spilled out, and I couldn't have stopped if I'd wanted to. She was probably the first person I told the whole story to. With others, it seemed like no matter how hard I tried or how well I explained, I just couldn't find the right words to accurately expound the way I saw it in my head. She somehow managed to see through my bullshit to understand my rambling.

"I'd goofed off most of my freshman year. Going to parties and sleeping in late, waking up with a hangover most mornings. Without the program, I don't know how I would've been able to afford another year. I was too proud to write home and ask for money, not because my parents really couldn't afford it, but because I knew they *would* send it.

"I'd been hoping that, due to trying to get a degree in writing, I would get assigned to one of the literature or writing professors, but no such luck. They either didn't need one or already had assistants. I ended up getting assigned to Dr. Carl Hofstadter, Professor of Early American History. He was a small man, maybe five-foot, tops. He was older than Methuselah and weathered like a twig."

She huffed a laugh at my description.

I smiled, even though my gut was in knots. "He always wore tweed, no matter the season, which had to be uncomfortable in the summer, but he never seemed to mind. He reminded me of Professor Plum from the Clue game."

"Love that game," she said with a grin.

I grunted. "He wasn't really that bad as far as workload. Mostly, it was just double-checking his appointments and calendar. The real work came when he assigned me to type up his manuscript. His sole ambition was to write a book about the post-Civil War era that would light the historian world on fire. The problem was, his writing was as dry as the Sahara."

She laughed again, and I truly loved the sound. It lightened the stale mood.

"He should stick to teaching then."

"Yup." If only. "It was all clinical facts and accounts. Nothing much beyond the dates and places. There was no imagination to it. Pouring through his notes and manuscript was like reading the phone book."

Another laugh. Success.

"So, after a few weeks of typing and retyping his work, I decided to get a little inventive."

"Uh oh," she mumbled.

I shook my head. "I didn't mess with any of his notes or facts. I just gave it legs and let it run. It was still very much based on his work. It just wasn't boring. It morphed into historical non-fiction that was equal parts 'Gone with the Wind' and textbook, retaining the historical accuracy of a documentary, but offered the reader something vastly more interesting than the arid bloated tome he'd written."

"Nice."

Running a hand over my face, I nodded. "I guess the real problem was that he didn't bother to read it himself after I'd typed it up. I dreaded he would tell me to go back and redo it the way he wanted. Which I'd already done, several times, as he'd kept adding notes during the process. If he'd just done that, none of the rest would have happened."

Her eyebrows shot to her hairline and her pretty green eyes widened.

Yeah. "Dr. Hofstadter sent the manuscript to the publisher, expecting his millionth rejection. Instead, he got a letter back praising the book. They wanted to get it into print as soon as possible, and did so. The book was well-received by Historian circles, especially the Civil War buffs, but it went beyond into the more commercial demographics. It even made its way onto the bestseller list, though very low, but far better than expected for an academic book. He was the talk of the campus History department. There were discussions of tours and lectures, and all of it was going to the man's head. His personality had changed from the distracted quiet professor into a slight egomaniac. He hadn't been the nicest person before. Rather gruff and dismissive, but not really mean. I guess money and success really does change everyone, and not for the better."

She grunted a sound of agreement. "Truth."

"I guess I was no exception. I was a grad student living on packaged noodles and whatever leftover food I could find in the cafeteria. I was getting pretty desperate. I needed money, and I had done most of the work on the book without even a by-line or thanks. I confronted him, probably with more greed in my intent than I would like to have admitted."

"A bonus or something."

I waved my hand to acknowledge her, but the worst was coming. "He was quite taken aback when I brought it to him. Once he recovered, he was furious. His gnarled old face turned beet red in anger. The way his remaining wiry white hair stuck out at the sides of his head, made him look like an atomic mushroom cloud."

A hand over her mouth, she seemed both horrified and amused.

"He pointed a gnarled finger at me and screamed, 'How dare you make such demands. It's imposturous that a mere student is responsible for one of the greatest works of significance to this university. You must be out of your mind to think you can take credit for years of my work.'"

Her brows rose again.

"I thrust a copy into his hand and said, 'Have you even read your book? Because, if you had, you would know it's not all your words. I rewrote it to make it more bearable. You didn't think it was strange that, after rejecting you so many times, with little more than a polite "fuck off" form rejection letter, the publishing company suddenly could not get enough?'"

She gasped. "What'd he say?"

"He sputtered in anger as he looked at the book in his hands. His demeanor changed as his ego shifted from attack to defense. He said, 'So, you're trying to discredit me, then? Well, your plan didn't work. Your little attempt at sabotage backfired on you. Genius can't be derailed by a child.'"

"What?" she screeched.

"Yeah. I shot back and asked if he was fucking insane or just delusional? Told him to read the book, and he'd see what I was talking about."

Jaw agape, she slowly shook her head. "What happened?"

"He ordered me out of his office and said he would take it to the Dean to get me expelled. Spit actually flew from his lips."

"Eww."

"I slammed the door as I exited his office. Mad as hell, I headed straight to the local bar where all the campus kids hung out. I spent the rest of the evening getting blackout drunk."

"I don't blame you."

"That Monday, I was summoned to the Dean's office. Dr. Hofstadter was sitting outside the office with a rather battered copy of his book. It looked as if he'd spent the weekend kicking it everywhere he went. He gave me a venomous glare as I was escorted into the office."

"Asshole."

"Yup." I cleared my throat and took a swig of beer, ignoring the riot in my stomach. "The Dean was an older woman with a gray bun at the back of her head. She looked more like a Headmistress from a Dickens novel than a college Dean who'd lived through the Disco revolution."

Another huffed laugh.

"As I stood in front of her desk, I felt like a kid about to get a dressing down from the principal. Amazing how some parts of our childhood stick with us, coloring our best and worst moments."

"I feel like that around Gran sometimes."

I nodded. "I had brought with me all the evidence I thought I would need to convince her of my side of events. Sadly, I never got that far. Due to Dr. Hofstadter having tenure, and the position the sudden success of his book had brought to the university, they felt it was best that I leave."

Her eyes rounded anew.

"I tried to explain my story, but it was no use. Their mind was made up. In order to save face and protect the college's reputation, they were cutting me loose. On my way out of the office, I lost my cool when I saw Professor Hofstadter's expression. I punched him in the jaw, sending him sprawling to the floor."

Lizzie didn't appear to know whether to cheer or fall over in shock.

"It really was a stupid thing to do, and I didn't stick around to see the aftermath. By the end of the week, campus security had escorted me off the grounds after watching me pack up my dorm. There wasn't much. It all fit in a few boxes."

I sighed, gaze lost in thought. It's kind of sad to see your life summed up in a couple of cardboard containers. All it would take was a single match to pretty much erase all evidence of my presence.

It didn't end there. I spent the next few years in legal battles with the college, trying to get my fair share. At that point, it became more about stupid pride than money. I was deluding myself, saying it was about what was right. In the end, I had no more funds, and they weren't budging. Every piece of evidence and point made was countered and tied up in bureaucracy. They had a team of lawyers, while I only had what I could afford, which wasn't much. What time I hadn't spent fighting a pointless battle was used busting my hump working whatever jobs were on hand, trying to keep my head above water. Every time I applied for a writing job, even the freelance stuff, I got turned down. Turns out, no one wants to hire a writer with less than two years of college and their only experience being highly contested in court, and not in their favor.

In the end, I'd decided I needed a change. I couldn't make it in New York, so I headed back home, because isn't that where they have to let you in? I tucked tail and ran home. I told as much to Lizzie.

"I'm so sorry."

I shrugged. They say confession is good for the soul, and it felt like a weight was lifted from my shoulders. Purging my mind of the events that had ended my college career in a blaze of youthful stupidity and pride had actually helped.

I've been trying to clear my head and put myself back together. About the only thing I've really been able to achieve is emptying bottles and ruining perfectly good reams of typing paper.

I leaned my head back, staring at the ceiling. It gave a subtle wobble, the telltale sign I was on the tipping point of classy drunk and sloppy drunk. No wonder, I had just spilled my guts to Lizzie.

I glanced at her, not quite sure what I was expecting.

She batted her eyelashes over those gorgeous green eyes. "So, you had a bad experience and a hard time of it. That doesn't mean you failed. You just need time to heal and learn to give yourself the benefit of the doubt. You've had your self-esteem shattered, and you just need a little recovery time before you try again. You know what they say—when you fall off the horse, you have to pick yourself up and eat that horse." She placed her hand on my chest as she leaned close.

My heart beat harder at her touch. "I'm not sure that's how that saying goes."

I was way too aware of her touch and its warmth. Her skin smelled sweet and flowery from whatever deodorant or shampoo she used. A combination of baby powder and rose petals. As I returned her gaze, I fell into the depths of her eyes. That's exactly how it felt. Like falling. We held one another's gaze for what seemed like eons, though it was probably only a few minutes.

Without warning, she kissed me.

My brain ceased to function, but then instinct kicked in. Her lips were soft. I wove one hand into her blonde hair, like cornsilk between my fingers, as I pulled her closer. My tongue found hers as the kiss deepened, losing ourselves.

It had been years since I'd been with a woman, and yet, here we were, sitting on my couch, necking like a couple of horny teenagers. As out of practice as I was, Lissie didn't seem to notice or mind. She took the lead without judgement, guiding me to her needs and wants.

Our little flight of fancy was interrupted by an annoyed chuffing sound.

We both turned to find Nimrod looking at us, confused. His head was cocked to one side as he seemingly tried to figure out why the two humans were eating each other's faces instead of giving him attention.

We burst out laughing, and just like that, the mood was gone. We sat up, trying to put ourselves together after our bout of hormones.

"Hey, about the Community Potluck this weekend, did you want to go with me?" She combed her hair with her fingers, all rumpled by my uncoordinated fumbling.

"Are you asking me on a date?" I asked coyly.

"Sure, why not? It's the 80s. Women can do that now."

"Oh, really?" I teased.

"Yes, we can even vote and drive and go to the store without a man holding our hand. If we can burn our bras, why not be able to ask a nice guy out?"

I laughed. "You don't know me that well. Maybe I'm just pretending to be a nice guy, but I'm planning on eating you like the Big Bad Wolf."

"Ugh, you make fun of me for my reading tastes, yet you read Thomas Harris. You're right, you aren't a nice guy, but at least your dog is cute." She mushed the dumb dog's face between her hands and made kissy noises at him. "Yes, who's a cute doggy? You are. Yes, you are."

He just slobbered in response, tail wagging.

"Well, since you asked, I would be happy to. Not like there is much else to do around here."

Looking at the clock, I realized it was a lot later than I thought.

Lizzie made suggestions that it was time for her to leave, but I could see in her eyes she wanted me to ask her to stay. What was more, I wanted to, but I couldn't. I liked her, and didn't want to ruin it by doing anything stupid. Like letting the head in my pants call the shots.

I walked her home since it had gotten dark. The night was lovely and warm. The western horizon still maintained a deep purple glow. Most of our walk was in silence, the two of us just enjoying the night air. I hardly noticed the absence of the feeling of eyes on us or my psychic shivers that had recently plagued me. We were purely alone.

We stopped at the foot of her grandmother's walkway. I felt like a teenager on his first date, standing there awkwardly.

"So, next weekend?" she asked shyly.

"Yeah, sure. I mean, you can drop by anytime, but yeah. I'll see you at the Community Center."

We said our goodbyes, and I watched until she was inside before making my way home. I was so giddy, I almost skipped the whole way. Had there been a lamppost, I probably would have swung around on it while singing like Fred Astaire.

CHAPTER 7

The week was a blur. As much as I tried to focus on my work, I found my thoughts slipping off to be with Lizzie. She didn't come over because her college classes had kept her busy. I made very little headway in repairing the house, but I did manage to cut back on my drinking. Though, I believe that had more to do with anxiety than self-control. It was, however, a small but welcomed victory.

Saturday evening finally rolled around, and I was ready to explode. We were going to meet at the Center around six, that way, neither of us had to go out of our way, and it really was just a short walk from each of our respective houses. So, around five, I threw on my cleanest pair of jeans and a button-up shirt, then spent about half an hour in front of the mirror trying to get my unruly brunette strands to look casual but not messy. My hair had grown out enough that it almost touched my shoulders. I had that typical beatnik style, sort of a composite between John Lennon and Bowie.

By the time I reached the Center, I was running about ten minutes late. Joey Akerman was manning the front door, handing out fliers about the new school year rules and requirements. Most of them were ending up in the garbage can from what I could tell. People would take them deftly and throw them away without so much as a glance. Same for the man himself. Most weren't even looking at or acknowledging him.

Then again, he had a certain way about him. A small town like Midnight Falls, stuck in its ways and highly religious, would not warm up a guy like Joey.

I said "hey" to him and patted his shoulder when he handed me a flyer as I crossed the threshold.

There were already a lot of people inside. I spotted Debbie Holmes from the Post Office, and her husband, Frank, I think his name was. There was Charlie Story, chair of the city council, who was talking to Marie Latterback, head of the school board, and Coach Littleton, who taught gym at the elementary school as well as coached the high school girls' basketball team. Coach Littleton's big belly shook as his booming laughter filled the room, evidently at something one of the others said.

No one stopped to talk to me, but the fine hairs on the back of my neck told me they were staring as I passed. I could almost feel the weight of their eyes. Being the new guy made me a bit of a curiosity. However, it did seem quite agnostic in tone tonight versus before. Ignoring the uncomfortableness, I glanced around for Lizzie.

The Midnight Falls Community Center was the center of the town, metaphorically. Physically, it sat more on the outskirts on the Fleming side. It was a large gymnasium that filled the role of a town hall, theater, and storm shelter. A multipurpose building. During school days, it would function as a sort of after-school rec center. On Friday nights, they hosted Bingo provided by the church, and occasionally, there would be a girls' volleyball game. It filled many roles for the community, allowing them to easily adapt to nearly any schedule or event. It did a lot of good for the neighborhood. It was currently filling up with my neighbors and other townsfolk who I didn't know by name, but by sight. Kids ran to and fro as their parents milled about, talking and holding paper plates of food.

I eventually spotted Lizzie at the buffet line, laughing and talking with Brad, who wore a white apron. He was handing out fried chicken, mashed potatoes, and rolls. There were crockpots filled with casseroles, pulled pork, green beans, corn pudding, and baked mac and cheese—the kind with the crust on top. The smell of the food was so good, my mouth practically watered.

Whereas I hadn't before, something made me notice tonight that Joey and I weren't the only ones being brushed off. Patrons were passing right by Brad as he served, barely nodding at Lizzie. Bigotry in action, right there, cult-like mentality raging. Brad being one of the only black people in Midnight Falls and Lizzie daring to have a mind of her own as a feminist would set the town's teeth on edge.

So be it. We could form our own mangy crew of outcasts.

I made my way across the room to join them, and Lizzie handed me a plate. "You look hungry, stranger."

We went down the line, loading our plates with homecooked food, and we made small talk while we ate. She told me about her classes at the community college. She was working in the nursing program, and her parents couldn't have been happier that their daughter was going into the family business, so to speak.

She seemed to be running from the boring expected life of following in her parents' footsteps. Staying with her grandmother and being a "liberated woman" was an act of rebellion. It's probably why she was drawn to me since I had escaped small town life, even though I'd returned.

Her father had been a doctor at the local hospital for several years before hanging out his own shingle as a general practitioner. He'd resigned before the hospital administration could give him the bum's rush for canoodling with one of his nurses. That nurse had been Lizzie's mother. She'd remained at the hospital, despite the gossip and rumors. Both had still had long careers in the medical field after this impasse. They'd encouraged their daughter to follow, though her father had wanted her to go to med school.

Lizzie had held no such plans, but due to a series of rejections from her colleges of choice, and her backups, the nursing program had been a fallback. While it had been a compromise to stop her parents from nagging her, she had no interest in becoming a nurse. She'd seen what her mother had gone through. Late nights, long odd hours, and endless complaints about demanding patients. A wholly unpleasant and undesirable prospect for one to consider spending the rest of their lives committed to, per Lizzie.

"So, what do you plan to do?" I asked between bites of corn pudding and mashed potatoes.

She took a swig of her soda before she answered. "I dunno. Once I get my RN license, I might just go for pharmacy tech so I can fill prescriptions." She finished off her drink while not meeting my eyes. She obviously had no interest in further pursuing the conversation.

I knew what she was doing, as I'd done more or less the same thing after being kicked out of college—pretending life wasn't a miserable pit of suck, and attempting to put off making the hard decisions until they could no longer be ignored. It's one of the follies of youth. You always think there will be time later, but time runs out.

After a few announcements from Charlie Story and Don Fields, several of the tables were cleared away to make room for a dance floor, and music started. The dance floor was made up mostly of young adults and older teens.

I was content to sit back and let them make fools of themselves, but halfway through the third song, Lizzie grabbed my hand and pulled me to my feet. She led me to the dance floor and turned to face me with a devilish, carefree smile on her face.

She began to move to the music in a very daring and primal way. In comparison to everyone else, who were fairly conservative, she was positively wild. They danced in that awkward style when worried others were watching. Even the teens were not as bold, probably because their parents were there, or someone who knew their parents, and would tell on them. Lizzie was not so inhibited. She slung her pretty blonde hair from side to side as her hips popped in opposition. Lithe was the only word I could think of to describe her in motion. It was less like she was dancing and more like she was caught in the midst of lust.

All I could think about was putting my hands on her, touching her, to feel every jerk and twist of her body as she gave herself over to the music. I kept my hands to myself, and though a little self-conscious, I tried my best to keep up with her.

A few songs later, I had worked up quite a sweat, though Lizzie's energy seemed to be boundless. On the last song, something fast and bouncy, the name and band I couldn't recall, she had all but mounted me on the dance floor. My blood pressure was through the roof and my brain had gone walkabout. I was now being piloted by that traitorous little organ that leads all men astray. It wasn't the scandalized stares and whispers that broke up our little tête-à-tête on the dance floor, but a garbled insult I didn't quite make out, except for one word.

Slut.

We whirled to a stop to address the direction from which it had been hurled. Standing on the edge of a small circle that had formed around us were Jarrod Earlywine and his two stooges.

The boys were nearly the same size. All three together looked like a mountain range among the sea of other kids. The teens had formed a ring around us while dancing, separating us from the rest of the floor, where the other adults were occupied. Through some sort of pack mentality, they seemed to be guided by a singular will and purpose. Drawn by the spectacle of what was to come, other occupants slowly took their cues from the imposing group of boys. Not sure if they were the ring leaders or if the crowd was just responding to the natural course of events, but this was clearly not going to end well for us.

"What a real slut she is to be with a faggot like that," said one of the stooges, whose name I think was Clutch. He, undoubtedly, had a real name, but I'd only ever heard the others refer to him by his colorful nickname.

"Bet she's never had a real man before, but we could show her a good time," guffawed Troy, the other one. "Think she can dance like that on my cock?" He gave his crotch a hike with one hand as all three cackled.

Neither Troy nor Clutch were as big as Jared, but all three were large for boys of their age. Each with the athletic builds of professional football players, they alone formed a seemingly unpassable, unscalable wall by themselves. Troy was the skinniest, but he still made the average person look anorexic at the birth of a refrigerator. Clutch, the shortest, his face pockmarked with angry red patches of acne, was head and shoulders above the rest of the group of jeering high schoolers.

I was getting sick of this punk and his friends constantly giving me shit. At this point, they were going out of their way, making a conscious effort for these schoolyard antics. Driving past my house just to yell at me out of their car windows was one thing, but this was taking the harassment to the level where things almost always ended up physical.

"Let's go," Lizzie whispered, giving the laughing idiots a contemptuous look and trying to pull me along by my hand.

I wasn't having it. I was tired of these bullies, and I was going to have the last word, at least.

"With as much as you guys seem to hate homosexuals, I would think you'd at least like some privacy when you circle jerk off into each other's mouths."

I let Lizzie tug me around to head out. I called over my shoulder, "Guess you thought it would be more fun with an audience rather than in the locker room like usual."

Though other patrons laughed at my barb, the circle closed ranks, not allowing us to pass. Like moths to a flame, teenagers are drawn to drama, the more humiliating the better.

They moved in tandem, controlled by some sort of mass hysteria or mob mentality that blinds the rational conscious mind of the individual, and gives over control to the collective. It was the same kind of groupthink dynamic people enjoyed at witch burning or southern lynchings. There was a palpable blood lust that hung over the crowd like a thick blanket. They were hungry to see either physical violence or psychological humiliation. Either will do, as that was the currency of their young social hierarchy. As pivotal to them as life-and-death gladiator battles. They would have blood in one fashion or another. One of us would leave this make-shift arena as a winner, the other, prey for the crowd. Licking their wounds, the losers would try to retreat before, like jackals, they would turn on them. The will of the crowd was as much my ally as his.

"What did you say to me, you hippie faggot?" Jarred snarled, clearly not used to his size and intimidation having no effect on others.

But then it happened again. That flicker behind his eyes I thought I'd seen before, and I abruptly straightened. It was so quick that even staring directly into his eyes I still wasn't sure I'd seen it. Once, I could've dismissed as a trick of the light, but...twice? It was as if his irises had...wobbled. Like a bad TV signal. It made my skin clammy and my blood cold. I didn't have the excuse of having a little too much to drink this time, but there was no way I could've seen that.

Right?

I let out a shaky breath, squinting. Was I losing my mind?

Lizzie's feet shuffled, drawing me back to the matter at hand.

Jarrod was a menace. Even adults were wary of him due to his father's position and their shared mean streak. No doubt, when he graduated, and his grades couldn't get him into college, he would seek out a position in law enforcement himself, justifying his need to bully others with a badge rather than his playground popularity. I had seen and dealt with his kind before.

My anger returned, in a hot rush of irrational testosterone.

All of this was just posturing, amounting to little more than pointless chest pounding. Not for me, but for everyone around him. Jarrod was suddenly faced with a challenger who didn't recognize his authority as king of the high school hooligans. Someone who was not impressed by his football prowess and unafraid of his threats of reprisals. His fragile, immature ego couldn't possibly comprehend this. It didn't jive with his sophomoric life view. So far, in his experiences, size and strength equated to power, and he mistook fear for respect. If he was lucky, he would never learn any different. If he was unlucky, one day, he would meet someone who actually *was* the malformed and disfigured ideal of masculinity learned from countless action movies and TV shows he fancied himself, and he would find himself on the wrong end of that stick.

The big lug was not intelligent enough to think around complex problems, to step back and take a few minutes to assess the situation before diving in headfirst. Like the bull in those Bugs Bunny cartoons, he was blinded by his own anger, and it only took a little goading from a clever wit to send him charging, head onto his own petard. When his anger boiled over, he would lash out, most likely, with his fists, and I would no doubt be the target.

He would throw the first punch, and I would have to be the bigger man and take it.

At that moment, I'd forgotten who his father was, and that a stint dealing with a serious assault charge wouldn't have much of an effect on him. One day, he would get into major trouble with the law, but today would not be that day.

I rolled my head to stretch my neck. "I said, it's weird such a big manly man like you would choose to take your boyfriends on a date in such a public forum. It's very progressive of you."

This earned a scandalized *oh* from the kids in the crowd, and only served to pour more gas on the fire.

Jarrod's eyes flared, and in them, I found the same blackness that was in his father's. An emptiness, belying a lack of conscience and a lust for violence.

The football star bared his teeth, an action which transformed his face from that of a dopey backwoods dolt into a mask of rage and humiliation. His huge hands knotted themselves into heavy fists, the knuckles cracking and popping audibly over the hushed noise of the crowd. He lowered his head as he charged the few feet that separated us.

The kids made a sound almost like a cheer as they recognized the start of the spectacle they'd been waiting for.

Even though I knew it was coming and braced myself when he cocked his fist to throw the punch, Jesus tapdancing Christmas, it still hurt. There was a dull thud as his fist collided with my nose and a blinding flash of light as my head snapped back.

For a few seconds, the world was confusion, and my vision blurred as involuntary tears welled in my eyes. Then, the pain hit. Hard. It began as an edgy drumbeat, and then exploded like a train coming out of a tunnel in a sort of Doppler effect of agony.

Something warm and wet washed over my upper lip, and I wiped it away with the back of my hand. It, unsurprisingly, came away covered in bright red blood. My sinuses were sending a warning to my brain that all was not well, but I mustered all my strength and pushed it out of my mind. I took a deep breath, and then forced it through my nose in a hard, painful snort. Gobbets of blood shot from my ruptured nasal cavities and splattered on the floor as I glared straight back into his eyes.

For a second, his expression shifted from one of anger to shock. He wasn't accustomed to someone just taking a punch. More than likely, he was used to picking on smaller kids who would fold or go flying when he hit them. Or, if they fought back, it was immediate retaliation. He clearly hadn't had someone just take a hit, much less shrug it off. Again, I had denied him what he expected and defied his victory.

As quickly as it had appeared, it was gone, replaced by false bravado and pleased self-confidence as if to say, "so there," now that he'd put the 'hippie faggot' in his place.

A baited *'Ooooooh,'* rose from the crowd, clearly impressed with my extremely stupid attempt at being macho. They'd been expecting a melee or, at the least, an entertaining one-sided beating. Now, they were held in suspense at what would come next. Was their promised fight just delayed, or had the moment passed and the window of opportunity closed?

I cleared my throat once, primarily just to choke down the whimper of pain and to keep it out of my voice. "For such a big strong football player, you sure have some pretty limp wrists," I said coldly, knowing it would sting him more than any punch I could throw. I was always faster and better with my mouth than I was with my fists.

More chuckles bubbled from the peanut gallery, and Jarrod's proud expression fell back into its angry one as he lunged at me again.

Our little scuffle had finally gained the attention of some of the adults, and several of them broke through the crowd, led by Coach Littleton. He of the large ass and ample belly, bulldozing kids aside as though it were a cow catcher on a train rather than the remains of far too many beers. Marie Latterback and Debbie Homes were in tow, hot on his heels with Joey Akerman and Brad Jefferson bringing up the rear.

They were, however, too late to stop Jarrod's second attempt at destroying a threat to his masculinity.

Time seemed to slow to a crawl as Jarrod's fist reared back for another punch. This time, he would not be satisfied with just one blow. I could see in his eyes that, this time, he was serious. He would continue punching until I either submitted or was physically unable to mock him.

There was no time for me to move or attempt to do anything other than brace myself for the assault, and hope the others would arrive to pull him off me before I was too badly injured.

As I held my breath, I caught Lizzie as she, who had been shunted aside by our pissing contest, stick out her foot. In an almost comical fashion of an old timely pratfall, designed to catch an unsuspecting foot and send its owner into a tumble, she snagged Jarrod at the ankle. It caused a hitch in his gate which sent him on a crash course with the floor that would've made Buster Keaton proud.

Clutch must have noticed Lizzie's attempt to trip up his buddy because he leaned forward, reaching out to grab Jarrod. Instead of the back of Jarrod's shirt, he managed to grab his pants, and as he fell, Clutch inadvertently pulled them down. In this accidental pantsing, somehow Jarred's underwear had gotten snagged, either by Clutch's hand or on Jarrod's own pants, and they, too, followed suit.

What felt like minutes of a slow reel took only seconds, and before anyone could help it, Jarrod Earlywine stood in the middle of the dance floor of the Community Center, everyone in the building now staring, with his pants and underwear pooled around his knees, his wedding tackle fully exposed for God and everyone.

A pregnant pause, and then the room burst out laughing.

It *was* kinda funny, not just from the breaking of the tension that had polluted the atmosphere, but because Jarrod's unmentionables looked like an acorn sitting on top of a wad of chewed gum. The juxtaposition of this big aggressive boy and his tiny genitals in all their embarrassing glory, or lack thereof, was hysterical.

My nose ached with each laugh, my terror of the past few minutes forgotten.

I was not the only one. Kids and adults alike were roaring all around us.

Jarrod's face turned a deeper shade of purplish-red with humiliation.

"No wonder you only hang out with your two cronies with a baby carrot like that," Lizzie called as the emasculated teen feverishly fought to pull his pants up, while Clutch and Troy danced about trying to apologize and shore him up.

Once he, more or less, had his pants back on, the trio retreated to the front doors, shooting dirty daggers and the occasional threats at onlookers who laughed at them. Over his shoulder, Jarrod shot Lizzie and me with an especially black glare, and the same menacing darkness moved behind his eyes.

"I'll fucking get you," he mouthed at us.

Jarrod's last threat hung in the air as Mrs. Latterback and Joey tried to get the teenagers calmed down and dispersed.

I knew Jarrod would not be humbled by this, and Sheriff Earlywine was going to rain down on everyone if Jarrod went crying to Daddy. Even if he didn't, it was unlikely his father wouldn't hear about this shameful event from someone, and once my name came up, I could bet my biscuits he'd be paying me a visit.

That was a worry for another day. For tonight, the dragon had been vanquished, and we could enjoy the rest of our evening.

CHAPTER 8

Lizzie and I hung out with Brad at the Center pretty much for the rest of the night, laughing and having a good time. The ugly business had been forgotten, and as the PTA and Women's Garden Club went on with their announcements or activities, the dance floor had been shut down to the chagrin of the younger crowd.

Parents, those of whom were here, had gathered their children, and had given Lizzie and me a wide berth. That was fine with us as we used the exile to raid what was left of the dessert table. The buffet, at least the main table, more or less had officially closed.

Brad had very little to do, and joined us in pigging out.

I had gotten through my fifth piece of transparent pie before Mr. Story called an end to the shindig, and people who were left began cleaning or gathering their belongings to leave.

Lizzie and I helped Brad clean up, though I had an ulterior motive, and that was to take as much leftover food home as possible.

We ended up walking back to my place with several tinfoil warming trays of leftovers and deserts stacked in our arms. It took a few minutes of juggling to get my keys out of my pocket. The entire time, Nimrod could be heard losing his mind on the other side of the door. The combination of us coming home and the food was causing him to switch back and forth between running the rooms and scrabbling at the door.

The minute the door was open, the dog danced between our legs, impossibly agile for his size. Hard to tell which he was happier to see, us or the food.

We somehow managed to get it all into the house while the husky was busy doing his business in the yard. Once we had put everything away, things suddenly turned into a mad scramble of hands and lips as Elizabeth all but jumped me.

There had been some electricity between us all night, especially during her rather suggestive dancing. I have to admit, part of me was more than into it. Which part should be obvious. Her arms were wrapped around my neck as she wove her fingers through my hair. Our kiss was deep and hard, and when she pulled away, her teeth bit into my lower lip, distracting me from the pain of my busted nose.

She pressed herself against me so adamantly, it was as if we were trying to merge into a single person. At the same time, my hands explored up and down her back. The chemistry between us at that moment had us drunk on our own hormones. We couldn't get enough of each other.

I ended up backing against the fridge as she climbed me, skin hot and heart thundering. Her leg somehow found its way between my thighs, and there was no longer any mystery between us.

A whine rent the air, and not from us.

We slowly ended our canoodling when we realized the dog was sitting in the middle of the kitchen floor, head tilted at an inquisitive angle, watching us. The awkwardness of the whole thing put enough of a damper on our little grope fest for us to think more or less straight. We looked at one another, embarrassed, a little red-faced, and laughed.

"Maybe we should take this somewhere a little more private and comfortable," she coquettishly suggested.

She took me by the hand and led me upstairs toward the bedroom. As we reached the top, Nimrod came galloping up the stairs behind us. He shouldered his way past us in the doorway and leapt onto the bed where he stood, grinning like a doofus.

I took him by the collar and managed to drag him out of the room. He whined and scratched at the door once I'd locked him out in the hall.

I returned to the bed, nearly out of breath, where Lizzie was perched on her knees. As I drew closer, she pulled her shirt over her head, leaving her in only a lacy pink bra.

Pale skin. Subtle curves. She stole the wind from my sails.

I pulled her close, desperate to touch her, and gently kissed the creamy skin over her collarbone as my fingertips traced her smooth, flat stomach. She ran her hands through my hair, lighting my nerves on fire, and arched as I nuzzled her neck. Her scent was sweet and subtle, that same baby powder mixed with roses, and it was all I could breathe with my face buried in her golden locks. She dropped her hands to lift the hem of my shirt, exploring my stomach, my chest, with her deft fingertips. My belly concaved at her musings as my air supply shrank.

A loud thud reverberated from the door. We both startled.

Nimrod had begun throwing himself bodily against the door. With any other dog, this wouldn't have been a problem, but the doofus easily topped a hundred and seventy-five pounds. Each time his furry shoulders hit the wood, it would cause the door frame to shake.

"Cut it out!" I yelled over my shoulder.

Lizzie, over the minor interruption, tugged my shirt over my head as she laid kisses on my chest. How I adored her mouth. Soft. Cajoling. I returned my attention to nibbling her earlobe, which made her moan. The rumble went through her and into me, heightening my need.

There was another crash, and before I could yell at the dog again, Lizzie grabbed my face.

"Shh," she whispered. "Ignore it, and maybe he'll stop."

She kissed me on the mouth hard, and it took my breath away. It was wonderful and succeeded in taking my attention off the dog trying to smash down the door.

Our hands free to roam on their own, mine found their way to her pert breasts. Firm, and just the perfect size to fit in my hands. I rubbed my thumb back and forth across her pink nipple, which instantly hardened with a little gasp from her.

Her hands had made their way to my belt buckle and she tried to undo my pants. Her breathing had become quick and shallow as excitement rose. Her green eyes shined from the room's dim lamp and sparkled as she looked up at me.

At that moment, we had forgotten everything. All was lost in the heat of the moment.

BLAM!

We jumped and craned our heads toward the sound.

The door frame had finally splintered under Nimrod's assault. The door flew open, the knob punching a hole in the wall and catching on the sheetrock.

Lizzie shrieked straight into my ear, the penetrating sound causing me to jerk away as she thrust out her arm, pointing.

I whipped my head around in time to catch Nimrod hurling himself across the room at...the window. I thought for a brief moment she was pointing at the dog, but no. She'd been pointing *outside*.

Then, for a fraction of a second, I saw *it*.

My heartbeat careened to a halt.

There had been *something* outside the window. It all happened so fast, all I made out was a big, dark shape. Only there for a flash before it disappeared, but I could have sworn it had...burning red eyes.

Nimrod jumped and snapped at the window, and I was afraid he would throw himself through it, as well. I rushed to grab his collar and tried to drag him away, but he refused to move. He had set his feet and squared his shoulders, making himself unmovable as he snarled at the window.

From outside, there was a ruckus. Something being knocked over. Trash cans? It was capped off with what sounded like a small explosion that punctuated the darkness.

My pulse pounded, making me dizzy and short of breath. What was going on?

The loud metallic *bang* finally broke through whatever had gotten into my dog and sent him scrambling into the bed with a wide-eyed Lizzie, where he cowered behind her like the big chicken he usually was.

Chest heaving, I sprinted for the door. "Stay here."

I left them both in the bedroom, rushed down the stairs, and out the back door of the kitchen. I only realized I'd forgotten my shirt when the cool night air hit my bare chest.

In my postage stamp backyard, I found Joey Akerman standing over something lying on the ground. He was shaking like a leaf, which didn't inspire confidence in me, considering in his hands he held the biggest revolver I'd ever seen. It looked ridiculously oversized when compared to the short, pudgy man.

Frantic, my gaze darted between him, the gun, and whatever was laying shapeless in the grass, mere feet from the house, under my upstairs bedroom window. I glanced up, the yellowish glow from my bedroom lamp piercing the night.

Brad's back door slammed open as he came rushing out, flashlight in hand. He jogged over to us, dressed only in his boxers and bathrobe. He at least had the presence of mind to put on slippers. I was standing in the cold, wet grass with my bare feet.

"Jeez-us Christ, what the hell was that?" Brad skidded to a halt next to me.

"I-I-I d-d-unno," Joey stammered. "I was in my kitchen, making a cup of tea, when I heard someone scream. I ran out my back door to find out what was going on when I saw some kind of animal jump off Josh's roof. I just shot it before I could think." He was so panicky, his words came out a mile a minute.

Brad spotted the gun Joey was barely holding on to. "Holy hell, where did you get a hand cannon like that?" He gingerly took the gun before a trembling Joey could accidentally shoot someone.

It was hard to imagine he'd been able to fire the behemoth, much less hit anything with it.

"The Second Amendment says I can own any gun I want."

"Yeah, well, as the only black man around, I'm gonna have to insist on holding onto your Second Amendment until you're in a calmer state." Brad looked over the revolver. "What the hell did you shoot at, anyway? A gun this big would vaporize a possum."

Joey pointed to the lump lying in my yard.

We all turned.

It definitely wasn't a possum. Whatever it had been, it must've been standing on the overhang above the kitchen, looking into my bedroom window. *My second-story bedroom window.* When Nimrod had scared it off, it probably jumped down the side of the house, landing on my garbage cans, putting it only a few feet from Joey's own back door. Where he'd shot it. The impact had most likely knocked it back into my yard, where it now lay on its side.

Brad shined his light on it as we all looked at the corpse.

I couldn't tell what it was, but it was big. Slightly larger than a mountain lion but smaller than a bear with elongated gangly limbs ending in wicked-looking claws. Its shoulders were broad and well-muscled like the rest of the body. The head was hard to make out as Joey's bullet had torn away most of the left side of its face. Brains and flecks of bone gleamed in the beam of the flashlight. It seemed vaguely canine, but malformed. I couldn't tell if it was like that naturally or if that was from the damage caused by the gunshot. Short, dark fur covered it, which was more like bristles than fur. Porcupine-ish. It was patchy in some areas, as though it hadn't fully grown in.

The whole thing was horrifying, like something out of a nightmare or a wicked sci-fi B flick. Its spike-like fangs seemed to glow in the dark as the light played off their whiteness in contrast to the inkiness of the night.

"What the hell is it?" I asked.

"It sure as hell ain't no possum," Brad replied, playing the flashlight over it.

"It kinda looks like a bear." Joey leaned closer and pushed up his thick glasses to get a better look at it.

"That don't look like any bear I ever seen." Brad shook his head.

I agreed. This thing was terrifying, too oddly contoured to be a bear, and I wasn't even sure we had bears in Fleming County. It looked more like a child's drawing with its exaggerated limbs and teeth like railroad spikes. The eyes were listless and dull, making it impossible to believe it had been alive. A chill ran down my spine as I recalled those glowing red eyes I thought I'd seen out my window. Nothing in nature I knew of had eyes that could literally glow, never mind red.

"Well, I think that's 'cause it probably has mange." Joey tilted his head. "Normally, when you see bears, they look fat and fluffy since they're covered in a thick layer of fur. I've seen pictures of black bears with mange, and they kinda look like this."

"Do we even have bears around here?" I asked.

"Yeah, black bears are native to Kentucky, but they're something of a rarity in this area in particular."

I'd seen pictures in elementary school of animals, bears included, with mange, and this still didn't seem to fit. For one, the body contour and fur were off, and what little there was left of the head wasn't the same shape.

"Well, whatever it is, it's dead now." Brad toed the dead creature with one slipper, his facial expression indicating he wasn't believing the bear story, either. The animal didn't respond. If it had, all three of us probably would have shit bricks and had simultaneous heart attacks. "Not surprising, since you blew away half its head."

"What do we do?" I asked. "It's too late to call Animal Control. Besides, Jeff is probably in bed at this hour."

Joey took off his glasses and wiped them on the edge of his robe. "We can cover it with a tarp for tonight, then call the Sheriff in the morning to see what he wants to do about it. If there is one...bear like this, there may be more, and he might want to put out an alert. That way, people don't investigate if they hear their garbage cans getting knocked over and find themselves face-to-face with one."

"Knowing the folks around here, they'd be more apt to shoot the critters than to be scared," Brad added, toeing it again.

"Yeah, and that's the problem. They might shoot without thinking and accidentally hurt themselves or someone."

"Kinda like you just did?"

Joey turned bright red at Brad's words, obviously a little embarrassed he had more or less just described his own actions.

Given the size of the gun, I was surprised there was any of its head left. Chunks of gore had splattered as far away as Brad's yard. It made my stomach a little queasy. The pie I had eaten earlier threatened to make a reappearance.

"Hey, Brad, if I grab one of my tarps, can I borrow some of those cinder blocks you got stacked in your garage?" I tried to suppress my urge to vomit.

"Yeah, I got some busted-up ones sitting to the side. A couple of them will do the job, and no one should walk off with 'em."

I ran back inside to fetch a tarp, and returned with the painting one we'd used for the living room and kitchen.

Brad and Joey helped to spread the tarp over the dead animal, and we pinned the corners with chunks of concrete. The job finished, we stood back to look at it all. It was like a scene out of a mobster movie, and we'd just buried a dead body. Something about it felt almost criminal in nature.

"In the morning, I'll call Animal Control, and probably the Sheriff. He may want to see this," Joey supplied, breaking the silent reverence of our quasi-funeral.

"Alright, I say we call it a night, gents. It's late, and my balls are freezing."

Brad was right. The night had taken a turn for the chilly in contrast to how warm it had been several hours ago. The weather had been absolutely bipolar—days boiling hot while the nights seemed to plunge to near freezing. My grandmother would always say that was a sure sign we were going to get an Indian summer.

I watched from my back door as Joey and Brad made their way back to their own homes. I kept watching until the doors had closed and their lights had turned out. I flicked off my own kitchen light and continued to watch in the semi-dark, even though I should check on Lizzie.

There was a bit of illumination cast by the streetlights out front of the gas station. Long, dark shadows fell across the back-yards. I peered into their depths for any sign of movement. The hairs on my arms and the back of my neck stood on end as a sense of dread fell upon me. An uneasy feeling knotted my stomach as paranoia sent my brain into overdrive. My nerves had become a tightly wound wire as I watched and waited. Even the slightest noise at that moment would have given me a stroke. I slowly counted my breaths as minutes ticked by, so slowly that they seemed to stretch for hours.

Once I had finally managed to calm myself, I headed back upstairs. In my bedroom, I found Lizzie and Nimrod sitting on the bed. She was practically wrapped around the big dog, looking like a child clutching a large stuffed animal. Her expression was pale, eyes round and frightened.

"What happened?" The catch in her throat indicated she was on the verge of hysterics, and I was not far behind her. Even Nimrod looked like his last nerve was fraying.

Guilt clawed at my gut because I'd left her unknowing too long.

"It's nothing, just some animal on the roof, and that's what was driving the dog crazy." I neglected to say what *kind* of animal, not just because we didn't know exactly what it was, but because it would've only panicked her more.

"But, what was that noise? It sounded like a gunshot."

"It was. It knocked over the garbage cans when it jumped off the roof. The noise caused Mr. Akerman to check it out. It scared him and he shot it."

"It sounded like a goddamn cannon." She pulled the dog closer, burying her face in his fur.

Nimrod let her and smiled his doggy grin, happy at the attention now that all the commotion was over.

I pried the doorknob out of the wall and made a mental note to add drywall repair to my list of things to fix. Once closed and locked, something about the idea of as many locked doors between me and the outside was comforting.

I got into bed next to them. There were no attempts to rekindle the passion that had been interrupted. The moment was thoroughly past, and there would be no more after our fright.

We tried to make ourselves as comfortable as possible. The problem being, there wasn't much room. It was a full-size bed that barely fit two people, much less two people and a nearly two hundred pound dog. Nimrod settled himself between us, and there would be no moving him unless he wanted to.

He didn't sprawl out like he normally did when napping. He lay between us, his head cocked back, looking over his furry shoulder, his eyes set on the window.

Lizzie threw one arm over him and pulled him close to her, but still, the dog kept looking at the window. Even in the darkened bedroom, he stood sentinel, solely fixated on it, his ears perked and swiveling like two radar dishes as he listened to sounds we couldn't hear.

As I started to drift off to sleep, I realized that, since I had returned upstairs, not once had he taken his eyes off of it.

Chapter 9

The next day was one of the worst of my life, and the apparent start of a downward spiral. I woke late enough the sun was pouring through my bedroom window. Having forgotten to pull the shades, it was positively blinding. I slapped a pillow over my face in an attempt to block out the invading light threatening to burn out my retinas.

My sleep had been troubled and all too brief. Fragments of nightmares filled with dark, shapeless shadows and burning red eyes slowly faded in the early morning light. The sun chased the monsters back into the shadows where they belong.

It slowly dawned on me I was alone in the bed, making it feel much larger and oddly empty. I lifted my head and opened one eye to look around. I was, indeed, alone. Bedclothes were left in a tangle, hanging from one corner of the mattress. Neither Lizzie nor Nimrod were to be seen. I assumed she'd gone downstairs, and the dog had followed her. Otherwise, he would have been sprawled out on the bed. Most mornings, he refused to budge until he heard food being put in his bowl.

I could hear someone arguing outside, even from upstairs in the bedroom, which was what finally drove me to get up.

I pulled a shirt over my head as I descended the stairs, having slept in my jeans. In the kitchen, I found Lizzie wearing one of my white t-shirts. The hem fell just below her ass, giving hints of her pink panties as she shifted her weight from side to side. She was looking out my back door, watching the activity going on in the yard.

I joined her, curious myself, looking over her head.

Brad and Joey were out back, the tarp pulled back, as they seemingly showed the dead animal to Sheriff Earlywine.

I sighed. He was the last person I wanted to see after last night.

Lizzie handed me her cup of coffee, and I took a sip.

It was still warm, and a dull brown color from all the added sugar and cream. It had been far sweeter than I was used to, normally taking it black out of habit and laziness more than preference.

I was going to have to go out there, though I really didn't want to. This was going to be a disaster of biblical proportions. From the sound of it, Earlywine was already in a foul mood, and my going out there was only going to serve to make it worse. The cords in his neck stood out as he and Brad had a shouting match in my backyard.

"How long have they been at it?" I asked as she took the cup of coffee back and drank from it.

"Not sure, but the Sheriff went postal a few minutes ago. He's been screaming nearly non-stop. If he isn't careful, he is going to have a coronary on your lawn."

Great, that's just what I needed, for the cop to vapor lock on my property. I have no doubt the town gossips would go nuclear at the idea of him having to be carted out by ambulance, the day after his son and I had made spectacles of ourselves in public.

I opened the door. I was planning on putting a stop to this, hopefully through de-escalation of the situation, however, it was more likely I was going to get punched again.

About halfway across the yard, I realized he could flip his lid completely and shoot me with that big gun of his, but at that point, it was too late. I was committed. Though stupidly approaching a pissed-off Sheriff after humiliating his kid was probably the kind of thing you get committed for.

The scene was not much better up close. Brad and the Sheriff were almost nose-to-nose. The brim of his bear hat was pressed against the big black man's forehead, causing it to bend skywards. They were locked eye-to-eye as Earlywine bellowed in the other man's face. Spittle flew from his lips as he yelled, and a large angry vein pulsed in his temple. It throbbed in time to each word as it approached its apex. It really did look like he was about to give himself a stroke.

The difference between the two men was very apparent due to their proximity, and if a fight were to break out, it was clear who would win. Both were tall, but the Sheriff still towered over Brad by a few inches, just enough so he had to look up to meet his eyes. The most notable difference was in their builds. While the retired electrician had probably been broadly stocky and strong in his younger days, time and one too many greasy meals had softened him. His paunch looked more pronounced in comparison. Earlywine, on the other hand, was like the side of a cliff. Solid bulk from his bull-like neck down to his overly ample ass. There was a mountain of muscle under that mass. The kind you get from years of bailing hay and plowing field harvest after harvest. Solid farm muscle. More powerlifter than bodybuilder.

His barrel of a chest seemed to expand with every inhale, testing the limits of his shirt. It was a testament to its quality the fabric didn't split along every seam. The gold star on his chest looked as though it was about to tear itself free of its mooring and go rocketing off into space, possibly taking out someone's eye.

I was struck by the sudden notion he looked like one of those spiny little puffer fish that suck in air to puff themselves up to look bigger and scarier than they are.

That, however, was not the case here. I was positive he was just as dangerous as he appeared.

In contrast to the two large men, little Joey Ackerman was running around them looking even more absurdly tiny. His attempts to intervene were dismissed and drowned out by all the shouting. Shouting, which I couldn't make sense of, due to its volume.

However, I was able to catch the last part, and my temples throbbed in sheer rage.

"...more pressing things to do with my time. I don't need to come running every time some faggot finds a dead badger. So, don't think affirmative action gives you the right to waste my time, you uppity nigger."

That last sentence landed like a bomb, putting an end to their conversation, if you could even call it that. The silence was nearly as deafening as the shouting had been. Their nostrils flared like angry horses as the two men continued their staring contest, neither refusing to give an inch.

I was shocked, for more reasons than one, but definitely at Brad's self-control. Granted, this was a lot farther south and antiquated than New York, and hearing someone using derogatory words like that one or even 'coon' was more common than it ever had a right to be, especially in front of black people. Not accounting for the homophobic slur directed at Joey. Sadly, it wasn't necessarily a voluntary racial slur in these parts, as people around here were ignorant, uneducated, didn't know any better, or cared. None of those were ever an excuse. At any rate, this was clearly not the case because the slur had been intentional.

And I'm not sure if Brad didn't punch the POS because he was the Sheriff or because he didn't think it was worth it. Whatever the reason, he had better restraint than if it had been me.

The tension between the two was broken when Sheriff Earlywine turned away, obviously feeling his dominance was established, probably thinking the 'black man' was too chickenshit to do anything.

This was not a good thing because when he turned around, he and I were now face-to-face. He didn't speak, but his whole body tensed.

When I met Earlywine's eyes, his pupils had contracted to pinpoints, nearly disappearing into the irises. I'm not sure if I'd ever noticed or if it was just a trick of the light, but they were a bright amber color. They didn't look human at all. Predatory and animalistic, they were deep and somehow cold, filled with that strange anger I'd witnessed before. The same darkness had been in his son Jarrod's eyes.

And...the similarities didn't end there. The madness in his eyes caused them to look like they were flickering. It must've been some sort of trick of the light because they seemed to flicker in time with the pulsing vein in his temple. As if spotting it caused it to cease to exist, it vanished.

Flick, flick, gone. So fast, I couldn't have said if it was really there or just my imagination.

I straightened slightly, my palms going sweaty, and couldn't stop my sharp inhale of surprise if my life depended on it.

Earlywine bristled, and for a moment, I thought he was going to lunge at me, based on his murderous expression.

Instead, he stalked angrily and stiff-legged around the side of the house. A few minutes later, his patrol car pulled away, tires scraping cement.

Only then did I realize I'd been holding my breath, and I let it out in a whoosh.

Joining Joey and Brad standing around the tarp, we all took a moment to settle ourselves.

"What the hell was that about?" I asked after a few beats.

"No idea," Joey squeaked, clearly still rattled. "He seemed fine enough when I called him out this morning." He shifted his weight to his other foot. "But when he pulled back the tarp, he went ballistic. Started yelling at us about wasting his time with dead coyotes and accused us of trying to start a panic. Not sure why."

"Man's got a bug up his ass." Brad cleared his throat. "We'll call Animal Control, which is what we should've done in the first place. Let them deal with his bullshit." There was a rough edge to his voice. Clearly, he was relieved the confrontation was over, but still irritated. He crossed his arms over his chest, but with his big belly, it just looked like he was resting them on it. "You got to see this, though. Joey, show him."

I cocked an eyebrow, confused at their worried expressions.

Joey motioned me over as he knelt next to the covered carcass. I hunkered down to join him, and with a flourish, he threw back the tarp.

The smell nearly bowled me over as it rushed out and hit me full in the face. It was a foul, sour odor, like rotten eggs and sulfur. My eyes started to water, and I had to turn away while suppressing the urge to vomit.

What was under the tarp was even worse. When I was able to look back, I was astonished.

The animal had only been dead a few hours, but the corpse was already badly decayed. The skin had grayed and pulled tight to the bones instead of bloating as fresh cadavers do. Each rib and the spinal column stood out starkly, the dense muscle it had been covered in last night now gone. In its shrunken state, it did look like a mangy coyote, except it was nearly six feet long. The eyes had sunken into the skull, leaving dark empty pits. The hole in its skull where the bullet had smashed the life out of the animal was flush with maggots, and the dried bits of brain underneath were black. What was left of the bristle-like fur was dried and brittle, gray in the areas that hadn't turned black from blood. Which was odd in itself because blood wouldn't coagulate that quick to turn black.

I had no words for what I saw. I couldn't explain it. My head was reeling from the stench and trying to comprehend what I was seeing. This animal had been rendered nearly skeletal in a few hours. This wasn't normal, and all I cared about was having it off my lawn.

Joey switched over to what I would assume was his teaching method. As though we were sitting in his science class instead of grown adults. "The level of decomposition is peculiar. Usually, animals bloat as they decay and fill with gas. That is what we should be seeing, but yet this one is emaciated and nearly gone as if it's been out here for weeks. This rate of decay should be impossible naturally."

He was far more interested in it than either me or Brad, who also looked a little green around the gills as he held his shirt collar over his nose as an improvised gas mask.

"I'll call Jeff over at the Road Department to come take this thing," I said as I stood, happy to have some distance between me and the dead thing on the ground. I wanted it gone as soon as possible.

I jogged back to my door, leaving the two men behind. The door banged closed behind me, and I felt a little better being inside and away from it.

Lizzie was no longer in the kitchen, having probably taken the opportunity to return to the bedroom and get dressed. I still had to fight my way past Nimrod, who was doing his excitement dance around my feet. It was hard not to trip over him or accidentally step on his paws or tail when he got like this. I finally managed to shove him away as I dug through the pile of detritus sitting beneath my phone.

I'd finally broken down and ponied up for the phone a couple weeks ago, though it had involved some begging for money from my parents. The begging came in the form of doing favors and chores as though I were a teenager asking for an allowance, despite being in my mid-twenties. Something about being in the presence of a childhood home seems to regress us all back to our formative years and the kids we once were.

Managing to find the dog-eared copy of the phone directory, I flipped it open to the municipal section and found the number for Fleming Animal Control. After about half an hour on hold, I was told they would be sending someone out after lunch, and asked if I would be present. I confirmed, and hung up.

Now, I just had to deal with Lizzie. Last night had been a comedy of elements resulting in, ironically, one of the best and worst dates possible. I had to have that awkward next morning talk, despite nothing having happened last night. That being the case, I had very little faith in a second chance, but it was entirely possible this could turn into one of those goofy stories we retell years later about how we met.

Romanticized notions aside, it was a mess I was not looking forward to dealing with. I was trying to think of ways to put it off when I noticed, once again, the notable absence of both woman and dog. I stuck my head into the kitchen to find it empty. There was a note on the table written on a page torn from one of the yellow legal pads I used to take notes.

Josh,

Took off. Sorry for not saying bye, but you were on the phone. Need to check in on Gran and assure her I wasn't murdered or kidnapped. I'll be back later, promise.

Lizzie

P.S., I let Nimrod out, he should be in the front yard.

Reading the handwritten note offered some relief. I had dodged a potentially awkward conversation, at least temporarily.

I let out a sigh and made a beeline straight to the fridge, fetching a bottle of beer. Before noon, be damned. It was either this or just counting off the day as a loss and heading back to bed. It was gone in two gulps, and the empty went into the bin next to the back door.

With a fresh bottle in my hand, I returned to the living room and let Nimrod back into the house. Even though it was October, the day was already gearing up to be another scorcher.

I settled onto the couch with my beer and turned on the TV. It was one of those large wooden paneled jobs where the television set was built into the cabinet. It didn't fit with any of the other mismatched furnishings in the place, and that somehow made it seem at home.

It had been a refugee from my parents' house when I'd visited to ask for money. Dad was all too happy to show off the new Sony they'd purchased. I'd asked why they just didn't stick one in their bedroom. They'd be damned if they'd become one of 'those people' who have a TV in the bedroom. Dad had helped me get it into the car, no small task.

I flipped channels. There were only three the rabbit ears would pick up, so I ended up whiling the day away watching trashy daytime television on the couch with my dog's head in my lap as he dozed. While he wasn't above eating poop, bad soap operas and talk shows were beneath his tastes.

The parade of shows and commercials marched on and, before I knew it, it was almost five o'clock. Looking away from the

TV, I noted a battalion of empty beer bottles had cluttered the coffee table.

Rising, my gait had a bit of a wobble to it. I managed to stagger to the kitchen, and looked out the window over the sink. The tarp and what was under it were still there. Definitely a lump, like a dune in the middle of that miniature blue desert. It sent shivers down my spine. Something about the situation just turned my stomach. I was about to call Animal Control again to see what was taking so long when there came the honk of a car horn from out front.

I nearly tripped on the coffee table on my way to the front door, sending bottles rolling across the carpet for the dog to gaily chase. Swearing and clutching my bashed shin, I managed to hop to the door without falling over. Hanging onto the jam, I threw open the door and looked beyond the screen.

At the curb sat a rusty white pickup used by the city as work trucks. The man hanging out the window was nearly as grizzled and weathered as his ride. I could just about make out a bright red ball cap perched on his head, which barely hid his wiry white hair, as sunlight flared off his windshield, blinding me.

Squinting, I waved an arm at him, signaling him to pull around back.

His head jerked in acknowledgment, and he pulled away from the curb. His truck spluttered around the corner, its tone changing as it turned into the alley that ran between our houses and the gas station.

The truck's engine cut just as I was exiting the back door. I had to fight the dog to stop him from bounding into the backyard. I didn't want Nimrod anywhere near whatever that thing was.

Jeff Helpenstein opened the truck's tailgate, where he fetched a shovel as I unlatched the back gate for him.

"So, you said you got a dead animal?"

"Yeah."

"And you said you didn't know what it is."

"Pretty much. Never seen anything like it. The neighbors don't even know what it is." I motioned to the tarp in the yard.

Jeff just looked at it as he took a cigarette from the pack in his shirt pocket, tucking it behind his ear.

"Whelp," he said with a grunt. "Let's have a look. Probably just a possum or something." He strode across the yard.

I moved one of the blocks holding the tarp and threw it back, uncovering the corpse.

"Sweet baby Jesus."

The stench that rolled out nearly knocked us over. I clasped my hands over my nose in an attempt to block out the sour odor. Jeff pulled his oil-stained shirt up over his mouth and nose.

The carcass was even more desiccated than I'd remembered. It was little more than misshapen bones, held together by ropy strands of tendons and skin, with sparse amounts of bristly fur that had gone gray. The grass beneath it, which had been lush and green, had turned a sickly yellow color, and the ground looked almost as though it had been scorched. The very defi-nition of desolation.

Jeff poked it with the end of his spade. "How long has it been out here?" He tried to lift part of the remains, and it pulled up chunks of the ground as if the rotting had adhered it to the earth.

"Just since last night. It was alive when the neighbor shot it. Any idea what the hell it is, or was?" I asked.

"No clue on God's green Earth. Kinda looks like it might be a big dog or somethin', but it shouldn't have this level of decay after just a day, even in this here heat. Heat speeds up decomposition. Seen it make deer on the side of the road bloat after about a day, but not like this. Sure it was alive?"

"Yeah, it wasn't this bad last night or this morning when the Sheriff was out here."

"And what did Doug say about it?"

He continued to pry the animal loose with his shovel, leaving divots where his blade separated it from the ground, taking portions of dirt with it. The man was already sweating from the work as the day was another record-breaking hot one. By this point, it was feeling less like summer and more like God had a personal grudge against the county.

"He didn't so much say anything. More like he went off on one of my neighbors for calling. It got a little heated."

I made sure to stand clear as he flipped the remains over onto the tarp, leaving a shallow crater in the lawn. The patch looked depressing, surrounded by the beauty of the rest of the yard.

Little white maggots squirmed in the dirt as they tried to flee from the sunlight.

"Don't right blame him, given the news he got this morning." Jeff stopped to take the cigarette from behind his ear and poked it between his lips. He offered me his pack, and I took one.

They were the cheap brand, but I wasn't picky. Being a broke college student teaches what you can and can't live without, and you learn how to compromise. Tobacco and Alcohol are two things you become very flexible on. I lit mine with my zippo and offered him the lighter.

He just shook his head and pulled out one of those Bics like from the gas station counter. He lit up and took a long drag.

"What news?" I asked curiously, but for some reason, I couldn't put my finger on why my stomach was heavy with dread.

His bushy eyebrows furrowed for a moment as he caught up to where he'd left off. "It was all over the radio this morning. Figured with the town gossips, you might have heard it through the grapevine. His deputy, Darryl, that simple boy whose eyes are too far apart? He found the Sheriff's boy's truck turned over in the Licking River just south of the quarries. They think he was drunk, rolled the vehicle, and drowned."

The bottom fell out of my stomach. Dizzy, my vision went gray. I had to put my head between my knees until the feeling of being violently sick passed.

Jarrod Earlywine was dead. It seemed impossible. I'd just seen him last night. Even though the kid was an ass, it was still a punch in the gut. There was a weight on my shoulders, and I couldn't help but think it was somehow my fault. That he'd gone out to drink off his humiliation, only to end up losing his life. I might as well have killed him myself.

Jeff's voice broke through my daze as my vision began to clear.

"I'm okay," I reassured him when I was positive I wasn't going to vomit.

"That's good. I was saying, I heard there was some kinda commotion over the Community Center last night with some of the kids. You suppose he had anything to do with that? He was quite a troublemaker from what people say, so it's not much of a stretch they kicked him out, and then he went and got plastered."

"You could say that." Again, my stomach rolled, threatening to send its contents back up. The heat wasn't helping, and I wouldn't have been surprised if I passed out at some point soon.

It was just a lot to take in the last twenty-four hours. I was physically and mentally exhausted, and the shock to my system had sobered me completely.

"It's gonna be a hell of a loss to the football team. They were looking good this year. The best season we've ever had."

Carefully balancing the carcass on his shovel, Jeff quick-stepped it across the yard, and with a simple deft motion, flipped it over the fence into the back of his truck as though it were a pancake. The bones clattered against the truck's steel bed. It was an unearthly sound. Not at all like the noise they made in old Mickey Mouse cartoons that were funny, made on a xylophone. This was somehow darkly final, a ghastly death rattle.

I suddenly couldn't get those words out of my head. Death. Rattle. Had Jarrod made his own death rattle when his lungs filled with water in the cab of his overturned truck as he drowned? Had he been scared? Angry? Or had he been thinking of how he'd been humiliated and who'd done it?

Satisfied that his job was done, Jeff tossed a tarp over the dead thing in his truck and hopped back into the cab. The old beater let out a belch of foul, greasy black smoke as it pulled out. It puttered down the alley, sounding as if it would stall out at any moment. It turned the corner and disappeared from sight, leaving behind only the grating of its struggling engine.

As if a magic spell had broken, everything came back into focus, and I was suddenly all too aware of the world around me.

Mowing lawns.

Kids screeching while playing.

Cars going by on the street.

Someone yelling a few blocks over.

The smell of fresh cut grass and someone grilling in their backyard.

It was all too much for me, overwhelmingly so, and I hurried back inside, making a beeline straight for the cabinet and something a hell of a lot stronger than beer.

CHAPTER 10

Two hours later, I found myself pacing the sidewalk outside Lizzie's house. She wasn't home yet, and I was angrily questioning why and who has classes on a Saturday. I had killed the better part of a bottle of Jack Daniels and couldn't get my brain to calm down. I couldn't stop thinking that I was somehow responsible for someone's death. Yeah, I'd wished people death before and threatened to kill someone in a heated moment, but it was so different when face-to-face with the actual reality.

While I was in the middle of a drunken panic attack, her Plymouth station wagon pulled into the driveway.

"Josh, what's wrong?" She opened the door. "You're pale as a sheet."

She led me inside as I tried to explain everything at once, but my foggy brain and clumsy mouth just jumbled everything around to the point any sane person would've had me committed. She took me by the hand and guided me into the kitchen. Pulling out one of the kitchen chairs, she sat me down at the table before going to the sink and fetching a glass of water.

"Here, drink this." She handed it to me.

I drank it in a single gulp.

"Coffee." The croaky voice made both of us jump. "You need to get some coffee into him. The blacker, the better."

Lizzie's grandmother stood in the doorway, and neither of us had noticed her. Not that you could blame us. The old lady could've been stomping around in wooden clogs firing a pistol in each hand, and we still might have missed her. Lizzie had been concerned about the state I was in, and I was three sheets to the wind.

"Jesus Christ, Gran, you scared the shit out of us."

"Don't curse in this house, and put the pot on. The boy is fully in the bag, and it's the middle of the afternoon. It's a shame, too many men are in love with the bottle instead of the Holy Mother these days."

She puttered across the room to where Lizzie had begun making coffee and motioned her out of the way before taking over the operation. Within seconds, she had the coffee maker chugging away, and before I knew it, a hot cup was shoved into my hands.

I sipped, my tongue blistering from the heat.

After the second cup, I was able to string enough words together to make coherent sentences. I told them what I'd learned from Jeff Helpenstein this afternoon.

Lizzie was almost as shocked as I had been, though it was clear she wasn't all that upset Jarod was dead. I guess she didn't feel as responsible as I did. Sobering had helped to take some of the edge off, but that hot ball of guilt sitting in the pit of my stomach was still there. Though it could've been the coffee, either way, I still felt sick about it.

Lizzie's grandmother sat across the table, sucking her teeth in the way people with dentures tend to do. It kinda made her look a bit like Mr. Ed, the talking horse.

"Bad blood," she said, breaking her silence. She hadn't said a single word the whole time I'd been rambling. "Bad blood," she repeated. "You can't get that kinda madness out of a family once it's set in. All them Earlywine men have been like that since Hector was a pup. Hot-headed, short tempered, always going off half-cocked, with a mean streak a mile wide. Men like them have always got to be top dogs, got to be the leader of the pack, but Mother Nature knows how to deal with them. Fools weed themselves out. They die in bar fights, kill each other in pointless squabbles, and yes, even drunk driving accidents." She put her wrinkled old hand on mine and gave it a light squeeze. "Don't beat yourself up over it. Men like that find one excuse or another for their own poor choices. If not last night, it would have been over one thing or another. Bad blood will out, in the end, that boy was heading for no good."

She rose from the table and shuffled over to the sink. Looking at the backyard through the window, she sighed. "That boy was trouble since he was born, and it didn't help his daddy done gone and spoiled him. Never let him face the consequences of his actions. It teaches kids the wrong lesson, and they pass it around. Spare the rod, spoil the child. If ever there was a child that needed his hide tanned, it was that one." She paused while rinsing out her cup. "It's always sad to lose a child before their time, but that's nature for you. Survival of the fittest, and all that evolution malarkey they teach in schools these days. I still say it's divine will, fools meet foolish ends. The Holy Mother knows what they're doing."

Lizzie rolled her eyes, hiding it behind taking a sip from her own coffee.

Apparently, her grandmother saw it. I have no idea how since she had her back turned at the time, and delivered a light smack to the back of Lizzie's head.

"Don't try me, child."

Which only caused Lizzie to giggle, earning her a stern, disproving look that the old woman must've used to stare down hundreds of students back in her teaching days. "If you're still feeling guilty about it, you should come to church with us tomorrow. See if praying for forgiveness doesn't ease that burden."

I couldn't recall the last time I'd been to church. My parents had drug me along every Sunday because that was just what you did. You got dressed up and went to church, whether you were a believer or not, and then you ate brunch at a restaurant.

In college, I once heard it said religion is not about getting answers, but stopping questions. The typical kind of naive cynicism you'd expect from kids who still believe they know everything, yet are learning that the world, in general, is out to screw them over. I couldn't help but think, what harm could there be in at least giving it a shot? After all, isn't that what hitting rock bottom was for? At the very least, the exercise could be cathartic if nothing else, and it would afford me a pretext to spend more time with Lizzie.

So, I agreed.

"Good, at least I'll have someone to be miserable with," Lizzie said later as I helped her wash dishes. "She drags me along every Sunday."

She'd managed to talk me into staying for dinner, which had been worth it. Though I still had plenty of leftovers we'd filched from the party the night before, it was nice to have a freshly cooked hot meal. After dinner, we sat in her grandmother's living room, watching reruns of the 'Andy Griffith Show'. For those few hours, I was able to forget the nightmare of the past few days.

I was up by seven the next morning, and I felt like hell. My head pounded like a drum and the inside of my mouth felt like it was coated with that sticky stuff they put on theater floors.

The sun was just coming up, turning the horizon into a pallet of oranges and purples. I was so hungover, even the sunrise was blinding. It felt like a railroad spike made of ice was being pounded through my eye socket directly into my temples. I poured myself two fingers as a medicinal precaution just so I could get out the door without bleeding from my retinas.

Churchgoing had never been a habit of mine, and I hadn't been since I was a kid. So, my wardrobe was lacking in that area. I just threw on whatever was cleanest, and wasn't my day-to-day jeans and t-shirt. I couldn't do much about my hair other than running a wet comb through it. The ending result was presentable, and I tucked a flask into my jacket pocket just in case I needed to ward off my hangover again.

The walk wasn't as bad as it could've been. I hadn't been able to find a pair of sunglasses. At this point, it would've just been advertising I was an alcoholic.

There are two churches in Midnight Falls. Something quite odd about the country itself, but seems to be even more pronounced in small towns. For a county of just a little upward of five hundred residents, two parishes seemed like more than enough. Just a mile up the road in Elizaville, there was another. Fleming was even worse, though it was much larger with a population of over two thousand. They had six, which seemed to me like overkill.

I had been so lost in my own thoughts on the subject I hadn't realized I'd walked clear across town. Granted, it's a five-minute walk, as the town is only a couple of blocks wide, but I had completely zoned out during the whole trek. Of the two churches in Midnight Falls, the Baptist was just across the street and two doors down, a block over from Lizzie's grandmother's house. Things, of course, are never that easy. Her grandmother attended the old First Church of Midnight Falls, at the other end of School Road.

It was ancient. It was nearly two hundred years old, having been built when early settlers had first laid the foundations for what would become Fleming County back in 1789. The original church had been burned down back in the late 1800s when lightning struck it, and the new church was built on top of its old foundation. I personally have to question the efficacy of rebuilding any structure God had already deemed to burn down himself. One would think it would be more of a middle finger to the Almighty rather than an act of praise, but one does not go looking for logic among fanatics.

The First Church of the Holy Mother was one of those Old Testament fire and brimstone fundamentalist types of congregations. I had agreed to come based on the assumption it was one of those toe-tapping psalms and hymns churches. Growing up, we'd been Methodist—of the proper bow your head and don't look God in the eye—Christians. Not like those tambourine-slapping, bound-for-hell Baptists.

This congregation was an entirely different experience, and I was surprised they were all locals. As far as I could tell, not a single person outside of Lizzie and myself was from elsewhere. I recognized almost every single one of them from the Community Center party Friday night, save for the handful of elderly people, who wouldn't miss an episode of Matlock even if they were having a heart attack right there on the living room floor.

Thankfully, Lizzie was there to get me through. She met me out front, wearing another of those adorable sundresses that showed off her long legs and highlighted her golden wheat hair.

She'd been escorting her grandmother, dressed in a robin's egg blue dress and matching pillbox hat that made her look like Jackie Onassis—if someone had run her through a food dehydrator a few times. I offered the old woman my arm in a mock gesture of chivalry, and she took it with a laugh.

As the three of us headed in, I could feel the eyes of everyone on us. Outsiders are always regarded with suspicion, even in some places as innocent as church, a holdover of tribal instincts designed to ensure the group's survival. Of course, in rural towns, it tends to metamorphose, becoming slightly to outright hostile xenophobia.

I blanked out again, lost in my thoughts as we took our seats in the weathered old pews. The place was little more than a giant shoebox. Not a lot of architectural imagination had gone into the rebuild. The walls were not insulated, and the windows were blurry and dulled with age. It was only eight in the morning, and it was already stifling. There was no air conditioning and barely any electricity. As a concession to the heat, the front doors had been left open, and a single old shop fan struggled to circulate air up the aisle. A door near them led to the balcony that overlooked the seating area. It was bolted with a sign reading 'Out of Order' taped to it. Rot had caused them to close it due to structural issues. The size of the congregation made me wonder if they had ever really needed that many seats. There were barely enough people to fill up two-thirds of the pews with several empty seats.

I could swear all of their eyes were on me, or it could be I was just more paranoid due to being visibly hungover and I had residual guilt.

Their eyes were cold and hollow, tracking our every movement, as we were clearly intruding into their territory. We were in the mouth of the dragon itself, the two people responsible for humiliating the town golden boy and, from their perspective, possibly responsible for his accident. I could swear I heard low whispers when our backs were turned. We were the outsiders. We were the invaders. We were the enemies here to upset their lives and destroy their way of life. Perhaps it was all just in my paranoid, addled brain. I had gotten little sleep over the weekend and was done in, but here I was, about to suffer through a stifling hot church service.

I was just about jitterbugging in my seat when the preacher and choir finally filed in. Minister Halworthy was a tall, skeletal man with sallow parchment-like skin stretched tight across his lanky frame. With his severely hooked nose and beady eyes, it wasn't hard to imagine him presiding over a witch burning. His unforgiving glare was like the desert sun, withering all but the toughest under his scorching judgmental gaze.

Everyone stood when he took his place at the pulpit, which was when I spotted Sheriff Earlywine towering head and shoulders over the rest. His broad back took up the space of three people. His size was the only thing that gave him away, and in his dark suit, he looked almost civilized.

I'd never seen him out of his uniform, though to be honest, I hadn't seen very much of him outside of our official interactions, and even that was more than enough for me. His face was stone, giving away no trace of emotion, even for a father who had lost a son. He stood like a lost mountain that had wandered in. I couldn't read his eyes from where we sat in the back, but his jaw worked as he accepted hushed condolences from nearby parishioners. Even though he'd probably shaved this morning, there was stubble on his chin. He was, undoubtedly, just one of those men with a perpetual five o'clock shadow.

The preacher told everyone to sit, and in near perfect unison, we obeyed. Halworthy greeted the congregation with a performance that reminded me of Christoper Lee in 'Dracula'. His voice was deep, and while he did not speak loudly, he was commanding enough it seemed to boom around the small church.

"We gather today, my children, in the house of our magnanimous God. Despite such a glorious day, there is a dark cloud hanging overhead, as we have lost one of our flock."

Dead silence. Not even the birds or bugs dared to interrupt his speech.

"It is with a heavy heart that I announce the passing of one of Midnight Falls's promising youth. Jarrod Earlywine passed away Friday night in a tragic accident. Tragic that this young man with so much of his life before him had to be cut short. So much promise and potential lost before its time to such...troubling circumstances." His eyes flicked in my direction.

I quickly looked down at my feet, severely uncomfortable.

"It takes a village to raise a child, and when a child is lost, the entire village feels that loss as though it were one of their own children. Mourn not the death of a loved one, but the life they lived, and rejoice as our son has been taken unto the bosom of the Holy Mother where she will care for this lost lamb. Know that our God is not just one of infinite love, but swift vengeance and justice, who rights the wrongs against all trespassers."

The bottom dropped out of my stomach. There was no pretense this time as the minister looked directly at me, and I could feel every single pair of eyes in the room join his.

Sheriff Earlywine's jaw worked as he ground his teeth and kept looking forward. He didn't glance back, as a few others had. His shoulders tensed and the pew in front of him gave a warning creak as his massive hands wrung the back.

I shot a look at Lizzie, but she didn't seem to notice. Perhaps it was all in my head, or maybe she didn't feel the same guilt I did.

Silence stretched, too long to be mistaken, normal, or comfortable. Not a cough, sniffle, or clearing of a throat filled the room. Time had stopped in a slow, drugging reel, letting the threat, real or imagined, hang in the air. Not a pause in service, either. A full-on stop to punctuate the subtle hostility. Despite wrath being one of the seven, I could feel it directed at me like a weapon, a loaded gun pointed at the back of my head.

I suddenly found it hard to breathe. The oxygen backed up in my lungs.

And then, the service commenced, and I flinched.

I tried to push it out of my mind as we were commanded to stand for the first hymn. I mouthed along with the words, but I couldn't help but look from one person to another. Were they really judging me, or was I just imagining it? Was I driving myself insane like that guy from the 'Tell-Tale Heart'? Hearing the still-beating heart as my guilt slowly ate away at my sanity? Would I soon be jumping at shadows and seeing phantoms around every corner?

No, I assured myself. The judgment *had* been there. There had been a cold edge behind their eyes, a secret hidden blade that remained veiled until just before it would be plunged into the soft lower ribs.

Though these people probably remembered the Hatfield and McCoy days fondly, killing over family honor was a rare thing. Not unheard of, but I doubt I really had anything to worry about from them beyond societal judgment and gossip. The grapevine was about the most dangerous weapon small towns wielded. Dirty glares and whispers would be the worst of it, but they would die down after a while, and if they didn't, there was nothing tying me here. Like with New York, I could just haul up stakes and go somewhere else. Maybe try my luck out west.

I was unduly beating myself up, letting my own inner demons call the shots.

The problem was, when I shoved those thoughts out of my head, I had to contend with the hellish din of collective voices, several off-key, droning their way through the hymn. It wasn't one I was familiar with, something about little children and the sleeping mother, and it played merry hell with my pounding headache. It was only compounded by the sadistic commands to sit and stand. It felt like no sooner had we sat for the benediction or scripture, then we were standing back up for another hymn. Up and down, over and over. I remember reading somewhere that hell is repetition.

Between the heat, the hangover, plus all the sitting and standing, it did feel like hell being here.

When we finally were seated for the sermon, I was relieved. It was a blasted furnace in here, the fan doing little to ease the torment, clearly losing the battle with the heat. I was soaked in sweat, like every other person. Several of the women fanned themselves with their pamphlets.

The minister showed no signs of it affecting him as he rose to speak. He started off by preaching of the unrighteous, who turned a blind eye to God and received, in return, a deaf ear as their enemies surrounded and crushed them. It quickly became a rambling diatribe about God punishing sinners, gnashing of teeth, and the fires of hell.

I tuned out and think I may have dozed off from the heat at some point. This wasn't the kind of church where people got emotional and randomly shouted out "Amen." They sat in dead silence as Halworthy thundered down upon them with the voice of God himself. Perdition would burn the trespassers and nonbelievers. The Holy Mother had ears only for her children, and only their cries and prayers would be answered. He filled them with the fear of an Old Testament God full of rage and wrath.

In the heat, it was all too easy to nod off. I have no recollection of when it happened, but suddenly the preacher was wrapping up, asking everyone to stand for the final hymn and dismissal.

My body ached, and I was sitting in a pool of sweat, my clothes sticking to the back of the seat. We stood and sang, in a hurry to get the hell out of that sweat lodge. Once finished, it was nearly a stampede for the doors. Even the Good Word can't compete with people being uncomfortable and bored.

In the mad dash, the crowd separated us. Lizzie and her grandmother were swallowed up by the throng and whisked away by the current. All I could do was go with the flow and, after a few minutes of scrabbling, and an elbow or two to the ribs, I was outside in the blessed air. It was still hot, but it wasn't stagnated, and a sweet breeze blew through my sweaty hair and across my neck.

Checking my watch, I was shocked it was a little after eleven. Three hours that could have been spent in bed asleep with air conditioning. Again, I found myself asking why anyone went to church.

I slipped my hand inside my coat, going for a bit of a pick-me-up, when I slammed into an unmovable wall. I hadn't been paying attention in the chaos, and was now face-to-face with big ole double ugly himself, Sheriff Earlywine. Face-to-face may have been a generous description, as the man towered over me like an angry thundercloud. He stared down at me with eyes that had been dead and listless in church, but were now burning with depraved intensity.

"I'm sorry about your son," I rasped as fear choked off my words.

I could see in his eyes that wild indescribable madness lay somewhere deep inside.

My skin crawled as a chill ran up my spine. Some small primal part of my brain started screaming, "Danger, Will Robinson," in that Robby the Robot voice, trying to tell my legs to bolt and flee in the presence of clear danger.

I'm not sure what I expected him to do. Scream and yell, probably punch me, break down and cry maybe, but he did none of that. Instead, he leaned in close and spoke to me in a quiet, level voice that was even more terrifying.

"I know what you did, and we will be settling up soon." With that, he straightened and calmly walked away.

Knees quaking in fear, I was frozen to the spot, unable to think or move.

Once I had some semblance of control, I fished out my flask and threw back most of it in the first belt. It burned my throat on its way down, bringing back some warmth and feeling to my body. Despite the hot day, the air around me felt cold. I took another swig in an effort to chase the sensation away.

"Hey there, sailor, don't hog the party all to yourself." Lizzie's sweet voice came from nearby, and she took the flask from me, raising it to her own seashell-pink lips. She gave me another of those innocent yet coquettish looks as she finished off the sip left in it.

I wasn't sure if she had witnessed my encounter with Earlywine or not, but it really wasn't an issue I wanted to get into. I just wanted to go home and try to shower the filthy off.

"Where did your grandmother get to?" I asked, looking around. I couldn't spot her in the dispersing crowd of people.

"She took off with her friends. They meet up after church for tea and to play gin rummy. Mostly, they just use it to catch up on the current gossip."

"Like Jarrod's death and me being responsible for it." I eyed her, as we both knew that was exactly what the ladies were going to be talking about.

"You mean *us* being responsible for it, and no, his death isn't either of our fault. People like to talk. It's all they got around here. Gossip and daytime soaps." She sighed, returning the now empty container, which I tucked back into my jacket.

"Sheriff Earlywine doesn't think that. I just had a run-in with him, and I'm pretty sure he just blames me."

"Well, that is sexist, assuming a woman can't be just as responsible as a man," she said in mock outrage.

"Yeah, it's funny because you aren't me. Best I can hope for is he just makes my life hell, and you know he can. But if a guy like that goes off half-cocked, he's capable of just about anything, and I would rather not turn up dead in some holler." I wasn't in a joking mood. I was far too sober. A problem I meant to fix at the earliest convenient chance, and the sooner the better. Thanks to that encounter, I was working with a dry socket.

"Well, what can you do about it?" She looked at me with those dazzling green eyes. They seemed to pull me into them as if they were tiny emerald whirlpools.

"Running like hell comes to mind. Head out west somewhere. Put all this far behind me." I breathed her scent into me. It was something flowery yet mellow, light and airy, but not overpowering. It was so subtle it could almost be mistaken for her natural scent. Lovely.

"You can't run from all your problems."

"Oh, but I can try."

She laughed at that, throwing her head back so her long blonde tresses caught the breeze.

I wanted to run my hands through the strands and feel them slip between my fingers. I could easily visualize her dancing through a field of wildflowers in a graceful fashion like some kind of nymph.

My fortune was to find such an oddity out of place in this dusty town. A snatch of some long-forgotten poem half-remembered floated into my mind.

"So, how about a distraction to take your mind off things?" She pulled away from me, holding onto my hand as she danced just beyond my reach.

"What did you have in mind?"

"I was thinking breakfast."

My stomach growled at her words as I realized how hungry I was all of a sudden. Food wasn't a bad idea. I had left the house in such a hurry, I had drunk my breakfast. On a hot day and on an empty stomach, it wasn't quite ideal. Though it had probably stopped me from vomiting on myself several times this morning.

"Did you have someplace in mind?"

She smiled devilishly and leaned into me again. "I was thinking your place, and you can have all you want. This time, with no interruptions."

With that, I forgot all about my hunger, and apparently, so did she.

It wasn't until much later that evening we finally got something to eat.

I was thoroughly exhausted as we sat on the couch, polishing off the last of the leftover food I'd brought home from the potluck, watching 'The Monster That Challenged the World'. Nimrod's big shaggy head lay in Lizzie's lap, trying to look his most pitiful and chuffing under his breath, in hopes he would get pity scraps. So far, he only managed to get head scratches.

"So, this is what you do on a Sunday?" I asked as I polished off my sixth piece of fried chicken. Grease streaked my mouth and fingers, and I wiped them on my shirt in lieu of a napkin.

"Yup, every single Sunday, like clockwork. Up at the crack of dawn to get right with the Lord, then straight off to do some good old fashioned sinning and corrupting of good innocent

Christian boys." Her reply was spoken around a mouthful of pie.

"And you decided to slum it this time with me?"

That got one of those rich honeydew laughs out of her. "Were you serious earlier, about just taking off?" She set her plate aside on the coffee table, keeping one eye on it in case the dog made a wild lunge for it.

"Why not? It's not like there's really anything forcing me to stay. If I had to, I could take off tonight." I watched as the giant caterpillar attacked Audrey Dalton on screen while idly picking at the label on my beer bottle.

She snuggled next to me, reminding me of the warmth and feel of her body on mine. The sex had been hot and furious, a quasi-mixture of that fumbling teenage first time and the experienced dedicated practice of two bodies knowing what the other needed.

"Yeah, but running all the time has got to be tiring. In the long run, wouldn't it be better to deal with your problems and be done with them? At least then you can still live where you want and enjoy the things and people you like."

Her breasts pressed against my side as she looked at me with those eyes again. Something about them just melted my defenses.

"I have tried it before, but problems have a way of multiplying. It's never that simple. I mean, right now, I don't have to deal with that little shit Jarrod anymore, but now I have his dad on the warpath and the entire town thinks I got him killed.

One problem solved, a dozen more pop up to take its place." I groaned and stretched. I was sore all over, and where I didn't hurt, I was stiff.

"Isn't that just what being an adult is?"

"Oh God, I hope not. I thought being an adult was having all this shit figured out. The older I get, the less I think I know or am prepared for."

"God, isn't that the truth." She laughed, causing Nimrod to prick up his ears. She scratched the dog's head and tossed his ears.

"At this age, I'd assumed I would have some kind of plan figured out and know what I was doing with my life. So far, everything has just felt like one big, slow backslide." For about the dozenth time, I tipped the empty bottle to my lips before remembering it was empty and setting it back down. That was starting to become a motion my arm knew on reflex, and that probably said something about my habits.

"I think we all expect that because our parents seemed so on the ball and had everything in hand, then we grew up and realized they were just playing it by ear and doing the best they could. In the end, all you can do is try your best to keep up the façade, and not let them see you bleed. It seems to me like being an adult is just walking around, trying to convince everyone else your world isn't falling apart. That kind of thinking has to take a toll on your mental state, and eventually, people have to find a way to cope, something to take their minds off things." She sounded so melancholy as she talked, so different and unlike the bubbly bright side of her.

"Speaking of things to take our minds off..." I popped the top off a fresh beer bottle. "When did you get to be such an old soul?" I took a sip.

This caused her to burst out laughing. Her laughter was warm and soft, a fresh blanket just removed from the dryer. Its effects were magical, and only made me want her more. Setting aside the bottle, I planted a gentle kiss on her forehead as she wiped tears from her eyes.

"I've been called a lot of things, but never an old soul. What does that even mean?" She chuckled.

I shrugged in response. "I have no clue, but I think I heard someone say it on TV once."

This only caused her to laugh harder. The dog gave us both a confused expression as our humor was lost to his apparent high-brow sensibilities.

"Well then, you know it has to be true." She wrapped her arms around my neck and passionately kissed me. Her lips were all-encompassing, bittersweet like wine as we drank each other in.

Breaking away, she got up from the couch and pulled me with her.

Nimrod used our absence to reclaim the couch. He turned circles a few times before settling down and returning to watching monster movies.

"I think it's high time for bed. It's been a long day." She breathed into my ear, her voice taking on a low, husky tone.

Taking me by the hand, she led me upstairs to the bedroom where we shut the door without interruption from the dog.

We didn't get to sleep until much later. We had other things on our minds.

CHAPTER 11

Lizzie turned out to be both right and wrong. The gossip going around regarding the Earlywine boy's death did, in fact, include our little escapade. It also seemed like it hadn't been just my imagination. While maybe not everyone in town, more than enough people felt the fault of his accident lay on my shoulders, due to prodding statements from his father, I'm sure. It was mostly in the way patrons looked at me with despise and whispered behind their hands as I passed by. Nearly everywhere I went, the atmosphere was positively chilly, despite the prolonged summer heat overstaying its welcome.

Debora Holmes had always been kind and overly bubbly to the point of being obnoxious. She was one of the few in Midnight Falls who didn't act as if I had the plague. I'd tried to keep our interactions brief whenever I went to pick up my mail because she would talk my ear off for the better part of an hour.

Every time I went in, without fail, Mrs. Holmes would be sitting behind her desk, chatting away with someone or another. There was always a friendly smile on her face and a *'hey, how are you'* for those coming in.

Yet, that following Monday, when I stopped in to pick up my mail, she ceased her chatting with a local woman, whose name I didn't know, but whom I recognized by sight, and both women gave me frosty frowns. The woman turned up her nose in disgust as though I had tracked in dog shit on my shoes. The postmaster jutted her chin in a clear indication of disapproval and dismissal. I hurriedly retrieved the few envelopes from my box and left. The entire time, I could feel their eyes follow me.

This pattern repeated itself all week everywhere I went in town. Even on the street, people whom I had never met or spoken to would turn their heads, and conversations would become hush as if I was being perpetually followed by a funeral procession. Post Office, grocery store, and even the girl at the In and Out gave me the stink eye when I bought gas. Which was shocking to me as I didn't think she really registered any-one. She'd always stared blankly ahead when ringing up gas and purchases, and when she wasn't, she had her face buried in the newest issue of whatever magazine was prominent on the rack next to her register.

I was now on the outside looking in at a community I had once considered myself a part of. It's a strange sort of isolation to be surrounded, yet boxed out, by people you used to know. Midnight Falls, like most small towns, didn't exactly take kindly to outsiders, but it had been amped to the Nth degree as of late. It seemed like I was one glare away from being six feet under. I just couldn't shake that feeling of something bad coming.

I would've chalked the whole thing up to my errant guilt or paranoia, if not for one thing—Sheriff Earlywine. Not every day, but more than was coincidental, I saw his cruiser sitting at the end of the street. It wasn't always in the same spot or parked in the same direction, but when it was there, I could make out his huge bulk in the front seat. I was guessing every spare moment he wasn't on a call was spent sitting there and watching me. Same for whenever I sat out on my porch, and he would drive by, or when I was in town, and he'd spot me. That wide Smokey Bear hat did little to shade his massive frame. Dark mirrored sunglasses concealed his eyes, but they still followed me as he passed. His thick bull neck strained at the collar of his shirt while his head swiveled.

A few times, I'd catch him actually following me. I'd spot his tan Sheriff's car about half a mile or so back in my rearview mirror. Whenever I'd head over to Flemingsburg to run errands—after only two weeks of being ostracized, I'd started doing my shopping there and handing in my articles rather than dealing with the Post Office—he would be following. Once, when I caught him, I took an impromptu trip to Maysville just to see if he would trail me that far. He stopped at the county line, or at least, that's when I'd lost sight of him.

Either way, it was unnerving and put me on edge. I became far too aware of my driving and extra cautious so as to not give the guy any reason to pull me over. Not that it would have done anything one way or another. Once you find your way onto a cop's shit list, they don't need a reason to give you a hard time. He didn't, at least, not that way. He just watched and seemed to bide his time. For what, I couldn't hazard a guess, but it didn't seem to be in my favor.

Earlywine was probably going through as many beers as me. I would've bet dollars to donuts that the floor of the car was awash in spent cans, and opening any of the doors other than the driver's side would send them pouring out in a tidal wave dedicated to alcoholism.

None of that was the worst part.

Someone had started violating my home. The vandalism began less than a week later. It had been rather mundane and childish shit for the first few days. Knocked over trash cans and garbage strewn across the lawn. Stuff like that. Some brave souls even graffitied the Charger, though they'd only been brave enough to use shaving cream. I would've been livid and homicidal if it had been paint. "Murderer" had been scrawled on the hood and an odd little doodle had been added to it. A crooked letter 'Y' with a hash mark nestled in the crook. No clue what it meant. A couple of passes with a damp rag, and it was forgotten. I started parking the car in the small garage that was little better than a shed.

Dead animals were next, and the worst of it thus far. Raccoons, opossums, rabbits, and even a few birds started showing up on my front porch. It was utter carnage. The carcasses had been gutted and torn open, left as a grizzly bouquet directly in front of my door. The corpses didn't bear the markings of a hunter prepping his kill or even eating it. Besides, there had been way too many to be coincidental. It had been done with pure malice, for the sake of killing, and left as a horrifying tableau from a sick mind. Grotesque and wholly juvenile. I would've hedged my bets on this being the work of either or both Troy and Clutch, avenging their fallen comrade. I hadn't figured either of them had the intellectual wherewithal to think for themselves, much less act on their half-baked ideas. They'd been a pack of hyenas, opportunistic, and going after the weak once they had them well outnumbered. Disturbing at a level that would've warranted reporting, had I not had the local Sheriff quite possibly contemplating doing the exact same things to me that had befallen those poor animals.

From there, it only escalated.

A few weeks later, I started finding dead cats, their eyes frozen in abject horror, heads twisted bonelessly to the side. They were all strays, just feral street cats from what I could tell, not pets. As I had with the other animals, I just scraped them with my shovel and pitched them straight into the garbage.

Brad had about the same position on the situation I did. He'd caught me at it one day when I'd slept in, trying to dodge a particularly nasty hangover. I hadn't gotten out to dispose of my latest ghastly delivery until nearly noon. Balancing the dead cat on the spade, I was making my way around the side of the house to the cans when he called out, causing me to jump about a mile and nearly dump the cat on my own feet. The guy was shirtless, as was customary by this point. The days were still so hot that just about anyone sweated through their shirt in minutes. Instead, he wore a blue bandanna about his bald pate, and in one hand, he'd held a half-eaten lettuce and tomato sandwich.

I had to wonder about how long this heat was sticking around. An Indian summer was a local sign of bad things to come. Usually, a really nasty winter, but that wasn't the vibe I was feeling.

"Got another one of them, I see." A bit of mayo clung to the corner of Brad's mouth as he took another bite.

I just sighed and tipped the poor dead creature into the can.

He shook his head in silence.

"This shit is getting old," I admitted. "Those little assholes are really making a nuisance of themselves. I would report them, but think we both know about how well that would go over."

"Uh-huh," he grunted around a mouthful of sandwich. "He still at it?"

He jerked his head toward the end of the street where the big Chevy Caprice slept in the afternoon sun. It was parked facing away from us so all we could see was the back end. Sunlight bounced off the wide chrome bumper. Its red taillights were like the eyes of a sleeping beast, ready to spring to life at a moment's notice and devour anyone foolish enough to disturb its slumber. I had no clue how he could see anything from there, but I was sure those mirrored shades of his were focused on our little fence-side conversation.

"You think he's in there?" It would've been a relief to just write all this off as something in my head, but Brad seeing and addressing it pretty much shot that all to hell.

"Yeah, the car is sitting pretty low, so I'd say he's gotta be in there. Damn shocks are gonna be shot on that side, big as that bastard is. Of course, our tax dollars are gonna go to fix 'em, if that alone ain't a kick in the teeth." Brad shook his head as he turned back to me. "Don't let it get ya down. Those little pricks will get tired of this shit sooner or later. If not, football season is going full rut, and they're gonna have their hands full between school and practice. Any luck, they'll be forced to pack it in and move on. That boy is dead and buried, wasn't nobody's fault but his own. But people don't like it when life screws 'em over royally, and they want someone to blame. Your bad luck is that it's you."

"Yeah, well, that's easy to say when it's not you," I mumbled.

"Boy, I'm a black man in the middle of the country ass sticks, and I've been one my whole life. You think I haven't seen it from one end to the other? As far as most of these folks are concerned, and most of them won't say it out loud, I'm a nigger from the moment I wake up, and it's nigger, nigger, nigger, until the moment I go to sleep. And you know what I am when I'm asleep?" His face came over all serious as he looked right at me, his eyes looking directly into mine.

"What?" I breathed. The derogatory term made me uncomfortable as fuck, no matter who said it.

"A sleeping nigger." He burst out laughing at some joke I apparently didn't get.

He was right. He'd probably seen more harassment than I would ever fathom.

"I remember Jim Crow and segregation, back when Whites had their side of town and Coloreds lived in the ghettos, and got their heads cracked if they so much as looked at a white man in a way he didn't like. I've had motherfuckers threaten to kill me and mean it. A few even tried. Now, I'm not saying it's fair the way they're acting, and for sure, you got the raw end of it. There are a lot of people out there with a lot of problems, many bigger than yours. Just because someone ain't currently in your shoes, doesn't mean they don't know what you're going through. Life isn't long enough to make all the mistakes yourself. You got to learn from other people, too. So, when I say I know where you're coming from, you can take it to the bank."

It was hard to argue with that. By and large, as twisted as some of this shit was, it was mostly just passive-aggressive. No one had thrown anything through my windows or set anything on fire. Even the graffiti had been, in a bizarre way, almost considerate. Being treated as an outcast isn't so bad with a little perspective on it. I'd been throwing myself a pity party since that night, trying to keep my head down and get on with my own shit. Between writing articles for the paper and the few remaining repairs on the house, I'd barely made time for anything else, sending me into a downward spiral.

Save for Lizzie's visits, which always made me feel worlds better. Something about being with her, bathed in her golden light, soothed my soul. After her visits, I would even attempt, ultimately in vain, to reignite my ambitions for writing.

No matter how I tried, it seemed that particular flame had been snuffed out for good. After banging my head, I would give it up and resign myself to the procrastination of what I considered 'real work.' Fixing up the house and writing those banal little fluff pieces had become my go-to excuse for pitching whatever abortion I was working on into the trash and drinking myself into a stupor. Nimrod did what he could to try to cheer me up, but the big furry knucklehead could only offer so much.

Things could always be worse, I'd told myself.

I was wrong. Things did get worse.

Everything snowballed the morning I woke to find Mrs. Thompson's dog dead on my front step. She lived up the street and owned one of those miserable little rat dogs. The kind that yaps non-stop and looks like a runaway mop head. I couldn't understand how anyone would want one of those ill-tempered little gremlins. Nimrod's opinion of it was along the same lines as mine. He didn't care for it, either. Yet, when it was lying lifeless on my front porch, I couldn't help but feel bad. A pet is a pet, and someone cared for it.

Strays and vermin were one thing, but this was taking it to a whole new level. The implications were terrifying. It made me wonder how far they'd go.

Its eyes bulged out of its head as its tongue hung limply to one side. Blood matted its fur in greasy clumps. The smell that came off it was inhumane. How that tiny thing made such a huge stink was a mystery. The smell of ruptured bowels had not been this bad with any of the other carcasses. My eyes started to water from the stench.

There hadn't been any real doubt it was her dog, but I had been holding out hope it was just a dead woodchuck until I spotted the little pink rhinestone-studded collar with its cheesy heart-shaped tag. "Scooter" was printed across it in bold block letters.

I couldn't just dump it in the trash bin and call it a day. I fetched a garbage bag and the shovel from the shed, and set to scraping the poor thing off the planks. It was stiff as a board, three of its little legs stuck out, the other missing. I was relieved after it slid into the bag, and I no longer had to look at it.

I didn't have to take the bag far. Mrs. Thompson's house was only a few houses down, past the corner on School Street. Most of the homes on that block all looked the same. A row of gingerbreads, identical prefab make and design, differing only slightly in paint scheme and upkeep. The lawns had more personality with their variances in fencing and walkways. The one I was looking for had an overcrowded postage stamp of a yard. What wasn't covered in flower beds was crammed with tacky lawn ornaments. I had to fight back a flock of plastic flamingos when I tried to open the front gate. Getting to the door was like navigating a minefield. Everywhere I stepped, there were potential tripwires of garden frogs and lawn gnomes.

The doorbell didn't seem to work, so I had to settle for pounding on the door until it opened. The woman was built like a washing machine, short and squat, and breasts with a berth you could launch ships from. Her wiry gray hair was done up in pink curlers and there was a swath of wax across her upper lip while a cigarette hung from the corner of her mouth. Smoke drifted up into her eyes, which were magnified by coke-bottle glasses to that of some giant insect.

"Waddya want?" Her voice croaked in a two-pack-a-day voice.

Even though the school buses had run, it was still relatively early in the morning before sensible people expected visitors. Clearly, she hadn't, as evidenced by her flowered moo-moo and run-down house slippers. I don't think I'd ever seen her out and about the neighborhood in anything other than one of those God-awful sweatsuits, her little dog on a leash. The woman before me looked like she would be more at home under a bridge somewhere telling riddles to goats.

"I, uh, found your dog, Mrs. Thompson." I braced myself.

"Oh, the poor thing. He got out last night when I was putting food out for the cats. He never leaves the neighborhood, and someone usually brings him in." She looked around, her big bug eyes squinting as though her glasses didn't help at all.

I don't know how she could've possibly missed the absence of the little yapping maniac. It's not like that damn thing ever shut the hell up.

I held up the garbage bag. "I'm sorry, but he's dead. I think some animal got him. I found him in my yard." I didn't know any better way to break it to her. I didn't know her, and I'm sure the last thing she wanted was to be consoled by me, of all people.

As I went to set the bag down in front of her, she snatched it from my hands and jerked the top open. What little color there was drained from her face as she saw what had become of her precious dog. A banshee wail I wouldn't have believed possible emitted from her near cancerous lungs as she beheld its gruesome fate.

I could understand her pain. If something happened to Nimrod, I would be just as inconsolable.

Her fat little fists shook in anger as she screamed her grief into the bag. It was so unsettling, I had to take a step back from the porch, and then another, and another, until I found myself well on my way home. Mrs. Thompson's screams could be heard even from down the street, and a few of the neighbors were looking out their screen doors.

I had mostly put it behind me and forgotten about it later that day when there came a knock on my front door. It was still quite hot, Indian summer was getting into full swing, and I was sitting in the kitchen typing up the last few paragraphs for the advice column the Gazette had me subbing. I was bare-chested, with the windows open to allow a cross breeze in a vain attempt to coax some relief from the heat. Nearly knocking my ashtray off the kitchen table, I tried to extricate myself from the mounting mess of papers, bottles, and spent cigarette butts as best I could. Sweat dripped from my neck, running down my back until it found its way into the crack of my ass. My hair was also a sweat-soaked mess, and every part of me probably stank to high heaven. I was not in any state to answer the door. Not that I cared. The only real visitors I had were either Brad looking for my help or Lizzie. Neither of them were strangers to my less-than-together appearance.

What I found on the other side of my door couldn't have been worse. Standing on my stoop was Mrs. Thompson in one of her ridiculous tracksuits that were a hodgepodge of clashing colors and shapes. With her was Jeff Helpenstein from Animal Control. He had one of those poles with the loop at the end in his hands. The worst part, which made my heart sink, was behind them both, leaning against his cruiser parked at the curb.

Sheriff Earlywine.

"That's him, Sheriff. That's the son of a bitch that killed my dog and had the sheer gall to gloat about it." She shrieked, jabbing one fleshy finger at my face.

I was confused and exhausted, but more than that, I was pissed off.

"What the fuck are you talking about?" I was about two seconds from slapping the old bat off my porch. My nerves were already strained from the heat and dealing with reading through people's inane whining letters. I hadn't killed the dog, and it had been more than nice of me to return the damn thing, though now, I was regretting not just dumping it like the rest.

Jeff stepped between me and the woman in an effort to head off any rash confrontations. "Betty here says you brought her dead dog to her this morning." He didn't address any of her claims, just a simple statement to get to the bottom of what was going on.

I nodded. "Yeah, found it dead on my porch this morning."

"She said it had been torn apart by some large animal, and sure enough, I took a look at it, and that's about the size of it."

"That's more or less what it looked like to me. That's why I took it to her, thought it was the least I could do." I wondered where he was going with this.

"Whelp, lotta people have been noticing animals going missing in the neighborhood. Mostly just yard cats and the like."

A hard lump began to form in the pit of my stomach as I connected the dots.

"Couple of people have also seen you tossin' critters in your bins. You know Tom Stetson? He's one of the fellers who works the garbage truck."

I didn't know the man's name, but I recognized the trash collectors by sight. Every Tuesday morning, their big truck would rumble down the street at the crack of dawn, picking up trash and waking everyone.

"Well, he said, just the other week, he saw two dead coons and a cat in your trash." Jeff gave me a look like he wanted me to come up with a good excuse for why I was suddenly flush with animal carcasses.

I sighed and decided the only thing I could do was tell the truth.

"Something has been killing them and leaving them in my yard." I left out the part where I suspected the some*thing* was more of some*one*, and they were a pair of high school football players.

"Yeah, that's about what I figured from seeing Thompson's dog. It was the work of a large animal, and large dogs are known to kill smaller animals from time to time."

I didn't like where he was going with this.

"And you know who has the only large dog in the Falls."

It wasn't a question.

"Jesus Christ, Jeff. You don't think my dog is capable of doing something like that?" I gestured over my shoulder to the screen door, where Nimrod was standing with his face pressed against the door. The effect pulled his upper lip back, exposing his front teeth and giving him a dopey and buck-toothed look. His eyes were pointed inwards as he tried to look at his own nose, making him go cross-eyed. The result couldn't have been more perfect in making him seem any more harmless. His long, flat tongue hung out one side of his mouth as he panted happily.

"You can't stand there and tell me you think that big dumb idiot killed that dog. Or any of those animals. Besides, he couldn't have done it. I've been keeping him in at night since the day I called you to haul that thing off my back lawn. Maybe it's another one of those things. Have you asked around if anyone else has seen one? You said it was some animal with mange or whatever. Did you ask anyone about that? Or did you just take *her* word for it that it was my dog?"

It was true I'd been keeping the big mutt inside at night, partially because of the diseased animal. The real reason, I wouldn't admit to, was that it felt safer to have the dog in the house with me at night, even if he did bark his head off sometimes.

"Look, Josh, I don't like this any more than you do, but it's the rules. I got to take the dog in."

"Fuck you! You are not taking my dog."

I squared myself, ready for a fight. I was not built, by any means, but neither was Jeff. He was much older, and I had him by at least ten pounds. Though, the second Sheriff Earlywine waded in, I would be done for. There were enough weight classes between us to make it clear there wouldn't be a fight. It would be a slaughter.

Since she'd been nearly silent after her initial outburst, Mrs. Thompson had escaped my notice, until she darted past me in a snake-like motion I didn't believe the doughy little woman possessed. No sooner had her pudgy hand grasped the screen door handle and given it a turn, than Nimrod seized the opportunity to make a bid for the freedom of the great outdoors. The husky shouldered the door with all his strength, and it nearly popped off its hinges. Bowling over the surprised old woman, he bounced down the steps and headed for the yard.

Jeff and I moved at the same time, however, he had reach with his pole and knew how to use it. In a single deft move, the loop was around the clueless animal's neck and pulled taunt. I was only a second behind and grabbed the pole with both hands, trying to wrest it from his grasp. He hung on with a vice-like grip as I cursed and tried to shake him free.

Nimrod only exacerbated matters, as he startled and began to panic due to the cord around his neck. He wasn't used to such treatment. Most people just patted his big dumb head or rubbed his belly. He hadn't ever had someone treat him so roughly. He began snapping his head back and forth with the weight and strength of his whole body, and he had a lot of both. For a few seconds, the three of us were trapped in a frantic bizarre waltz on my front lawn.

Someone called out, and all of us looked up.

Joey slammed the door of his car, having just gotten home from school. The little man had a concerned expression, but given who all was involved, he looked like he didn't want to be a part of it.

"What's going on here?" he asked again.

"These assholes are trying to take Nimrod because this dumb bitch is blaming her dead dog on him," I yelled angrily. My blood was boiling, and all restraint had been tossed to the wind.

"It's not just that, and you know it. I don't want to do this, but it's city policy for Animal Control to investigate." Jeff gave another tug on the pole, and I jerked it back.

Nimrod didn't appreciate either and gave his shoulders a shake forcing the both of us to hang on tighter.

"Well, what proof is there that his dog did it?" Joey crossed the lawn as he spoke. He held his briefcase in one hand, and for some unfathomable reason, a jacket in the other. Keeping his distance from the scuffle, he tried to mediate. He wouldn't fare well if it turned into a free-for-all.

"We have some people who've seen dead animals on the property, and from the marks on Mrs. Thompson's dog, it had to be done by a large animal." Jeff hissed through gritted teeth, trying to maintain his grip.

"There have to be a number of large animals capable of killing a small dog around here, even other dogs."

Joey was just retracing the same arguments I'd used, and I doubt he would get any further than I had.

The Sheriff hadn't moved from his position, just stood there, silently watching us.

"Not in the Falls, and the only large dog around is this one."

"Come on, Jeff. You can ask anyone around here, and they'll tell you that is the friendliest dog in the state. He wouldn't hurt a fly. And how can you say you know for a fact there aren't any other animals who could've done it? A raccoon is more than capable, especially if backed in a corner. Maybe it was another one of those mangy coyotes like the one from last month. At the least, you can't say for certain it was *this* dog." Joey spoke to Jeff in a very rational and soothing tone that one might use for unstable individuals.

I have to say, he was very convincing, and had I been the one he was addressing, it would've worked on me.

"I know, but it doesn't matter. The Sheriff has ordered me to take the dog in, and that's what I got to do. I don't mean no harm by it." His apology seemed sincere, but Jeff's grip never faltered.

"Okay, you take the dog in. Then what? Are you going to conduct tests? Measure bite patterns? What is the next step?" Joey asked.

We all knew Jeff hadn't any plans to do any sort of testing. He'd confiscate my dog, and go back to whatever business he had that didn't involve what little work the city paid him for.

He was hesitant with his answer. "Yeah, we can do some tests, and if they don't pan out or more dead animals turn up in the meantime, you can have your dog back. No problem. Just pick him up at the vet's office over in town."

It was bullshit, and I wasn't buying it. I was sure this was just the Sheriff taking advantage of an opportunity to hurt me because of his son. I wasn't going to let them take my dog without a fight. He'd done nothing wrong, and they had zero evidence. This was revenge, plain and simple.

I relaxed my hold just a bit and let the pole slip toward Jeff before jerking it back with all my strength. The feint had thrown him off guard, and as I pulled, I threw a shoulder check into his chest. The older man released the pole as I drove the air out of his lungs and sent him sprawling on his ass.

My victory was short-lived. Before I could free Nimrod from the snare, Sheriff Earlywine heaved himself off his car and covered the distance between us with deceptive speed for his size.

With one massive hand, he seized my arm, and it was as if it were encircled by a band of iron. He spun me around with just a twist of his wrist. His other hand grabbed the back of my head, and the ground was suddenly rushing up to meet my face with a sickening thud. The right side of my head throbbed to the tune of my heartbeat.

I tried to cough, but found myself unable as something incredibly heavy and sharp pressed into the middle of my back. I struggled to breathe with the cop's knee crushing me. Through one blurry eye, I watched as the dog catcher dragged my husky to the back of the old beater pickup. He forced the poor confused animal into a wire cage, his eyes filled with sadness and confusion.

Hot salty tears began welling up in mine as my anger and frustration mounted. I tried to fight, but I could barely move. The weight pressing down on me was unshakable, no matter how much I thrashed and kicked. I was less than helpless as I watched the truck pull away.

I wanted to scream and fight, but pinned as I was, all I could do was rage silently. My own heart pounded in my ears, reducing all other sounds to a muffled din. My vision retreated to a pinhole as the pressure on my back and my pained sobs made it hard to breathe.

It was only a few minutes, but it felt like ages. I barely noticed it when Earlywine released me.

Joey's faint voice made it to my ears as he scolded the Sheriff for the rough treatment and something about excessive force.

I just lay there, limp and defeated. I assumed this was how those hippies from that college video must've felt when the police had just rolled over them. It was unfair. I did nothing to deserve this, and things kept getting worse. Life had become a repeating pattern of getting kicked when I was merely trying to live my life and be left alone.

Then, when I was down, life kept kicking me.

When I managed to sit up, I wiped my forearm across my eyes. My shirt was covered in grass stains. I was a mess, and I was pissed. I wanted nothing more than to bash Earlywine across the back of his fucking head with a blunt object as he walked to his car. I hadn't asked for any of this. He and his bastard son had started this ridiculous pissing contest, and I wanted to put an end to it. The more violent, the better. The caveman part of my brain wanted blood and rage, smashing all the things that hurt and angered it. All I could do was sit there like a sulking kid, impotent and weak. The powerlessness filling me was like a stone chained around my neck, dragging me down into the depths of the ocean.

The cop car pulled away, tires crunching over wayward gravel and sending it spraying in its wake. The dull taillights glared at us as they pulled away as if to say 'so there'.

I thought about flipping him the bird as he drove off, but the last thing I needed was to give him a reason to come back and stomp my ass again. A lucid part of my brain found it odd the asshole hadn't taken the opportunity to tune up on me any more than he had. Had our situations been reversed, I probably would've kept kicking until my legs gave out.

Of course, having someone witness you beat a helpless punk to death over a dog might not get smoothed over as easily. Joey being there might've just saved my life.

As I picked myself up, he tried to give me a hand. I raised mine in a silent no-thank-you, too pissed and ashamed to want anyone touching me.

"Aw, man." He winced. "That bump looks pretty bad. I'm not a doctor, but maybe put some ice on it."

Shrugging off his words I tenderly touched my temple. A dull pain sent blinding flashbulbs across my vision.

Great, just what I needed. The day couldn't possibly get any worse.

"What the hell happened, Josh?" Joey was still trying to be helpful. The tiny little guy had tried to stand up to the Sheriff, despite the fact the brute could've punted him like a football.

I sighed. "I found Mrs. Thompson's dog dead on my porch this morning. I tried to do the right thing and take it back to her. She ran to the Sheriff, blaming me and my dog for killing it. They showed up just a few minutes ago, and started this shit when you drove up."

"What makes them think it was Nimrod?"

"It was mauled by an animal, and it turns out, I'm the only person in the Falls that owns a large dog." I still doubted that claim.

"That's nuts. Huskies aren't vicious, and I've never heard of them attacking other pets or any animals. They're lovable dogs." He sat on my front step.

"Yeah, well, I don't think that matters to a crazy old bat and a man who hates me." I joined him on the step, wiping my nose with the hem of my shirt.

"Why does Earlywine hate you?"

He had to be the only person oblivious to the last few weeks.

"Remember when Lizzie and I embarrassed Jarrod at the community potluck the night before he died? Some people seem to think that was the reason he got drunk and crashed. So, I've been kind of getting the cold shoulder from everyone."

"Oh, that makes sense, but you can't beat yourself up over that. It wasn't your fault. Dumb teenagers have always been dumb teenagers, and they do stupid stuff. I remember back when I was in school, some local kids got killed in a car accident. They were reckless, racing, and didn't see a truck coming around a blind corner, and *boom*. Major pile-up. Only the truck driver survived, because he'd been driving one of those huge pulpwood trucks. Those sons of bitches are built like tanks. He didn't get a scratch. It wasn't his fault, but that didn't stop him from blaming himself. And yeah, a couple of the parents blamed the driver. They just didn't want to face the fact that life can be unpredictably cruel. That's just human nature. They'll get over it and realize how foolish they are to be angry over something they can't control. Of course, it did royally screw up the football season."

I snorted a laugh that was cut short by another twinge of pain from my noggin.

"I'm afraid he's gonna try to use this to have Nimrod put down just to hurt me." As I said the words, my heart dropped again at the thought of losing my dog.

"I doubt he would go that far. There doesn't seem to be any real evidence to back up Mrs. Thompson's claims. I'll keep an eye on it and make sure that doesn't happen." Joey patted me on the shoulder in a fatherly manner. "Besides, there are plenty of other possible culprits. You said you've been keeping him in since the other night, so in case there were any more of those diseased animals, he wouldn't catch it."

"That, and so you don't blast him by mistake." I joked.

He rolled his eyes and threw his hands up in mock exasperation. "You and Brad are not gonna let that go, are you?"

"Not any time soon, Dirty Harry."

He just shook his head as he got up to leave.

I felt a bit better, or at least, not wanting to set the entire neighborhood on fire.

But this wasn't over by a long shot.

CHAPTER 12

I didn't feel like being alone. I probably would've gotten drunk and done something stupid. So, I took a shower and changed clothes, planning to head over to Lizzie's. At least I would have someone to commiserate with, and then maybe we could come back to my place for the night.

My reflection looked like hell when I got out of the shower. My nose was still slightly swollen from the night of the potluck, and the yellowing bruises under my eyes made me look jaundice. The bump on my head was red and angry, roughly the size of a golf ball, and throbbed to no end. Lizzie was studying to be a nurse and would know what to do. Maybe she'd even have some good drugs or at least something stronger than Anacin.

Kids were shrieking and running about as I walked to Lizzie's. After-school activities had just finished, so the children who were finally relieved of Little League and other clubs were turned loose on the community at large. In a small town where everyone knew everyone, it was safe to let your kids run free. Mothers just warned them to stay out of the street and come home when it got dark. Other than that, they could roam. It was so different from the city with its constant hustle and flow of people or traffic.

Nostalgia took me back to my own childhood for a moment. Running home from school to ditch my bag and books, grab a snack, and then head off to the city park for a pickup game of baseball or basketball. Playing horse or home run derby when there weren't enough for teams. Splashing in the creek next to the park that cuts through the middle of town whenever there was a practice or the high schoolers wouldn't let us "babies" play with them. Having delirious fun over the fact that we were free, with no cares, then losing track of time and rushing home in a panic, afraid our parents would skin us alive.

By the time I got to Lizzie's place, I was in a far better mood than I would've believed an hour ago. The air was filled with the scent of freshly mowed lawns and dinners cooking. Carried on a breeze was a hint of approaching autumn. Cicada's sung somewhere in the distance, mingling with the sounds of tractors as they hauled their harvests off to housing. Everything was so alive. It made me forget my problems, to want to just sit on the porch with a pitcher of tea and watch the sunset.

If I hadn't just had my head kicked in and my dog kidnapped.

Lizzie came out of the house as I mounted the steps. She looked gorgeous, even in a plain t-shirt and jeans. Her lovely hair was pulled up in a messy bun under a faded bandanna. There was a stained rag in one hand and a pair of heavy-duty yellow gloves in the other. I had obviously interrupted her cleaning, and she looked happy for the excuse.

"Wow," she greeted me with raised brows. "Looks like your day was worse than mine. What happened to your face?"

"You should see the other guy."

"Oh, I'm sure, mister tough guy." She laughed.

"The other guy was Sheriff Earlywine," I said.

"Jesus Christ! What the hell happened?"

She ushered me inside and sat me at the kitchen table, examining my head as I told her about everything that had happened. When I was finished, she seemed as shocked and just about as pissed off as I had been.

"That is bullshit!" She handed me a couple of little yellow tablets. "Take those. They'll help with the swelling. I can't believe that vindictive asshole would do something like that. That bitch, Mrs. Thompson? Gran says that woman is a walking drama house who makes like the whole world is out to get her. She should be the one locked up, not your poor dog."

I popped the pills dry and swallowed. "He's been stalking me for the past several weeks," I told her.

I had no idea where we stood. Lizzie and I hadn't put a label on what exactly we were. Were we convenient or casual, merely using each other for physical pleasure despite genuine affection? It was almost self-serving in a way. I wasn't sure where the line blurred, so we hadn't chatted as often as a normal couple would have, and it dawned on me how much she probably didn't know about the past couple weeks.

She frowned. "Really? When did he start doing that?"

"The day after the funeral, maybe? I don't know, but he's been parked down the street often, watching the house, and follows me when I go into town."

"Isn't there someone you can report him to?" She paced the room with her hands on her hips.

"Not really. In small towns like this, everyone knows everyone, and they all grew up together. He's a good ole boy with the Flemingsburg police, the DA, and probably every judge in the surrounding counties. So yeah, pretty much screwed here."

"There has got to be something you can do." She crossed her arms, causing her shirt to pull tight across her pert breasts, making it obvious she wasn't wearing a bra.

"Joey Ackerman said he would take care of it, at least, as far as Nimrod is concerned." The pain in my head was down from a constant ache to a dull throb.

"Good, 'cause if anything happens to that dog, you won't have to worry about Sheriff Earlywine. I'll kill him myself." She huffed.

She looked cute, biting on one thumbnail in her anger. Her righteous fury made me feel less alone. Misery loves company, especially when it looks like her. I somehow found it hard to stay mad or upset whenever she was around. Something about her approach to living just softened my cynicism. Life hadn't yet made her as jaded as I was, I guess.

"Sorry I had to bring all this in on you and your grandmother." I sighed.

"No, it's okay. Something like this is important, and I'm always here if you need someone. Besides, Gran is down for her nap. She's having one of her bad days."

"Well, that's too bad. I thought we could go back to my place." I stood and pulled her against me.

"Oh? And what did you have in mind?" Her tone was shy as she formed herself to my body.

"We could hang out on the couch and watch TV? Maybe order a pizza and you could *console* me."

"Really? Using your dog to try to get into my pants." She laughed.

"Yep, since day one, he's been my accomplice." I nuzzled her neck and kissed her gently on her earlobe. She smelled warm, and there was a lingering hint of some flowery perfume or shampoo on her.

"I knew that dog was too cute to be innocent." Her hands crept up the small of my back as she looked at me. "Well, I have some ideas of things we could do here instead."

"What did you have in mind?" I tried to give her my sauciest and most suggestive smolder. Though, from her expression, I guess I just looked constipated.

"You can help me take care of our mouse problem." She pulled away from my embrace with a laugh. "Saw one of the little critters last night, and it nearly gave me a heart attack. It ran under the basement door, so I wanted to put some traps down there."

"Don't tell me you're scared of creepy basements," I teased her.

"No, there's a padlock on the door, and Gran said she didn't know where the key was. Not that it matters because it looks like the lock is rusted shut."

She led me to the door. It was set in between the kitchen and living room. Just above the knob, sure enough, there was a padlock that looked like it had been there for ages. It had turned reddish brown from years of neglect and lack of use. I gave it a tug, and it didn't give at all.

"So, I figured you could hit it with a can of WD-40 and get it in working order while I look through the junk drawer. There must be a million keys in there, and I'm sure one of them has to fit." She looked over my shoulder as I continued to fiddle with the lock.

"No need," I replied. "Get me a flathead screwdriver. I can just remove one end of the hasp. The door should open right up. As long as it's not painted shut or something, and I don't see any kind of door lock on the handle. We can have this knocked out in just a few minutes."

"Ooh, cute dog *and* handy. Very sexy."

"You forgot funny, smart, and good-looking," I supplied.

"Did I?" She gave me a smarmy grin, clearly pleased with herself.

"Keep it up, and you'll be putting your own mouse traps in the basement, missy."

"Well, in that case, *very* handsome."

She crossed the kitchen and opened an end drawer. After a few minutes of rummaging around, she came up with a long-barreled flathead screwdriver with one of those clear acrylic handles. She brought it back and handed it over.

In a matter of seconds, I had the screws holding the hasp to the door frame out.

"This is why you nail your latches, not screw them."

I tucked the screwdriver into my back pocket. The loose screws I dumped into my front pocket for safekeeping. I didn't really have any plans for them. If Lizzie asked, I would end up just replacing the whole thing and putting on a new lock. That way, they would at least have use of the basement again.

I tried the door, and it resisted. I put my shoulder to it, and with a little weight, it popped open. The hinges squeaked in protest as the door swung wide, revealing dusty wooden steps down into the dark basement.

The stairs groaned with each step we took. They were little more than single boards suspended in mid-air with no banister to hold on to. I was a bit worried one of them would break, sending one or both of us tumbling down the remaining stairs to the bottom. It was hard to make anything out. What little light there was came through a single grimy window. It turned everything in the basement into hulking shadows.

The air was stale with a heavy, earthy smell. It was so musty, I could taste it on my tongue. Every movement set off another cascade of dust, thickening the air. We were both coughing and sneezing before we reached the bottom. The basement floor was an old dirt cellar design, the kind you read about where serial killers buried their victims. I was fairly sure Lizzie's Gran wasn't snuffing people and disposing of them in her basement.

Well, reasonably sure, anyway.

Cobwebs hung from the rafters. Lizzie screamed and jumped when one touched her face, nearly causing me to do the same. The basement did a better job of blocking outside noise than the upstairs. It was deathly quiet, making her scream all the louder in the small, isolated space. I was pretty sure I was now deaf in the ear she had inadvertently wailed into. Digging one finger into it, I tried to get it to work again while we looked around for a light.

We eventually found the chain hanging from a single bare bulb on the ceiling. To my amazement, it clicked on when she pulled and bathed the room in dull yellow light. It wasn't much, but we could now make out the room a little better.

Near the base of the stairs was a stack of old cartons, and along one wall were a bunch of shelves, piled with odds and ends. Jars of preserves probably canned around WWII. Cans of rusted nails and screws. Boxes and containers that had held God knew what. Motor oil bottles and mechanical parts I couldn't identify. There was also a long-barreled flashlight.

I picked it up and tried it. It came on, but the light was so weak, I could barely tell. Smacking it against my palm a few times caused whatever loose connection there was to sort itself out and the beam became somewhat brighter. It wasn't much more illumination than the bulb afforded, but it was something. I handed it to Lizzie so she could light our way while I set the traps.

Taking up the largest area was the furnace. They probably had a coal furnace when the house was first built, but had swapped it out for an electric one at some point. I thought it was a good thing they hadn't had any issues with it in a long time. If her grandmother was right and they lost the key for so long the lock had rusted shut, there was no other way to get into the basement and fix it if it crapped out. We really hadn't had much trouble getting in, but for an old lady living alone, that seemed a bit dangerous.

"What's this?" Lizzie moved around the furnace and was looking at something obscured from my line of sight.

I moved around the monolith, being careful not to knock over an old bicycle propped against it I almost hadn't seen in the poor light.

One back corner had been walled off by boards into a little cubical, and she was playing the beam of her flashlight over a door set into one side. There was no handle, knob, or lock, just a board nailed on one side that spun a makeshift latch. The paint had been scratched in a circular pattern, giving it away. A square shovel with a short wooden handle was leaned next to the door, and I would've bet it had been used to shovel coal into the old furnace.

"It's a coal bin," I said.

"A coal bin?"

"Yeah, my grandparents' house has one. Back when my grandpa built the house in, I want to say either '42 or '45, they had a coal furnace. About once a month, a truck would deliver coal, and they funneled it through a back window into one of these small rooms. When they swapped the furnace out somewhere in the late 60s or early 70s, my grandmother had him convert theirs into a storage room for the food from their garden that she canned. It was pretty common back then." I made my way around and closer to her.

"Think there's still coal in there?" She reached for the latch.

"I doubt it. Probably just stored junk."

I was wrong. I was so very wrong. What was in there was horrific beyond description.

The latch turned easily with only the barest whisper of noise. She tried to push the door, but when it refused to move, she instead dug her fingers into the groove between the door and the jam. With little effort, the door swung out on well-oiled, noiseless hinges. Odd, considering everything else in the basement was dirty, dusty, and succumbing to entropy.

When the door opened, out rolled a powerfully sour, almost greasy odor. I covered my nose and mouth as I fought several gags to not vomit.

Lizzie pulled up her shirt to cover her lower face in an improvised mask against the stench and shined the light beyond the entrance.

Inside was something I couldn't quite get my mind to comprehend. It was as if my brain was trying to protect me by refusing to accept what my eyes were seeing. I don't exactly know how to describe it.

It was some sort of altar, and it was extremely primal. Made from twisted tree limbs and roots, decorated with deer antlers, hides, hooves, feathers, and things I didn't want to know. The walls were covered with symbols and glyphs. I couldn't be certain, but it looked like they were painted in dried blood.

Laying upon the altar were several bones I couldn't identify, but part of me worried they were not from animals, along with several canine teeth, and a rough hue stone knife. The blade was made of obsidian with a deer antler hilt. The chipped edge gleamed in the light from the flashlight and shone all the colors of the rainbow like an oil puddle after a rainstorm. To one side sat two large leather-bound books with cracked covers.

"What the fuck is that?" I was at a loss for words, and that was all that would come out when I opened my mouth.

Lizzie merely shook her head by way of an answer.

It was wrong. Just...whatever it was, it was wrong. I don't know why, but something about the whole thing seemed blasphemous, almost perverse. An affront to all that was natural and normal. What was it, and why was it in Mrs. Sexton's basement?

Looking at it made my skin crawl, and the little hairs on the back of my neck stood on end.

I couldn't tell if it was having the same effect on Lizzie with her shirt covering most of her face, but I could swear she was fascinated. She had recoiled initially, as I had, but had recovered much faster and moved in for a closer look.

I didn't want to go anywhere near it. I wanted to slam the door shut and run screaming from the house. This was the kind of sick shit that they found in the lairs of devil worshippers.

Lizzie picked up the book on top and blew a thin layer of dust off the cover. It had black leather binding with faded gold leaf edges. A thin, dull red ribbon hung from between the pages. It looked to me like a family bible until Lizzie flipped it open. The pages turned stiffly because every page had photos pasted to them. They seemed dated, all in black and white. The people wore simple clothing from around the turn of the century.

"I wish you hadn't found that."

We both jumped.

I struck my head on one of the furnace ducts, sending more dust avalanching down on us.

We turned to face the person who had spoken, and were shocked to find Mrs. Sexton standing at the bottom of the steps. In the light from the door at the top, all we could see of her was her silhouette.

"Gran? What is all this?" The fear in Lizzie's voice mirrored my own.

"I really wish you hadn't found that," the elderly woman repeated as she stepped forward.

In the light of the naked bulb, it was obvious there was something wrong with her. Her eyes were bloodshot, but they had gone over all white like someone who had cataracts. Which wasn't the worst part. The skin of her face was...*moving*. Not muscular as with expressions or speech. No, it was more like something was underneath her skin, shifting, like insects crawling or burrowing.

Lizzie gasped, palms extended in a paused motion somewhere between wanting to reach for her grandmother and push her away.

I couldn't move. This was the thing B-horror flicks were made of, I thought as my brain tried to reason with reality. An allergic reaction. She'd fallen and hit her face. Anything to explain the sight before us. My heart pounded in my ears, and I could feel it pulsing in my temples as my head swam.

Then, the elder woman's face bulged as if her head was made of clay, and someone had shoved their fist into the back of it. It made a sickening crackling sound like dry wood in a fireplace. My breath caught as I recognized it as the same sound I thought I'd been hearing off and on for weeks, making me questioning my sanity.

Her head then abruptly jerked to an inhuman angle, jaw sideways and the top of her head nearly flush with her shoulder. Her whole body began to shudder as it contorted in alien, horrific ways, accompanied by the same terrifying dry snapping.

Neither of us shifted an inch. Fear trapped us in place as our minds struggled to witness the horror. Lizzie let out small pathetic whimpers. My own throat clenched as my lungs forgot how to breathe. The sheer terror made me feel so small and helpless before the grim display.

Oh God, and then it got worse. Her pale insipid skin began to stretch taunt across her body, forcing a spider web of black veins to protrude. She shifted and behaved as if there was something inside her that was far too large for her frame, and it was struggling to emerge. Her clothes tore apart mere seconds before her flesh followed suit. Her skin split open and pulled away from grayish flesh with patchy, wiry white hair.

Eyes wide, jaw agape, I emitted a sound somewhere between a gasp and a curse. Blindly, I reached for Lizzie's arm while keeping my eyes glued to the nightmare before us.

A beast tore its way out of Mrs. Sexton, shedding its little old lady disguise with a sound equivalent to pitching wet laundry onto the ground.

Thwap.

I shuddered. From my roots to my toenails, a full-body shudder.

Its lanky body was emaciated to the point its bones and the tight whipcord of its muscles were exposed. Every single one of its ribs stood out behind the saggy pair of breasts that hung like a pair of windsocks on a calm day. Its large bat-like ears brushed the cobwebs from the rafters as it straightened to full height.

The thing peered at us through milky eyes as it sniffed the air with its crinkly black nose, scenting us, looking for prey. It opened its long, wolf-like snout in a terrifying snarl, revealing blackened gums with rows of teeth that had more gaps than teeth. The remaining fangs it did have were long and sharp, and more than capable of tearing apart soft human flesh.

What the actual hell? This wasn't possible.

It rushed us, shouldering aside anything that got in its way, and my gut bottomed out. Despite its deceptively frail build, it moved faster than I would've thought possible. Its head plowed through furnace ducts, crumpling them as though they were tin foil.

Panicked, I ducked left and ran. In my haste to get away, my legs got tangled in the shovel that had been leaning against the bin, and I fell over backward. One of its gangly arms swiped at me, missing by inches. Its paw, tipped with thick dull nails, slammed into the wooden wall of the coal bin, smashing the boards to match sticks.

Lizzie screamed as she dove in the other direction, going down on her hands and knees, crawling behind some cardboard boxes in the corner.

A brief moment of relief filled my chest when the creature went after her instead of me, but I had almost no time to absorb the thought because sheer unadulterated panic for her clawed at my windpipe.

Disgusted with myself, I shoved the thought of running out of my mind and grabbed the shovel in both hands. Wielding it like a baseball bat, I wailed on the thing's back. Reverberations vibrated up my arms with every blow. The creature barely seemed to register the assault as it swatted boxes aside, trying to get at Lizzie. My ears were ringing from the combination of her screams and the animal's baying. In there, somewhere, mixed in, was my own yelling. In my frenzy, I managed to nail one good lick upside its broad head.

All that did was piss it off.

It swung one of its arms back, cutting my legs out from under me. The world became chaos for a few seconds as it sent me flying head over heels, and I landed hard several feet away on my back.

Oxygen whooshed from my lungs. Something hard and sharp jutted painfully into my lower back. Jagged. Throbbing.

It took me a few seconds to realize the pain was from the handle of the screwdriver sticking out of my back pocket. I pulled it out, noting the handle had cracked from the impact.

Panting, getting to my knees, I held the screwdriver like a dagger and lunged. With all my strength, I plunged it into the creature's thigh, just above the knee joint.

It let out a wounded howl and swatted at me. Its backhand caught me full in the face, and pain exploded as I felt my nose break again with a distinguishable *crack*.

On my knees, disoriented, I closed my watering eyes and covered my nose with my hand. Stinging radiated through my sinuses, agony I couldn't breathe through for several elongated seconds. Spots dotted my peripheral. Blood gushed and splattered all over the dirt floor.

Lizzie's horrifying wail snapped me back.

Blinking the tears from my eyes, I looked for the shovel I'd dropped when the beast had flipped me like a pancake. *There.* A couple feet to my right.

Without thinking, I grabbed it. The beast had lost interest in either of us for the moment, distracted, and struggling with the screwdriver still sticking out of its leg.

Arms raised, I drove the shovel at the monster like a spear. The edge of the spade caught it in the throat. Between that and its injured leg, my charge bowled it over, the momentum propelling it into the back wall. Leaning my full weight into the tool, I was able to pin the thing.

Hopefully, I could keep it trapped long enough for Lizzie to run out of the basement before it tore my head off. Heaving air, I glanced at her.

She didn't leave.

Screaming like a banshee, she shot to her feet and ran straight at me. Throwing her full body weight into the handle of the shovel, we drove it forward and deeper into the creature's neck.

It made a surprised strangling noise, and its milky eyes bulged from its eye sockets. A long black tongue lolled out of the side of its mouth as blood sprayed from its throat.

We thrust our weight into it again, driving the edge deeper into its flesh. It continued to emit choking, gagging sounds and spit up gouts of blood. We rammed it home again, this time causing its limbs to tremble and convulse.

Panicking, we thrust it one more time with the last of our strength. There was a sharp *crack*, and the thing's head drunkenly listed to one side. A blood bubble slowly grew from one flared nostril as the body finally went limp.

Panting, we stayed frozen in place a few beats, eyes wide. My heart was pounding in my chest on the verge of a heart attack.

Eventually, we slowly removed the shovel, and the head came with it.

Lizzie shrieked and jumped back, arms wrapped around herself.

I recoiled.

We'd managed to sever its head, and it now sat in the spoon of the shovel like some grotesque memento. I turned the shovel, dumping the head unceremoniously into the dirt with a wet *plop*.

We stared at it. Now dead, it just looked like someone's discarded Halloween mask.

It didn't seem real. It was lying right there in front of us, and it still didn't feel real. That didn't just happen. Elizabeth's grandmother didn't just turn into a monster and try to kill us. We didn't just chop its head off in the basement. None of this could be real.

I dropped the shovel from my lax fingers as Lizzie threw herself into my arms, sobbing. My shirt was drenched in blood that was still pissing from my nose. I couldn't tell if she was hurt or just hysterical, but I thought it best if we got upstairs before sorting that out.

I led her back up the steps, her supporting me as much as I was supporting her. Back in her kitchen, I eased her into a chair. She seemed shell-shocked and shook uncontrollably. Other than a few scratches, she didn't appear to be harmed.

I grabbed a hand towel, wet it under the faucet, and held it to my nose. Hot pain bloomed once again, and I quickly pulled the towel away. Instead, I snagged a bag of frozen peas from the freezer, wrapped it in the towel, and applied it to my nose again. It was better, but still made my sinuses sting and my eyes water. At least I wasn't dripping blood everywhere.

Once I had that handled, I began searching through the kitchen cabinets, praying the old bag had enjoyed the occasional snootful of booze. I was about to give it up as a dry hole until I found a bottle of cooking sherry in the pantry. I spun off the cap and downed about a fourth of the bottle.

It burned and tasted vile, but it was better than nothing. I got a glass from the cupboard and poured some into it before handing it to Lizzie. She was nearly catatonic, just sitting in the chair, faintly rocking back and forth. Her eyes were glazed, staring at seemingly nothing across the room.

I put the cup in her hand, and she automatically brought it to her lips. After she drained it, I topped her off again, and she managed to get that down, too.

"You okay?" I asked.

Her wide, watery gaze lifted to mine. "Josh, what the hell was that?" Her voice came out several octaves above normal and cracked in the middle of her question.

"How am I supposed to know? She is—was—*your* grandma."

"Not really. I mean, not biologically. She was a distant relative by marriage or something. We just called her "Grandma" because it was easier than 'that old bag we take care of out of obligation'." She sounded on the verge of hysterics again, speaking rapidly. "It's not like we get together at Thanksgiving and discuss if turning into a monster runs in the family or reminisce about slaughtering people. She tried to *kill* us!"

Seeing she was about a hair's breadth from losing it again, I poured her another finger of sherry. There was barely any in the glass before she slugged it back.

I thought I had a drinking problem, but it was nothing compared to Lizzie in state of shock.

CHAPTER 13

Once the cooking sherry was empty, Lizzie fetched a bottle of scotch from the living room. After finishing off half the bottle, we were both about as balanced as we were going to get.

She was calm enough to examine my nose again, declared it definitely broken, and set about straightening it.

That was a truly unpleasant experience. Grinding the bones against one another—both in sound and sensation—almost made me vomit. I'd gritted my teeth, but still flinched and dry heaved.

Even though she announced the operation as a success, my nose was still slightly crooked. My eyes had gone fully black, making me look like a raccoon, and once I realized it, I noticed it was impeding my vision a bit, too. I only hoped I wouldn't wake up tomorrow with them swollen shut.

Lizzie got a bag of frozen vegetables from the freezer to put on. I wrapped it in a towel and placed it over my eyes. The cool relief was much welcomed. What wasn't welcomed, however, was when I closed my eyes, all I could see was that thing in the basement as it came at us, all fangs, fur, claws, and burning glare. Involuntary shivers of fear ran down my spine in waves, and the edges of my mind began to blur as it threatened my grip on sanity.

"What do we do now?" Her voice trembled, though not as badly.

I had no idea. There wasn't a precedent for this kind of situation. If she hadn't seen it, too, I would've had to question if I'd just gone insane. The whole thing didn't make sense, or more accurately, my brain didn't want to make sense of it. The dark basement, the weird altar, and the nightmare that attacked us. Pieces my mind couldn't put together in any way that made sense without both of us being insane.

"I don't know," I eventually responded.

"Should we tell someone, or call someone?"

"Like who?" I answered. "And what do we tell them? Oh hey, you know sweet little old Mrs. Sexton? Yeah, well, she turned into a beast and tried to kill us, so we chopped off her head, and now her body is in the basement. Wanna come take a look?" I was being sarcastic, probably cruel, but the look she was giving me had me worried that was exactly what she'd been thinking.

"Why not? It's the truth."

"Because at best, it sounds nuts, at worst, we'll be labeled serial killers."

"I think you have to kill more than one person to be a serial killer."

"The fuck does that matter? There is a dead...*thing* in the basement, and the cops aren't exactly my favorite people right now. So, who do you propose we tell? Honestly, the only rational plan I can come up with at the moment involves burning the house down and leaving town in the middle of the night." I was starting to become hysterical myself. There wasn't any way I could see us getting out of this that didn't end with one or both of us in a jail cell. No one was going to believe what happened, and after the past few weeks, they probably wouldn't want to.

We were royally fucked.

"What about your neighbors?"

"Who? Joey and Brad? Why would we call them?"

"Well, I thought after that thing you guys killed in your backyard, they might be more receptive than anyone else. Plus, they don't seem to have a grudge against you like you say everyone else does."

"Because they do!" I screamed in frustration. "Why does no one else see it?"

"Look, I am not saying you're wrong. I mean, they are people you would trust, right?" Her tone had taken on that of someone talking to a deranged lunatic about to fly off the handle.

Given how the day had gone, that wasn't too far from reality.

But, she was right. Brad was an outcast, too, if for no other reason than his skin color in a racist small town, and Joey had backed me up when they'd taken Nimrod from me. They'd been more than neighbors lately, and they *had* seen the thing in my yard.

"Okay, but I'm not sure why a dead coyote or whatever would convince them that we aren't making this all up." I mean, they *had* seen what I'd seen, and they clearly didn't buy that it was a coyote any more than I did, but did that mean they would go out on a limb and trust me? The thing in the basement was pretty damning evidence that these things were no normal animals.

"No, we tell them one of those things got into the basement, and we need them to come over and look. Once they see for themselves, we tell them the truth, then they'll have to believe us."

It seemed a bit thin, but it could work. I mean, Joey, at least, would be curious enough to take a look. Brad, on the other hand, was just good-mannered enough to lend a hand in almost any situation.

Tentatively, I rolled the plan around in my head. "So, we tell them one of those things got into the basement through a window, we killed it, and need their help deciding what to do because it's too late to call Animal Control."

"And you don't really want to call Animal Control after the incident this afternoon with Jeff and the Sheriff over your dog," Lizzie added.

"That actually sounds like it would work." I was impressed in our state we managed to think of something halfway plausible. We had about a bottle each in us, but apparently, the sheer terror we'd faced was still keeping the effects of the booze at bay. Well, almost. My gut was feeling like it wanted to wretch at any moment between pain, our fight or flight, and the alcohol.

Which didn't sound like that bad of an idea, really. I rose, rushed to the kitchen sink, and vomited the contents of my stomach.

After about five minutes of puking, I felt remarkably better. My face still throbbed like a mother, though.

We called Brad and Joey, and both agreed to come over with far less hassle than either of us had anticipated. My body was zinging with nervous energy, and I paced back and forth in the kitchen. Time stretched out forever as we waited. Every time I looked at the clock, I could've sworn it hadn't moved. It got to the point where I checked its batteries twice.

Lizzie tried to get me to sit down by pouring me another drink when the doorbell finally rang. It had been only an hour since we'd called, but the two of them had shown up in short order.

Brad was carrying a shovel and several heavy-duty black trash bags, clueless as to what we were about to spring on them.

They seemed to notice how frazzled and nervous we were by the wringing of Lizzie's hands and averted gaze, not to mention my tightness and pacing. Their gazes fell on the bottle-laden table.

Without a word, Lizzie and I led them to the basement door. As I reached for the knob to open it, her hand fastened around my wrist, her expression a mask of fear and concern.

"Wait," she whispered. "What if its...you know..."

"What?" I was confused at first, but then it dawned on me what she meant.

"In the movies, they always, you know, turn back once dead. What if we go down there and it's gone? It's just Grandma down there? What do we do? They won't believe us."

Brad and Joey exchanged quizzical glances.

She made a good point, and my brain started to go into panic mode before seizing upon a simple realization.

I shook my head. "That thing in my yard? It never changed."

That seemed to calm her down, and she let out a sigh of relief. Her hand fell away and allowed me to turn the knob.

I glanced over my shoulder at Brad and Joey, who were equally confused at our pause. They had no clue what they were walking into, and the way we were behaving only served to exacerbate their confusion.

I gritted my teeth and opened the door. A musty sour smell rolled up from the basement.

A flood of decay and rot hit us all in the face as, one-by-one, we descended the rickety stairs. In the dim light of the bare bulb and what little light came in through the dirty basement window, they could now see the full horror of the truth.

Our fear the creature might turn back into a little old lady was alleviated, as the remains of the thing's body and head were where we'd left them. In the time since we'd fled the basement, the remains had undergone noticeable change as though rapidly decaying, just as the one in my yard had done.

The body looked like a shriveled balloon someone had let the air out of. It was nothing more than papery skin and fur, propped up by the framework of bone beneath. The skin on the face had gone slack and was peeling off the skull, leaving behind a patchwork nightmare of gleaming white bone and blackened rotting meat. The eyes were dark sunken pits in which small black insects crawled in a singular undulating mass. The earth beneath the creature's body was stained black with the ichor that escaped it. I swear, there was some kind of steam or gas coming off it in the dusty light, carrying with it a rank stench.

Lizzie and I stood clear, far too intimate with how dangerous it had been while alive.

Joey, however, didn't share our dread, and instead hunched next to the thing, picking up the broken screwdriver and poking the carcass in curiosity. Where he prodded with the tool collapsed like poorly constructed papier-mâché. For a moment, I was worried he might think this was all just a joke.

Wrinkling his nose, he stood, wiping his hands on his khakis.

"Whatever it is, it's been down here for a long time. I thought you said you killed it this afternoon, but you don't see this level of decomposition for weeks." His tone suggested he knew we weren't telling the whole story. "What really went on here?"

Here goes nothing. "Sorry we didn't tell you the truth at first, but you wouldn't have believed us, and you still may not. Hell,

I can barely believe it and we were the ones who survived it." I paused, sighing. "It was alive about an hour ago, and it tried to kill us. We managed to cut its head off with a shovel and then called you guys because we didn't know what else to do."

Joey opened his mouth and closed it again. "Well, where did it come from? You said it broke in through a window, and the only one I see looks fine."

He seemed puzzled and was still not fully grasping what I was trying to tell him. In his defense, I wasn't doing a very good job of explaining.

"That thing is—or was—Mrs. Sexton. She turned into...*that* when she saw what we found in the coal bin."

"What coal bin? What do you mean that animal is Mrs. Sexton? Josh, you aren't making any sense."

Brad remained mute, hands on his hips, but he had an eyebrow quirked like he figured he was being pranked.

Lizzie crossed her arms. "Me and Josh came downstairs to place some mouse traps. We were looking around, and noticed that door. It's an old coal bin. We found an altar and weird stuff, like bones and symbols in there. While we were looking inside, Gran must have heard us or the door, and come down. She caught us, and then...and then..." Her bottom lip began to quiver, and her eyes started to tear up. She'd been seemingly numb until now, and relaying the details aloud must've made it all real to her for the first time.

Witnessing her vulnerability and her on the edge of a breakdown made me want to hold her. I ran a soothing hand over her blonde locks instead.

Joey poked the carcass again, causing part of its ribcage to collapse in on itself with a hollow rasp like sandpaper against pine. It had become dried out and desiccated. More of a withered and smashed pinata than a fresh corpse. In that state, it was hard to believe that, just a couple of hours ago, it had been a powerful beast trying to kill us.

"Is that thing real?" Brad asked, despite our protests to the contrary.

Joey frowned. "Well, there *is* some sort of cellular activity. I mean, it's decaying at a rate I've never seen in anything before. It's as if the air is cystic to it. It seems to be as if the dead cells are imploding on themselves, but it's almost identical to that thing we saw in Josh's backyard weeks ago. I just have no clue what it is." He stood, finished with his examination.

Brad shook his head. "How did that come out of an eighty-year-old woman?"

I still couldn't wrap my mind around it, and I'd witnessed the horror. "I don't know, but it was something from a sci-fi flick." I gave them the short version of bones cracking and skin tearing. How fast it had moved and the strength.

Joey scratched his chin. "Like a moth in a chrysalis or perhaps more like a horsehair worm inside of a mantis?"

"Yeah." That was a good way to describe the situation. They appeared to believe us, and I was grateful. "More like an alien leaving a host, except...an animal."

"This is crazy." Brad, wide-eyed, locked gazes with each of us, and said what I'd been fearing. "How many more are out there? I mean, there was one of these in your backyard awhile back."

No one answered, and the silence hung.

Finally, Joey spoke. "So, what do we do with it?"

"I don't care, just get it out of here." Lizzie hugged herself, her tone robotic. She was stoic, eyes glazed, and she refused to look at the corpse for longer than it took to cast a glance.

Brad and Joey helped me make short work of it. They voiced no problems in stomping the dried husk almost into powder before bagging what was left with heavy black bags from the kitchen. Surprisingly, it only took three not quite full bags.

We hauled them off in the back of Brad's pickup to a holler as far away from town as we could. As the sun set, we took turns digging a grave.

Tossing the bags into the hole and covering them with dirt, I couldn't help but feel there was something criminal about our actions. Burying evidence of crimes at night like common mobsters. Lizzie's grandmother had been nice to us, and monster or not, she deserved something better than a lonely, isolated, shallow grave in the middle of nowhere.

We drove back to town in silence. There wasn't much for us to talk about, seeing as we were in shock and had no answers to our plight. Neither Brad nor I wanted to talk, anyway. Joey tried to turn on the radio, but Brad stopped him with a shake of his head. Given what we'd just done, it wouldn't have felt right.

So, we sat in quiet contemplation, rationalizing and coming to grips with what this meant in our own ways. That we couldn't trust anyone because who knew how many more of our neighbors were monsters. That underneath the thin disguise of humanity, they were hungry beasts, hunting us like prey.

CHAPTER 14

"Hey, Josh, meet us at the library as soon as you can."

It was almost one in the afternoon, and I had been in bed, still asleep. The incessant ringing of the phone had finally forced me to get out of bed just to shut it up. I had been finding it hard to sleep without Nimrod. The dog had been such a part of my life that I hadn't realized just how much I would miss him. His big shaggy bulk was comforting, and without it, I spent most nights tossing and turning in the couple days that had passed since he'd been taken, and what had happened the other night still gave me nightmares.

I could barely bring myself to look in the mirror because seeing my broken nose caused me to remember. Even when I wasn't sleeping alone, what rest I did get was fitful and broken. Lizzie had been staying with me. She didn't want to stay in that house alone, and I wouldn't make her. She spent the nights in my bed, and when we made love, there was no love to it. It was just a desperate, sweaty distraction. The sex had become something primal and life-affirming. We fucked to forget our fear and remind ourselves we were alive. It had become about survival and nothing more.

Though we went to bed together, it was always empty when I woke up. Lizzie was what I considered to be the most obnoxious kind of human—a morning person. There is something very wrong with people who can't wait to wake up and get their days started. For me, a new day was something to be despised and only begrudgingly accepted when one could no longer feint sleep.

The morning also brought with it demonic hangovers. I was drinking too much. I knew it, but given the circumstances, I felt it was an appropriate response. Lizzie must have agreed because she kept pace with me for the most part, save for the fact it seemed she was immune to the consequences of alcohol. Maybe she was just better at hiding it than I was, but I never saw any signs of her suffering skull-shattering headaches or aches from dehydration.

I had nearly fallen down the stairs as I pulled up the second leg of my jeans while trying to navigate the stairs to get to the wall where the phone hung between the kitchen and living room. When I had safely made my way to the bottom, I answered to Lizzie's voice on the other end.

"What?" I said dully, sleep still clouding my brain, making everything fuzzy around the edges. It sounded as if she was speaking from down a long hallway. There was a delay between what she was saying and my brain comprehending it.

"Sorry, what?" I said again, clearing my throat as the cobwebs in my brain slowly lifted.

"Can you meet me at the public library in town?"

"The one in Flemingsburg?" It was the only one around I could think she meant, but with the goblins wearing pointy shoes and doing the dance of the Cossacks in my head, she could have been talking about a library on the moon.

"Yeah."

"When?"

"Now."

I rolled my eyes and nearly passed out as my hangover took the opportunity to kick me between the ears.

"Or as soon as you can." She paused. "Josh? Can you hear me?"

"Yeah, yeah," I mumbled, hunched over the kitchen sink with the phone still to my ear, waiting for the dry heaves to either turn wet or subside. "Give me a few minutes, and I'll be there as soon as I can."

"Oh, and Josh?"

"Yeah."

"Make sure you aren't followed." That last part she added in a conspiratorial whisper as though she expected the line to be bugged.

I knew what, or who, she was hinting at. I started to roll my eyes again, remembered what that had caused a few seconds ago, and stopped myself.

"Yeah, I know." I wiped my mouth as I straightened.

She said goodbye, and we hung up. I could already tell today was not going to be a good day.

Half an hour later, I was showered and changed as I headed out the door to the Charger. I barely paused to glance at the corner to see if Sheriff Earlywine's cruiser was there. These days, I just assumed it always was, so it was a bit surprising when I wheeled the muscle car around the corner onto the main street, and it was missing.

I knew it wouldn't be long before I picked up a tail, and sure enough, as I crossed over the bridge which acted as an unofficial line marking the edge of Midnight Falls, I spotted his cruiser pulling out from a side street. The sun glinted off the windshield, making it impossible to see who drove, but I could tell from the way the driver's side of the car sat lower it was him in there.

So, I made sure I was a soft touch on the gas, not to give him a reason to flip on the red and blues. He didn't need one. If he wanted to give me a hard time, there was nothing and no one to stop him.

Which was why it bugged me he never did. He could've pulled me over every time I got behind the wheel, he could have been handing out tickets and harassment non-stop, but he didn't. He just watched and waited. Waited and watched. It sent chills up my spine. Abusing his power and position I would have understood, and expected, but this was odd, almost creepy, and somehow worse.

He never got close when he followed, never more or less than half a mile back. He had to know he wasn't hiding, but I suspected that was the point. He wanted me to know, be on guard and nervous. I refused to give him what he wanted. If there was one thing I hated, it was bullies, and no wonder his son had been a Grade-A shithead. Never show them fear. That's what they want, but contrary to what my parents had always told me, you can't ignore them, either. I learned that from Seth Woodrow in the sixth grade.

Seth had been held back a year due to being quite a bit dimmer than your average hijack. Which was saying something since Flemingsburg wasn't exactly an intellectual haven. I don't remember why he'd decided to single me out to pick on. I hadn't been the smallest or even the nerdiest kid in class, but for some reason, he got a bug up his ass about me. I just tried to ignore the big oaf, until one day, someone told me Seth was waiting for me to go to the restroom before lunch where he was going to beat me up so bad, they would have to call an ambulance, according to the gossiper.

Well, I had thought the best thing to do was just not go to the restroom. That had been a mistake. Our sixth-grade teacher had taken to standing outside the restroom door to stop kids from horsing around in the bathroom, and ironically, this would have prevented a fight.

I didn't care who called me chicken, I just wanted to avoid getting beaten up. Seth should have been in the eighth grade. He was not only a head taller, but had me by at least fifty pounds. I was maybe eighty pounds soaking wet. No bookie in the world would have taken a bet on that fight. Seth could've easily broken a couple of my bones. Not fighting was the smarter choice, or so I'd thought.

Once the teacher had left the room and positioned herself by the bathroom door, Seth seized his opportunity, snuck up behind me, and hit me with a sucker punch to the ear. It did exactly what you would expect, and I was thrown sideways off my chair with the force of the punch. I busted my lip on someone's chair on my way down. My ear stung as heat radiated. It didn't hurt so much as it pissed me off in a way that I'd never felt in my life. It would've been smart to stay down, but instead, I jumped back up and screamed he was a coward at his retreating back.

He'd whirled around, face blazing red with anger as he came back to finish what he'd started. I don't know if he was too stupid to realize he'd already won or was just a lot braver since he'd gotten in the first shot, cheap as it had been. More likely, he was just pissed and decided to finish what he'd started, even if the teacher caught him.

Unfortunately for him, things didn't go his way. Before he could even wind up another punch, I hit him in the mouth with all the strength my little string-bean arm could muster. It must've caught him off guard because he stumbled. I would like to say I was methodical and did it on purpose, but I was operating on blind rage. I shoved him while he was off balance, and he fell against the blackboard. Grabbing him by the ears, I proceeded to bang the back of his skull against it until the blackboard had cracked.

Somehow, the teacher had missed my screams and the commotion at the start of the fight. It was the sound of the blackboard cracking that had brought her running. When she reached the room, she'd found me astride the bigger boy, wailing on him with all the fury I could rally. By the time she and the assistant principal, whose office was right next door, managed to pull me off him, I had beaten him bloody and broken two of my fingers. I got two weeks of in-school suspension, and my parents had to replace the blackboard. Seth had been taken home by his grandmother.

It wasn't the last time I got picked on by a bully, but it was the first time I'd stopped letting them get away with pushing me around.

This was nothing like the sixth grade. I couldn't exactly punch out a cop. Not because I would get worse than detention, but because Earlywine was a hell of a lot bigger than Seth had been, and he'd already proven that, physically, I was no match for him. He was too well connected for me to go 'running to a teacher,' even if I knew who to report him to. There was only one thing I could think of doing. Give him what he wanted, and see who called whose bluff.

As I drove up the hill towards Elizaville, I dropped the hammer. The big block engine let out a throaty roar like a waking dragon. The back end shimmied as the tires fought against torque for traction. I was thrown back into my seat when they caught, and the beast took off, leaving behind a trail of pale smoke and long black tire marks. By the time I hit the top of the hill, she was hitting her stride, and I felt myself go weightless for a second as the car crested the hill and escaped gravity. At the bottom of the other side, the street became an intersection with the buildings on the corners so close, I couldn't see around them. Holding my breath, I cut the wheel as sharp to the left as I could, and the car coasted around the corner almost sideways, nearly clipping a sedan that had just pulled up to the light. The little old lady behind the wheel had a look of sheer terror on her face as I struggled to dance the Charger around her.

I checked my rearview mirror before the house on the corner blocked it from my vision. The squad car hadn't even topped the hill yet. That had been my plan as soon as I was hidden from sight of the main road. I took a right at the first road I came to, then whipped onto the first farm drive.

I pulled to a dead stop behind a fence row, overgrown with weeds and kudzu, hiding the car from anyone following me. I killed the engine and held my breath as I watched through my rearview mirror. Sure enough, a few minutes later, the Sheriff's cruiser blasted by. It didn't have the Charger's pickup, but it was made to haul ass, and he had it going flat out. Exactly as I had hoped. I'd planned to panic him into chasing me, and after breaking lines of sight, trick him into passing me on a fruitless search, to follow a trail that wasn't there.

Grinning like a fool, I waited a few seconds to give him time to get far enough down the road he wouldn't see me pulling out in his review mirror before firing the engine back up. The Charger purred like a jungle cat, pleased with itself, as I backed out onto the road and pointed it the way I'd come.

As I made my way back to the main road, I turned on the radio and sang along all the way into Flemingsburg, feeling quite clever, thinking my luck was beginning to turn around.

CHAPTER 15

The Fleming County Public Library had originally been the Post Office when I'd graduated high school. Sometime while I was away, they'd built a new Post Office, and the Library had moved in. The building wasn't any bigger than the house I rented. It was a one-story affair, with a basement that was used for public functions from time-to-time. Despite that, I liked it. When walking through the door, I was assaulted by the smell of old paper and leather binding. Not exactly musty, but that aged aroma books get after several decades. I found it comforting, as my parents had always encouraged reading, especially over television.

Our home was always laden with books, mostly paperbacks, everything from John Steinbeck to EC Comics. My mother had disliked them, calling them gratuitous gore and trash, but my father had told her to leave them be. After all, they were no different from the penny dreadful of the Victorian era, now regarded as literary classics, like Shelly's 'Frankenstein' or Stoker's 'Dracula.' As an adult, I wouldn't have gone that far, but I did see their value in getting my younger self interested in not only reading, but writing. I'd wanted to be the next H. P. Lovecraft, but as they say, the best laid plans of mice and men often go astray.

The library itself was the most accurate representation of the inside of my head I had never known existed. The small space had been expertly used to maximize shelf space, and every shelf was crammed from end-to-end with books from floor-to-ceiling. It was chaotic, yet organized. A beautiful mess, my mother would have called it. I'd spent a fair amount of time in the NYU library as well as the New York Public Library, the one with the lions out front, and those felt like libraries. Sterile and stern, unforgiving to those who dared cause disruption within their walls. The Flemingsburg Library was more like an overcrowded used bookshop, the kind owned by a little old person with a cat who lives in the stacks.

I was wondering how anyone could find anything in here when my name was called. Following it, I found Lizzie at a small table, crammed in a back corner, piled with books. She wasn't alone. Joey and Brad were with her, and the bottom dropped out of my stomach as I started to get the feeling I wasn't going to like what she wanted me to see.

As I moved through the stacks to join them, I absentmindedly stretched out one hand and let a finger drift lazily along the spines of the books as I passed. There was a dull, barely audible thud with each passing book, sending vibrations along my forearm. It was comforting, and the whole thing conjured up the ghosts of memories and echoes of nostalgia. The corridor between the bookshelves seemed to stretch on forever as my vision reduced to a pinhole, creating a tunnel effect. As though I was walking my own Bataan Death March, or what prisoners on death row call The Last Mile. That one final walk to the electric chair where they took their last seat.

Then it was gone. The spell broken when I reached the end of the row. Reality, which had been stretched thin, snapped back like an elastic band, and I found myself in a small nook, barely large enough for the table, let alone for people to sit around. This was only compounded by the mountain of books it strained under. I glimpsed a few of the titles, and they were all various things like 'The Beast of Bray Road' or 'The Michigan Dogman and Other Monsters.' They all sounded like Vincent Price films, the kind of black-and-white movies I used to love as a kid.

There were no more chairs available, so I pulled up a round step stool that was used to reach books on the higher shelves, and plunked myself down at the end of the table, completing our little circle so the pow-wow could start in earnest.

I held up my hands as if to say, 'now what', and addressed the group. "Okay, I'm here. Now what?"

Everyone just kind of looked at one other with skeptical, almost ashamed expressions. No one wanted to be the one to come out and say something that would make them look or sound foolish, or crazy.

Crazy was about the be-all and end-all that would describe what had been going on for the past few days, if not months. No, it went back further than that. Ever since I'd returned and settled in Midnight Falls, something had felt off. I'd written it off as some form of jet lag, or civilization whiplash, going from the extreme urban jungle of New York City to a hard dive into the absolute asscrack of rural Kentucky. I knew, just knew, I was about to learn it wasn't, that there really *was* something wrong, not just with us, but the town itself.

"Ever since...you know..." Lizzie stumbled over her words, seemingly trying to force herself to say what she needed to without having to relive it. "The other day, when Gran...when we encountered *that thing*, I haven't been able to really sleep. My brain just won't stop, you know? So, I put it to use trying to figure out what we saw. What happened in that basement."

What happened had hit us all, but me and her harder than Joey or Brad. She did look a bit rough around the edges, but nothing like me. She had a sort of nervous energy about her. She was practically vibrating in her seat, not from fear or anxiety, but from excitement. It was like she was a child who'd learned some new mind-blowing bit of information in school, and couldn't wait to share it with whomever would listen.

"Remember those books on that weird primitive altar in the coal bin?" She didn't leave time for a response, she just held up the two leather-bound items to underline her point. "So, I looked through them, but this one..."

She thumped the cover of the older of the two books. It looked positively ancient, and despite being old, dry, and dusty, it gave off a sort of greasy, somehow foul aura which made me uneasy.

"Well," she continued, "I couldn't read a thing in it. None of it is in English. Most of it isn't language, it's just bizarre markings." Holding up the book, she flipped pages to show what she meant.

"Glyphs," I said.

"What?"

"They're called glyphs, or pictographs. I don't know. They're early proto forms of written language, meant to stand for words or meanings. I didn't really pay that much attention in History Lit class, but those scratches and hash marks look similar to examples of ancient Sumerian or maybe Cuneiform. It kind of looks more primitive than that, actually."

"Yeah, that's what I thought." She picked back up on her original line of thought. "It all looks primitive—the writing, the book, the altar. So, I started looking into sightings of any such creatures in America."

Joey rolled his eyes with a sardonic grimace on his face. "Jesus Christ, please don't say Bigfoot. If you're about to say Bigfoot, I'm sorry, but as a man of science, I will have to walk away."

"Really, Mister Science? You want to explain that thing you saw in the basement," Lizzie snapped.

Joey shut his mouth and dropped his eyes.

We all knew we had long since passed beyond the rational world and into the looking glass where nothing made sense. Bigfoot made just as much sense as anything else.

She gave us all a no-nonsense glare that dared any of us to interrupt. "I started looking through anything I could find on wolf-like creatures. Dog boy, wolfman, anything. Most of what I found was, more or less, along the lines of Bigfoot nonsense, until I started looking into Native Americans. Now, I didn't really find anything that matched in Native American tales from the U.S., but when I started looking into Inuit mythology, I came across this."

She held up another book. It was rather new, with a glossy plastic jacket cover. The title read: "Myths and Monsters of Canada." I was about to make a joke about being killed with politeness by a weremoose, but I caught myself. She was taking this seriously, and given that none of the rest of us had any answers or had bothered to research, why shouldn't we take it just as seriously? She, at least, had something tangible.

She leaned in, and in a conspiratorial whisper, said, "What I believe we're dealing with is the Adlet."

We all just blinked in dumbfounded bewilderment. It didn't register anything to us.

"I'm sorry, what?" Joey asked.

"That doesn't ring a bell for me," added Brad.

I was just as lost. If it wasn't in a Hammer film, I had no clue as far as monsters go.

Lizzie rolled her eyes at us, opened the book to where she had the page marked, and started reading.

"The Adlet is a creature of Inuit legend often also referred to as an Erqigdlet." She stumbled over the pronunciation of that last word, but picked it back up. *"The Adlet are a race of dog or wolf-like creatures that are part beast, part human. The offspring of an Inuit woman named Niviarsiang—"* again she had trouble pronouncing the non-English names *"—who rejected all the human suitors her father Savirqong arranged for her, she instead married a dog named Ijirqang. The two had ten children, five dogs and five Adlets. After Niviarsiang's father killed Ijirqang, she ordered her Adlet children to tear Savirqong apart. Fearing for their lives, the dogs were sent overseas to settle Europe, while the Adlets turned inland to plague and ravage mankind. The Adlets were brutal and warlike. Cannibalistic and blood trusty, the Adlets preferred prey is that of humans."*

Silence resumed as we stared at her.

"Now, listen to this part." Her voice barely contained her excitement at what followed. *"Depiction of these creatures varies. Most commonly, they are described with the hind legs and long tails of wolves, with the upper torso of a man, and claws for hands, but it also has the head of a wolf with a pronounced snout, long fangs, pointed ears, and glowing red eyes."*

A ghastly chill ran down my spine. She had just described exactly the creature who'd attacked us, and it was nearly identical to the thing Joey had shot in my backyard. I could tell from their expressions they'd realized this, as well.

"That isn't the worst part. Listen to this. *The Adlet is not a solitary creature, and hunts in packs like regular wolves. The packs are usually led by an alpha male, who is larger and more aggressive than the rest."* She paused for a moment and looked poignantly at us. "Does that sound like anyone you know?"

"You aren't suggesting..." I trailed off, hoping against hope she wasn't saying what I thought she was implying.

"I'm not. It's pretty clear when you look at this."

She pulled the other book from under the ancient tome and held it up so we could all see it as she flipped through the pages. It was an old photo album, with each page carefully and me-thodically laid out and put together. Unlike other scrapbooks that had fancy lettering, doodles, or glitter and knick-knacks pasted into them, this was plain. Each photo was fastened se-curely, and below it in spidery handwriting, too perfect to be human, were dates. No names or locations, just dates.

Each photo showed several kids in their mid to late teens, all standing side-by-side, center focus of every shot, their proud, beaming parents standing behind them. With each page flip, the decades passed, and time marched forward, changing clothing and hairstyles, but the subjects never seemed to change. They were different children, obviously, but paying closer attention, generations grew and had offspring of their own, and the family patterns repeated. The dates were roughly every seven to eight years or so. The oldest photos started sometime around the Civil War, from appearances and dates. The newest ones all seemed to be instant photos taken with a Polaroid, probably sometime in the 70s. But no matter the era, the kids' faces were all the same—smiling and their chins coated in blood.

Lizzie flipped back to a particular page featuring images from the 50s, and my blood ran cold. In the middle of the group of kids, nearly a head taller than everyone but his father, stood the ghost of Jarrod Earlywine. They were nearly identical, and if I didn't know better, I would have sworn it was him. Young Sheriff Douglas Earlywine was nearly his son's doppelganger. The difference was in the facial shape, or more so the eyes. Where Jarrod's had been piggy and mean with a hint of madness, his father's held no trace of his son's daftness. They were the eyes of a sharpshooter, cold and black. The eyes of someone who had not only killed once or twice, but could do it with emotional detachment as well as enjoyment.

Predator's eyes.

"What the fuck am I looking at?" Brad's tone was solemn.

He'd been quiet for most of Lizzie's grotesque little show and tell, but now, even he was at attention. He'd gone ashen, but was still better than Joey, who was a bit green around the gills.

"From what I can tell, about once or twice a decade, when the children come of age, they have a little induction, similar to Native American's rite of passage when they formally join the tribe. I think when their kids get old enough, they join the pack with a ritualistic feast. Based on the dates, usually on All Hallows Eve."

"Oh, my God" Joey slapped his forehead. "The Harvest Welcome Feast! Of course, now it makes sense."

We all just stared at him, nonplussed, while he gave us all an expression of, *well, duh* as though it was the most obvious thing in the world.

He became exasperated when none of us caught on. "Okay, you know how Midnight Falls doesn't officially celebrate Halloween?" He explained that it was kind of an old story, but everyone in town knew about it. Some time back in the 1800s, the religious fundamentalists banned the celebration of Halloween as a demonic Pagan holiday. The tradition had never really been lifted, though people in Midnight Falls still trick-or-treated.

"Well, instead, they formally celebrated something called the Harvest Welcome Feast. Today, it's treated more like a quasi-Founders' Day/Halloween celebration hybrid. The Welcome Feast used to be a big tradition in the days when agriculture was the primary backbone of America. Back then, people would be hired on by farms as seasonal workers to help bring in the harvest. Most of them were transients and passers-through. It was a major thing up through the Great Depression, and is still kind of a thing going on today with migrant workers. At the end of the harvest, the community would have a big celebration and formally welcome into the community those workers who had done especially good jobs or had become seasonal regulars. It was seen as an honor to be accepted into the community as one of them. The Harvest Welcome Feast is still celebrated in Midnight Falls every year, and every year, it's only by invitation."

Brad jumped in. "And you think this Harvest Feast is where these..."

"Adlets," Lizzie added.

"Yeah, Adlets. Where these things, what? Baptize their young into the pack?"

"Yeah. If you think about it, it makes sense." Joey nodded. "They invite the newcomers, always people fresh to the area, who won't be missed if they just disappeared, and the new Adlets feast on them to prove themselves to the pack."

"So, you're saying every few years, the whole town of Midnight Falls holds a murder party." Brad stared deadpan.

"Not the whole town, I wouldn't think." Joey mused, rocking back in his chair.

"How many, then?" Brad questioned.

I'd been mulling over in my mind, doing arithmetic in my head, counting backward the ages and generations. The answer I came up with was—too many.

"Not all, but most of them, and definitely everyone in here," Lizzie said, tapping her finger on the photo album.

"How do they do it? How do they keep from getting found out? In all these years, all these people, how has no one discovered them?" Brad leaned forward, a hushed tone in his voice, as though he was afraid one of them might be in the next row over, listening.

For all we knew, they could've been.

We all leaned forward into a huddle, the better to whisper.

Joey sighed. "What would they say if we said we found out about a wolf monster murder cult? You and I have seen the bodies, and even I don't fully believe it. All I keep thinking is, there has to be a scientific explanation for all this, and I think that's the problem. Science and the modern age have convinced us there are no monsters, that they're all fairytales and Hollywood movies. Drop Dracula in the middle of goddamn Boston, and no one would believe he was a vampire. David Copperfield made the fucking Statue of Liberty disappear while everyone watched. People can and will explain away anything that conflicts with their view of reality. From the most rational skeptic to the extreme religious fundamentalist, if it doesn't fit into the neat little boxes we can label, it doesn't exist."

"But what about the disappearances?" Lizzie asked. "Wouldn't the police at least have to acknowledge and investigate them?"

Joey shook his head. "Setting aside who is on the police force for the moment, let's take any given year. The number of people who vanish—not counting those who run away, fugitives, anonymous drug deaths, or are found later—but those who *really* disappear and are never found? Ever? Those numbers, when put up against general population statistics of their geographical region, roughly two to ten percent of their populations vanish without a trace. These rates are nearly identical in predator/prey populations, which is the ratio of prey animals needed to support any given predator population. Something *is* hunting us. The numbers don't lie. We just don't know who or what is doing it. It's a statistical fact no one talks about."

We all sat in stunned silence after that little diatribe. The Midnight Falls elementary science teacher had just dropped a major bomb on us, upending the world we thought we knew. He just drove home the point we'd all been tiptoeing around—that the monsters under the bed were real, and comforting lies we told ourselves about turning on the light or hiding under the covers didn't do shit.

"So, how do they perform these rituals? They just kill anyone who shows up to their party?" Brad asked, finally breaking our melancholy.

"No," replied Joey. "It's by invitation only, which is brilliant, in part. They send invites to their victims like, 'Hey, welcome to the neighborhood. We want to formally welcome you to town,' and newcomers unknowingly walk right into the trap."

"What if they don't show up?" I asked.

"Poland," he replied.

"Poland?" Lizzie asked, confusion wrinkling her brow.

"He means they come to get you, like the Nazis in WWII when they invaded Poland." I frowned.

"*Oy gevalt*." She groaned.

"Pretty much." I agreed.

"What do these invitations look like?" Brad asked. "Are we talking fruit baskets or stripper-grams? I mean, yeah, they're trying to kill ya, but they could at least do it with a nice piece of ass. I'm just saying, if you're going to bait a trap, use the right bait."

He was joking, but I could tell he was just as nervous as the rest of us. He was dealing with it using humor, otherwise, he'd probably be doing what the rest of us felt like doing—running from the building, screaming until the men in white coats and butterfly nets were called.

"They send out their invitations in little red envelopes, or so I have heard." Joey shrugged. "The Community Committee has been working on it for the last month. I offered to volunteer like I do for the Community Center events, but they said they had all the volunteers they needed."

I didn't hear most of what he said after the part about the envelopes. The world seemed to go eerily silent. All I could do was picture my coffee table at home where I had dropped the mail without looking at it. The stack of envelopes had been casually tossed aside until I could bother to go through them. The small bright red one that was in the bundle had caught my eye when I'd picked them up from the Post Office.

There was an invitation sitting on my coffee table in my house right now, and it was all my brain could focus on as alarm bells of panic started clanging in my head.

"Holy shit!" I shot to my feet.

Everyone looked at me with alarm.

Suddenly remembering where I was, I clapped both hands over my mouth and slowly sat back down.

"What's wrong, Josh?" Lizzie asked tentatively, as though she were trying to talk a suicidal person off a ledge.

I leaned forward into our little solitary circle. "There's an invitation in a red envelope at my house right now!" I whispered furiously, trying and mostly succeeding in keeping my voice down. "I think it came in the mail yesterday. I've been putting off looking at the mail since I missed my last two deadlines, and I'm pretty sure the Gazette will be sending me a pink slip any day now." After missing two of my last three deadlines, assignments had been steadily falling off in both quality and frequency. Soon, I would be out on the street if things didn't pick up or change, but it looks like that might not be an issue.

I was going to be murdered before they could fire me.

"I think I got one of those, too." Brad scratched his massive chin.

"I've been too busy to check the mail lately, but I bet there is one in mine, as well," Lizzie added.

We all looked to Joey expectantly.

The guy shrugged. "Since I'm on the volunteer committee, I believe I'm already invited to all functions, but this time, given that I've been kept out of the loop, I'm not sure I would get one. They may just expect me to show up." He sighed and wiped his glasses on the hem of his shirt.

Stunned silence held fast in the air, and none of us had anything to add.

"So, what now?" I asked.

"We come up with a plan. We stop these monsters before they kill us," Lizzie said.

"I cannot believe we're actually talking about this," Brad mumbled.

"Ugh, not this again." Joey rolled his eyes.

"Look, I know we've been through a lot, and we can't pretend we don't know this is real," I admitted, "but we can't possibly tackle this ourselves. We should tell someone. The police, the government, something."

"How would we do that? We don't have a lot of time, and we already know at least one of those things *is* a cop. Who knows how many more there could be." Lizzie huffed.

"Judging by the photos in the book," Joey interjected, "quite a lot. A conservative estimate, based on the time periods cataloged and standard generational deviations or trends, is roughly sixty to seventy percent. Maybe higher. But, for sure, everyone who attends will be a monster."

"So, as far as we know, the entire town is setting us up to be...what? Murdered? And your plan is to murder them before they murder us. That's insane." I shook my head. "The smart thing is to run."

"We can't run, Josh. In every account I could find, from the Dogmen to the Dwayyo, it's always the same. These creatures, once they've seen you, and you've seen them, they stalk you and they keep coming after you, until..." She let the unspoken sentiment hang in the air like an ominous storm cloud.

The unpronounceable death sentence weighed heavily upon our heads. I wondered if this was how soldiers in WWI or on D-day felt, knowing they'd soon be walking into certain demise.

"Between running and dying, I say run," I repeated for what felt like the millionth time.

"Run, and you will only die tired," Joey replied. "I can't remember where I read that, but it seems apt. Wolves are persistence hunters. They chase prey down until it's too tired to run anymore, then they move in for the kill."

"Jesus Christ, the Harvest Festival is just a few days away, and you guys want to go off half-cocked with this? Fine, but I'm out. I'm gone. I'm packing up tonight and heading anywhere but here."

I stood, and couldn't help but shrink at the hurt on Lizzie's face. It had to be hard for her to watch me flee like a coward, but better a live coward than a dead idiot.

Dead was exactly what they were going to be if they went with her naive power trip. There'd been no hint of fear in her eyes when she'd exposited all of her findings. The opposite. She'd been excited, wired almost, at the idea of riding to the rescue like some hero in a book, but this wasn't fiction. In the real world, heroes usually died.

I stormed out of the library, leaving her behind for what felt like the last time. My mind was made up. I guess you could call it my pattern of behavior. Run and leave my problems behind me, and just pick up somewhere else to start over.

No matter what guilt followed.

CHAPTER 16

Before I could get halfway across the parking lot, someone called my name, and against my better judgment, I turned.

Joey had followed me out of the building and was hailing me.

"Hey, Josh, hey!" He jogged after me. "Hey, man. I know this is all kind of...much, but you've got to hang in there and not do anything rash."

"I meant what I said in there. I'm out, man. There is nothing you can say to me to change my mind. I'm heading home, then I'm getting out of here."

"You have to do what you think is right. I know there isn't anything I can say to make you stay, and I don't want to. You probably have the most rational head on your shoulders of all of us right now. Things haven't been easy on you these past months. Trust me when I say, I know what it's like to feel like an outsider with everyone against you."

"Yeah, and what's that got to do with any of this craziness?"

I took a beat-up cigarette pack from my hip pocket. I stuck one of the bent coffin nails between my lips and lit it with a flick of my Bic before offering Joey the pack. It was an automatic reflex from practiced habit, but to my surprise, the guy took one. I passed him the little plastic lighter, and he lit up, as well.

He took a long drag before looking at me. "I'm not going to dump my purse in your lap, so to speak, but as far as this 'business' goes, well, I don't think anyone alive has a frame of reference for it. You're young, but you're not dumb. At least you're a lot smarter than I was at your age. I did a lot of stupid things, but I also saw a lot of things. And I know when you see a, let's call it an injustice—"

I laughed at the idea of comparing shape-shifting monsters to an injustice as though we were discussing civil rights, racism in America, or the Vietnam War.

"You can't leave them be," he finished. "They don't solve themselves. Lord knows, I wish they did. So many lives were pointlessly lost or irrevocably changed because good men stood by. Have you ever heard the saying, 'The only thing necessary for the triumph of evil is for good men to do nothing'?"

I nodded, thinking I'd seen it on some TV show or another. A sappy speech delivered to fire up a crowd by a Jimmy Stewart type. Not really something I'd ever put much thought into myself.

"Do you know who said that?" he asked.

"Nope, guessing someone in the Bible?"

"Edmund Burke, eighteenth-century philosopher," Joey answered as though he hadn't really heard my reply. "Right now, there is a crisis in the U.S., that people, especially the government, are only too happy to be silent on because it serves their agenda. To marginalize and destroy a demographic of the population who deserves to exist. And yet, here I am, the good man, doing nothing. Saying nothing. Hiding out of fear, allowing the injustice to continue while others fight."

"And what does that have to do with the price of tea in China?" I was annoyed he was going to start haranguing me to stay and join their little crusade.

"Not a thing, not a thing at all. Only, you're not as alone as you think you are. Everyone likes to romanticize their problems as if they're the only ones who've ever had them. Many men have hoed that road before." He shook his head and pitched what was left of the cigarette butt into the gravel. "You do what you have to, and I am going to do what I have to. This, here? This is an injustice I can do something about. This is an evil I will fight."

I was about to tell him to take a flying fuck at a rolling donut, but something in his eyes stopped me. They were suddenly so old and weary. He was maybe in his late thirties to mid-forties, but in that moment, he looked sixty, at least. He wore the sad, beaten expression of a man who had lived through one heartbreaking circumstance after another, like the very definition of an old soul in a young person's body. Or maybe, better yet, old before his time. Like those pictures of men during the Depression, tired and worn, all the hope crushed out of them.

He sighed, and it was gone.

"All right, enough preaching. I promised I would help you get Nimrod back, yeah?"

I nodded, the afternoon sun causing sweat to bead on the nape of my neck. The parking lot blacktop had grown hot, and was throwing the sun's heat back at us.

"Whelp, let's head over to the Animal Control office and put a bug in Jeff Helpenstein's ear."

With that, we piled into my Charger and headed over to the City Utilities office on Rail Road Street, behind the Flemingsburg Fire and Police Stations. It was a large metal warehouse and garage where the city vehicles and equipment were kept or maintained.

We found Jeff in the back in a small closet that had been converted into a makeshift office.

Joey went in to talk with him, probably afraid I would brain the man with whatever I could get my hands on with as worked up as I was. He was probably right, given that, in the short drive over, I had smoked all four of the remaining cigarettes in the pack.

They came out of the office, both men red-faced, and a vein bulging in Jeff's neck. Whatever had been said, the two had clearly been arguing, though I hadn't been able to hear them over the roaring of machines in the garage.

We were led through the door into another back room I had no idea was even there. Inside, along with several pieces of road equipment, was a stack of kennels.

My poor buddy looked so sad with his furry bulk squished into a metal cage too small for such a large dog. It was heartbreaking to see the goofy mutt who bounced around open yards or sprawled out on the carpet or couches confined to such a tiny cage that he couldn't even turn around. His ears pricked up when he saw us enter. Nimrod nearly burst through the cage door before Jeff could get it open. The big mutt could've broken out if he'd really wanted to, or had been smart enough to realize the flimsy wire mesh couldn't hold him.

Once freed, he was all over me, jumping up and licking my face, nearly knocking me over as I fought to keep from falling on my ass and being buried under the furry behemoth. There are no words to express the unbridled joy one feels from such an animal relishing its freedom and being reunited with their owner, and that feeling is very much infectious. I'm not sure which of us was happier and more relieved.

He was overjoyed when we took him outside, dancing back and forth on his leash. I'm sure it was much better than being trapped in that hot smelly back room. He even happily hopped in the backseat for the ride back to the library to drop Joey off.

I thanked him as he got out. Without his help, I'm not sure I would've gotten Nimrod back, or something even worse might've befallen my dog. Things were not okay, but better than they'd been.

As Joey headed to his car, he looked back one last time and said, "Josh, I know you're a good man." And that was the end of that.

Nimrod hopped into the front seat and stuck his big head out the window. I knew he wanted a long ride with the wind in his face, and he deserved it. He was going to get a lot of it as we had plenty of miles to put between us and the town of Midnight Falls.

Once at home, I began packing the Charger. I could've sworn it all had fit in the car when I'd arrived in town months ago. It's amazing the junk we accrue just by settling down. All of it parts of our lives, and in a way, it was life itself. All the little things, from takeout menus to that cluttered notepad next to the phone, the socks and shoes kicked off by the door, and stacks of magazines next to the couch—all of it speaks of life. Signs that someone is living, not just existing. It's all those little things we don't think of that really make a house a home. A place to relax, kick your feet up, and stay awhile. Where you're safe.

Something that's proven a contradiction when one is in a hurry to leave, and quickly, you realize just how much you're willing to give up in the name of survival. Man is nothing if not adaptable. If the goal is just survival, then one needs nothing more than a place to eat and to lay their head. In the greater scheme, if the goal is just to stay alive, nothing matters other than that. If caught in a trap, a coyote will chew off its leg to get free.

I guess my survival instincts were not as good as a coyote's. I couldn't just light out. I had to make something of an attempt to salvage my belongings. That boiled down mostly to my clothing and my dog. Nimrod sat on the passenger seat, his knucklehead laying on the windowsill, eyes disappointed he'd been in the car for almost fifteen minutes, and yet, he was not zooming down the road with the wind in his fur.

I was running back and forth between the house and the car, stuffing what I could in the trunk. My mind ran in circles, counterproductive in its panic, racing as I tried to plan and sort through what I needed and what to leave behind. TV? Too big. Books? I loved my books and I could buy more, but I also had a limited budget of whatever was left in my bank account. Clothing? Yes, obviously. Dog dish and food? Of course, Nimrod needed to eat.

I was debating the food in the fridge, weighing having to buy more over risking it going bad in the car, when Lizzie showed up. She leaned against the rear bumper when I came out of the house with another load of stuff.

"So, you really are just leaving?"

I ignored her, opening the car door and muscling the load into the backseat.

I think of myself as the nice guy, but in reality, I'm just as shallow and self-interested as the next jerk. I was putting my own survival over doing the right thing. As Joey had said, *a good man doing nothing,* no matter how much I cared for someone. Lizzie included. I was choosing to run.

She reached out and put a hand on my arm. I hadn't even noticed it had been shaking, but something about her soft, familiar touch seemed to calm my mind, and the shaking stopped.

Oh God, I wanted to hold her to me in that moment, to feel her body pressed to mine. I would've clung to her like a life raft in a storm. I wanted to grab her and plead with her to come with me. I would've gotten on my knees and begged if I thought it would've worked.

But she had a look in her eyes that proved she was dead set on going through with their plan. She wanted this, wanted a mission that would break apart her boring provincial existence in a little town, where people spent their entire lives without ever being noticed. A desire that's seemingly universal to the foolishness of youth, seen in nearly all teenagers and young adults who hadn't learned how vulnerable they were or how cruel the world could be.

She wasn't jaded yet. Despite seeing real danger and facing her mortality in that basement, she still thought she was invincible. I wished I still shared that belief, but I'd learned the hard way trying to fix problems only made them worse. I lost the words, if I'd ever possessed them, to persuade her to join me. All the outcomes I foreshadowed for her ended poorly.

"You should leave, too. Just pack some clothes and get out of town. Go...somewhere, anywhere but here."

She shook her head. "They'll just track us down if we run."

"You don't know that."

"The book says they will—"

"You don't know that!" I snapped.

She flinched, backing away from me. Hurt and real fear lanced her eyes.

"You don't know that," I repeated in a calmer tone. "We don't know if any of what the books say is true. We're in the dark here, trying to understand and deal with something we've been told to believe was a fairytale for hundreds of years."

"It's better than nothing," she shot back. "We have to take anything we can get because you're right, we don't know what we're dealing with, not really. So, isn't it better to accept any help at this moment? We need all the advantages to fight these things, and that's what we have—an advantage. They don't know we know about them, and they aren't expecting their victims to fight."

"These monsters have been here since God knows how long. They've been doing these rituals and hunting for hundreds of years without anyone ever even suspecting them. You think they haven't dealt with threats before? They know what they're doing, and they know they have nothing to fear from us."

I thunked my head against the roof of the car in exasperation. How could I make her realize how much danger we were in?

"We've managed to kill two of them already. They aren't immortal. They're flesh and blood. They can be beaten. We can beat them." She huffed. "But we need you, we need all the help we can get."

"We got lucky. We can't count on getting lucky again, much less lucky enough to kill...how many? We don't even know."

"Yes, but now we have a plan."

"No." I shook my head. "You are talking about a suicide mission."

It was frustrating how dead set she was on going forward. I knew arguing with her wouldn't work. The deadline was closing in, and every second I spent trying was time wasted, better spent getting out of Dodge, but I couldn't help myself. If she would just get in the car, she could pick any random spot on the map, and we could start a new life there. Hell, it could've been Albuquerque or Timbuktu.

For her, it would be worth it.

"Go then," she spat, the wind whipping that gorgeous straw-colored hair of hers around her face. "Go ahead and run, but just know, you'll be running for the rest of your life. It doesn't matter how far you go or how fast you drive. Until you face your problems, they will always be chasing you. You ran away from your problems at home to New York, and when that didn't work out, you ran here to get away from the city. You ran away from that asshole Jarrod's bullying, and he was just a kid. Then, you tried to run away from thinking you were responsible for his death. You've been distant and withdrawn since we found out. You think I haven't noticed how much you've been drinking? Writer's block and booze are just you refusing to deal with your shit. You're a grown man, Josh, not a kid, so stop acting like it. You aren't the person I thought you were. You're a fucking coward. So, go ahead and keep running, but don't bother to look back, because there won't be anything here for you anymore."

She turned on her heels and walked away.

Somewhere, deep down, a primal anger reared its head, and I had an urge I hadn't ever felt before. A violent one because she was correct. It faded quickly, buried by shame.

I watched as she left, and all I could think was a snatch of poetry from my college days. Something about how regrets are made in the smallest of moments, but have an infinite existence. I should've stopped her from leaving. I should've grabbed her and kissed her. I should've told her how I felt, and that she was right. Small moments of infinite regret, a life half-lived, and a love half-loved. Regrets that would follow me for the rest of my days.

The sun had nearly set when I tossed the last of my possessions into the Charger and slammed the trunk. With Nimrod in the passenger seat, I reversed out of my driveway with a squeal of tires. I told myself not to look back, but I couldn't help it. As if possessed, I looked at the darkened windows and empty yard. Memories of evenings spent with Lizzie on the couch, sharing laughs. Days spent fixing up the place with Brad's help while my dog played in the yard. If only time could've stood still, and those memories could last forever.

I punched the radio knob to try to drown out my thoughts, only to be treated to Bonnie Tyler soulfully singing about her broken heart. Proof that God has a sick sense of humor. In the rearview mirror, I caught Joey standing on his front porch, holding a coffee cup in one hand. He tipped me a farewell salute with the hand holding the mug.

I dropped the hammer on the old girl, and laid a cloud of smoke and rubber the length of the street. Seconds later, I was crossing the bridge and heading out of town. My headlights carved a never-ending down in the night air as the car passed through it.

I drove all night in a hypnotized state. No matter how many hundreds of miles between me and Midnight Falls there were, it never seemed like enough.

In the early hours of the morning, exhausted, I pulled into a truck stop and shut the engine off. In the absence of its powerful rumble, the silence was so heavy, it was oppressive. The world seemed empty. For the first time in months, I truly felt alone. I had no plan or clue what I was doing, other than to just keep driving. Everything I had was left behind me and, unlike the other instances, there was nothing ahead of me. Before, there had been relief or excitement when I'd fled a bad situation. Now, all that lurked was guilt and anger. Anger at myself for being a coward. Lizzie had been right about that. There was nothing I could do now, I told myself, but just keep going and figure something else out.

Nimrod laid his big head on my lap, looking up at me with his startling blue gaze. He kept giving me those big sad eyes. He was just a dumb dog, for Christ's sake, one that forgot where his food bowl was half the time, and even he knew what a loser I was. It was as if he was silently saying, *Hey, dumbass, what are you doing? The pretty girl is back there. Your friends are back there, where the monsters are, and you're leaving them to save your own skin. I may eat my own poop, but you're a fucking idiot.*

"Jesus Christ, not you, too." I moaned. "You think I'm a piece of shit, too, don't you?"

The husky just blinked in response, still judging me with those eyes.

"You probably think we should go back."

He sat up and grinned in that goofy way of his.

"Well, shit. I am an asshole, aren't I?"

He put one paw on my leg as if to say, *Well, duh.*

"Fine, let me get a quick nap, then we'll head back."

I'd never felt so low in my life. She'd been right. I was a fucking coward. I'd been acting like a child, running away from my messes instead of accepting and dealing with the consequences. Like I was special and somehow above it all. The sheer immeasurable immaturity of my entitlement made me sick in the pit of my stomach. I had to grow up. I had to stop acting like a dumb kid and do the things I didn't want to. No matter how much it scared me, I had to go back and face my problems head on, and hopefully, I wouldn't be alone.

Nimrod danced around in a circle on the passenger seat before curling up.

I laid my own seat back and closed my eyes. Maybe it was time to grow up and face my problems. Given what waited for me back in Midnight Falls, it made my past struggles seem small and petty. I was choosing to do the brave thing and knowingly walk into danger to try to save my friends.

It would probably be the dumbest decision of my life.

Chapter 17

I had only managed to sleep a few hours, and what sleep I did get was fitful. It had nothing to do with trying to doze in my car. Anxiety refused to allow me to even reach a place where I could have nightmares. After several attempts to go back to sleep, I finally gave it up as a bad job and began to make my way back to Midnight Falls.

Somehow, I'd managed to almost make it to the Kansas state line, and the return trip seemed to be much more daunting and take longer than it had the night before. I'd pushed the speed limit most of the way. Even then, I barely made it in time.

I pulled up in front of Lizzie's house with only an hour to spare before the Festival at the Community Center had been set to start. The drive past it on my way back into town had shown their parking lot was already almost full.

My heart was pounding in my chest and my panicked brain pummeled me with horrible thoughts of missing my friends just seconds before they left. I got lucky, and Lizzie opened the door in surprise after I pounded on it. Her face was pale as she timidly peeked out, obviously fearful of just who might be on the other side. Those emerald eyes filled with relief when she saw me.

We didn't say a word. She threw her arms around me and held on as if she were afraid if she loosened her grip, I would run away again. Her fear was probably justified, as I can't say I wouldn't have. It felt good, like coming home. The smell of her and feel of her blonde hair in my hands fed some waning part my soul and filled me with a warmth I hadn't known I was missing.

Nimrod let out a booming bark from the open car window to let us know he was there, too.

Lizzie let out a hysterical giggle of relief.

"I'm glad you came back," she said, her face buried in my chest.

"Me, too. I couldn't let you do this alone."

"I'm not alone. We have to hurry and get to Joey's place. He says he has a plan all set up that he thinks is going to work. He hasn't shared the details yet, but you'll be impressed with what we came up with so far."

She sounded confident and, in that moment, I started to believe maybe we could make it through the night alive. We wouldn't let the monsters win.

Brad met us at Joey's house and let us into the garage where Joey was waiting for us. There was barely enough room in the garage for the four of us, a big dog, and Joey's small Honda. We managed to crowd around a workbench that looked well-used. Above it was a large hand-drawn building blueprint. Several Polaroid snapshots of the Community Center's front and back entrances were pinned up with the map. It reminded me of that scene from the 'Thomas Crown Affair' with Steve McQueen. Though, I didn't feel much like McQueen. Maybe if I had a leather jacket, it would've been better.

"Hey, man. I'm glad you showed up. I thought maybe you had skipped town." Brad greeted me with a wide grin.

"Well, that had been the plan," I admitted.

"Yeah, then what happened?"

"Best laid plans of mice and men."

"I hear that. So, you came back." He shook his head as if he couldn't believe it. "Leaving was probably the smart thing to do."

"Yeah, probably," I agreed.

"Glad to have you with us, Josh. Not sure what else we could've done. You know how insane all this is, right?" Joey looked as if he couldn't believe it himself.

"We *are* planning to kill a bunch of people, who turn into monsters, and who are planning to kill us. Pretty much the definition of insane." I nodded. "What *is* the plan, exactly?"

"Well, if we do this right, hopefully, no one actually has to die. Or, at least, we don't have to kill anyone directly." Joey pointed to the map. "Here on this side of the auditorium, there's a door that leads to the basement. It's always locked and only the council members have keys. The basement is supposedly mostly for storage and the boiler room. However, from the research Elizabeth and I have done, we suspect it's the Adlet's lair—a sort of central hub for the pack's power where they keep their kills and main altar to their mother. Now, according to the lore, destroying the lair should destroy the pack. Or, at least it does in all the old Inuit legends. I don't know how this is supposed to work, but erring on the side of caution, this does have real-world parallels with actual wildlife. Hunters who are dealing with coyotes will burn the den to drive out the pack, causing them to move on and find a new home. This is the same tactic hunters used back in the frontier days for dealing with wolves. Killing off the leaders of the pack and burning their dens would cause the pack to fragment and disperse. Hopefully, we burn down the Community Center and, in the chaos, anyone left will panic, forget about us, and instead focus on relocating to keep themselves hidden. This is the best chance to wipe as many of them out in one shot as possible."

"And if it does work like the books say?" Lizzie asked him.

Joey shrugged. "They all just magically drop dead? I would say that's a net win for everyone, but I'm not holding out hope."

Everyone just kind of looked at each other, clearly thinking the same thing.

"How does this actually work?" I asked. "How are we supposed to get in there and set the place on fire? It's crawling with people already."

"That's both the tricky and the easy part." Joey sighed. "We're going to walk right in the front door."

The three of us looked at him like he was insane.

"Just hear me out." He pointed to the front and back doors on the blueprint. "These are the only ways in or out of the building. The three of us, you, me, and Elizabeth, will go in normally and act as if nothing is wrong, like it's just a regular party and we don't know what they're planning."

"Your plan is to walk right into their trap? Okay, that's insane," Brad said. "You know how dangerous and stupid that is."

I was thinking the same thing.

"Yes, but it's the perfect cover. While the two of them act as a distraction, I can get ahold of one set of basement keys. Marie Latterback always leaves her purse unattended at these events. It's like the woman is practically begging people to steal from her. I can sneak into the basement. While that's going on, Brad, you will chain the front door closed once everyone is in, then wait around back by the doors to let us out. We lock them in."

"And how are you going to guarantee the basement fire will spread fast enough before the fire department shows up?" Brad stroked his chin, seemingly mulling over this information, acting more and more confident in the plan as Joey elaborated.

He ducked under the worktable and lifted a couple of clear glass containers. They looked like large mason jars filled with dirt and oil. Their lids had what appeared to be the guts of a digital alarm clock taped together. Our friendly elementary school science teacher had managed to make himself some homemade bombs.

"These are a couple of napalm bombs."

"Holy fuck, my man. What are you, some sort of terrorist?" Brad's jaw hung wide as he picked up one of the jars to examine it.

"Well, I wouldn't go that far. Mostly, it's just basic science and some improvisation." He took the jar back and put it down gently. "It's pretty stable, but best to err on the side of caution."

"Where did you manage to get explosives like this?" I was as shocked as Brad, and a little scared at what Joey could apparently make in his garage on short notice with a little motivation.

"It's not difficult. These are all household items." He pointed to the cloudy liquid at the top of the jar. "That's the napalm. It's a mixture of Styrofoam and kerosene, which will stick to walls and floors to make sure they burn. This part is just run-of-the-mill fertilizer from my garden." He indicated the dirt that took up the bottom half of the jar. "The high nitrate level will combust when exposed to the flames of the napalm, spreading it over a good distance. I didn't get a chance to test it, but if my math is correct, it should cover a good distance. The rest is just a clock radio attached to a spark plug to ignite the mixture on a timer."

It was an impressively simple and nasty little device. It reminded me of photos I'd seen of the kinds of devices that the IRA was currently using in Ireland to protest the British government. If something like this could blow up a café, it could easily cause enough damage to burn down the Community Center.

Something about seeing and holding it in my hand suddenly made it all too real. What we were planning was domestic terrorism, plain and simple. Even if they were monsters, what we were doing was no different from the justifications of extremists across the globe. It turned my stomach and caused me to ask myself if we were sure we should really proceed.

"What if it doesn't work, or someone stops us?" Lizzie faced Joey. "We need a backup plan in case you can't get to the basement, or they catch us first."

"We do." Joey took out what looked like a road flare with a wire connecting it to a small black box. "This is an ANFO charge. I was able to steal it from the Road Works Department. On its own, like this, it still packs a punch, but it's not enough for what we need. But tomorrow is Sunday, and you know what that means."

Brad and Lizzie looked puzzled, but after a few seconds, I realized what he was getting at.

"Sunday morning, while everyone is in church, the gas station across the alley refills their underground tanks," I answered.

"How do you know that?" Lizzie still seemed lost.

But a light bulb seemed to go on in Brad's head.

"Every Sunday morning, we can hear that gas tanker." Brad crossed his arms. "It's sitting out there right now, full of fuel, waiting for tomorrow. So, you want to steal the truck, stick the ANFO in the tank, then blow the entire building sky high?"

"It doesn't have to be the tank, anywhere on the truck will work, really, but yeah. We park the truck right behind the building where the propane tanks are, which will add to the blast. When it goes off, it will level the Community Center, the Post Office, and wreck anything within a block. Originally, that was my first plan, but that level of destruction I think makes it a better backup plan."

"Jesus Christ," we all chorused.

Joey nodded. "That's why we should hope we don't have to resort to that. In the short term, we have other ways to discourage people from stopping us. Thankfully, I already had all of these." He turned from the bench full of explosives to his car. Taking out his keys, he unlocked and opened his trunk. It was full of firearms. There had to be more than a dozen guns, several of them appeared to be military-grade, along with boxes of bullets. You could fight a small war with what he had in his car boot.

"Joey, you're starting to scare the shit out of me, man. Just who the fuck are you?"

Brad's hushed tone echoed my own thoughts.

"What do you do in your spare time, knock over banks?"

"The Second Amendment says it's my right to own all these. A man has to defend his home. You think it's bad being a black man in a backwater like this? Try being gay."

He'd never come outright and admitted his sexuality before. The only thing shocking to me was the fact he did. To us. And I realized, right then and there, each of us had something we were running from or battling. Monsters not withstanding.

Joey took out an AK-47, loading a magazine into it before handing it to Brad.

"Oh, hell no, scary white boy. I know you just did not hand a black man a machine gun in a town full of hillbillies. Are you trying to get me killed?" He handed the gun back and pulled out the Dirty Harry gun he'd taken from Joey weeks ago. "If it's all right with you, Rambo, I think I'll just stick with this one."

It didn't look as big in his hands as it had when Joey had first used it in my backyard.

Joey started to pass it to me, but I shook my head and picked a .45 handgun out of the pile. It was a 1911. I checked the slide to make sure the chamber was empty like I'd seen Magnum PI do. Loading one mag into the gun, I put two extras into my pockets before stuffing the gun in the waistband of my pants.

Lizzie eyed a shotgun. "Are you sure these will kill them?"

"They should. After all, I've already shot one, and Josh killed another with a shovel. So, it stands to reason, if we put enough bullets in one until it stops moving, it'll do the trick. For obvious reasons, we can't just shoot them all. Even I don't have that much ammo. For anyone else, just waving these around should send them running."

Lizzie shrugged and dropped the shotgun to pick up a small machine pistol. A MAC-10, which I recognized from old episodes of 'Miami Vice.'

Fully locked and loaded, we were ready to put our plan into action.

CHAPTER 18

Lizzie and I entered the Community Center fifteen minutes later, and the handgun in the back of my waistband felt really conspicuous. Despite her reassurance it couldn't be seen under my shirt, it felt to me that it stuck out about a mile, and there was no way everyone else couldn't see it. It was extremely uncomfortable and awkward. I wasn't a gun person, and walking around with one just felt wrong. I also wasn't sure that, if it came to it, I would be able to use the thing, never mind hitting something. I grew up shooting rifles, but this wasn't the same. This wasn't hunting, it was about killing people.

I couldn't get rid of the lump in my throat.

We were stopped at the door by Coach Littleton, who was checking invitations. Tonight's party was an adult-only by-invitation affair. A great way to ensure only the right people were there to enjoy a mauling.

Lizzie had her invite, but I'd thrown mine away the second I'd found it in my mail stack.

Littleton just laughed and shook his head, letting us through as if we were the guests of honor. I breathed a sigh of relief. I hadn't even had time to make up an excuse, but we'd breezed right on through.

Inside the building, the atmosphere was very different from outside. The night had been slightly cool, as fall had finally managed to overtake Indian summer, but the air inside the auditorium was warm and heavy. It was an oppressive, almost jungle-like environment, decorated with lots of leafy plants and streamers. There were props and stands all about the place, made in extremely primal designs. Many were similar to fodder shocks, the bundles of corn decorated with animal bones and symbols from twigs and twine. I recognized the most common one—a warped-looking Y with a hash mark in the crook of the arms. They were everywhere, turning the usually wide open space into a claustrophobic obstacle course.

There were patrons everywhere. It was a sea of bodies, shoulder-to-shoulder, wall-to-wall. Not just the usuals I'd seen at Center functions before, but others I knew not by name, just in passing. Old and young alike, from a handful of high schoolers to senior citizens. Even though the lights were low, I recognized a few of the elderly bunch as friends of Ms. Sexton from church. It looked like most of those churchgoers were here, which was odd because a lot of them, like Lizzie's grandmother, hadn't liked the place. I once heard her call it garish. Yet, here they were, as if it were just another Sunday picnic.

Every step felt like it took us deeper and deeper into some primeval darkness. I could hear my own heartbeat as it weighed upon me. Clenching my teeth to keep from screaming, the anticipation was nearly unbearable, hanging over our heads.

The party atmosphere was no different from the last time Lizzie and I were here together, but there were slight notable differences. There was no buffet table or dancing, and even the music was resolute. Despite that, there was the same excited buzz of energy running through the crowd, like everyone was waiting for something to happen.

I looked around for Joey, but I couldn't spot him. He'd entered through the back staff entrance, claiming it would be easier to slip in unnoticed. After all, he had to smuggle in two bombs and that ridiculous rifle, if he could manage it.

I found Marie Latterback and Charlie Story talking at the edge of the stage, but no Joey.

Something we'd overlooked in our plans was we had no way to communicate. I guess we'd know when the bombs went off, but we were supposed to cause a distraction, and we had no idea when we were expected to do it.

Shit. We had no plans for *how* to distract everyone.

I turned to Lizzie, whispering, "How are we supposed to get everyone's attention so Joey can sneak into the basement?"

She leaned in and whispered back, "I don't suppose you can just pull down someone's pants again?"

I rolled my eyes.

"Exposing one minor's penis is an accident. Exposing multiple penises tends to be one of the things that gets you locked up in jail. And the last thing I want to do is give Sheriff Earlywine a reason to arrest me."

She snickered at my attempt at humor, but I was seriously worried about the Sheriff catching us. It was bad enough he hated me for personal reasons, but after finding out he was one of those...things, and the purpose of tonight was to use us as sacrifices, it would be like putting a welcome mat at my backdoor.

I looked around and couldn't spot him, either. The man was a giant. It wouldn't be hard to miss him, and I knew he'd be here. There was no way he'd miss out on watching us die, even if not partaking.

I didn't have long to wonder.

With a loud *snap*, the lights went out. A single spotlight buzzed on above the stage. There stood Charlie Story, Marie Latterback, Coach Littleton, and Debbie Holmes. Charlie stepped up to the mic and thumped it several times to check that it was working before he spoke.

"Good evening, everyone. I'm glad to see almost everyone could make it. I know some of you have other obligations and family who couldn't be here tonight. I know my wife, Laurie, would love to be here, she never misses a Harvest Festival, but she had to stay home and take the kids trick-or-treating. So, I'll try not to have too much fun tonight without her." A chuckle ran through the crowd, and he waited for it to die down before continuing. "That's what tonight is all about—family. That's what our community is—it's a big family. And tonight, we're welcoming new members to our family and community. Every year at the Harvest Festival, we welcome new blood. That's what the Harvest Moon symbolizes—renewal and new life. On this night, we honor the Holy Mother in bringing new members into our family."

Yeah, I thought, but he left out that those 'new members' were their children, and they do so by watching them slaughter people. I had a flashback to all of those pictures of smiling kids, standing with their parents, mouths smeared with blood.

I was trying not to glance over at the basement door, in case anyone was watching that way, they wouldn't be inadvertently tipped off to Joey. Out of the corner of my eye, I caught a glimpse of the door swinging shut. I hoped it was Joey, then we could slip out before anyone truly noticed us.

We were not that lucky.

Another spotlight snapped on right above the two of us, bathing Lizzie and I in brilliant dazzling light. Blinded, I had to hold up my hand to cover my eyes. Lizzie clung to me, clutching my arm in a death grip.

After a few seconds that stretched on for decades, my vision started to come back, and the entire crowd was facing us. There were hungry grins on every face. Even without having fangs, I could see the beasts beneath their masks. Punctuating the air was the low, constant, popping and snapping sound, like they were impatient and couldn't wait to tear themselves free of their human skin suits.

Crunch, crackle.

It set my teeth on edge. The sound I thought I'd been imagining was of bones and muscles moving and rearranging beneath flesh as the monsters fought their own instincts to say hidden.

"We would like to ask our guests of honor to please come and join us on the stage." Charlie's voice boomed even louder in the silence, and while the tone was jovial, there was something in his inflection that made it clear we didn't have a real choice.

Didn't mean we were going to comply.

Lizzie and I tried to resist, but it wasn't long before hands were roughly shoving us along, passing us from person to person, before we found ourselves thrust on stage.

"Ladies and gentlemen, it looks like some of our guests couldn't make it. That's okay, don't worry. We'll bring the party to them soon enough. After all, that's what community is."

Charlie laughed jovially, and had we not been in the know, I'm sure we would've missed the sinister undertone of his words and laugh. A chill ran down my spine as though I couldn't get warm.

"Well, let's get on with it, then. I know how anxious some of you are. Our youngsters have been waiting for this all year, and it's been a hard one with the loss of one of our most promising young men. But, as the good Reverend teaches us every Sunday, we're never alone, as even in death the Blessed Mother takes us unto her bosom, and we are forever a part of the greater whole.

With the Holy Communion, we partake of the blood and the flesh to consume the soul, and embrace Her divinity. I invite our new members to shed their adolescence and partake in our oldest sacred rite, a duty passed to us by the Holy Mother, to become full members of the pack. Tonight is your first feast!"

As he bellowed those final words, something in the air finally gave. It was like a wire under high tension giving way.

Looking over the crowd, their faces all hidden in deep shadows, I saw dozens of glowing eyes. Like pairs of shiny coins, they threw back a yellowish light. Deer in headlights, yet way more sinister. Underneath the reverberating silence was a low growl. In unison. A deep rumble I could almost feel in my feet, and it slowly escalated.

Lizzie grabbed my hand, crushing it in a vice-like grip with a strength I wouldn't have guessed she possessed, while I struggled to breathe.

One of the teenagers from the group at the front of the stage let out a snarl that couldn't have come from a human throat.

My stomach clenched.

Clutch, who'd been one of Jarred's friends, leapt on stage with zero effort at all despite it being at least waist height from the floor. The way he moved was far too graceful for his stocky build, and almost feline in nature.

Now bathed in the stage light, we could see him clearly, his body twisting and shifting as though something under his skin was trying to tear its way free.

Together, Lizzie and I took a step away in retreat. All the air my lungs fled.

Clothing strained and split at the seams as misshapen muscle covered in fur ruptured through human flesh. Sharp, wicked claws had replaced his fingernails as he stretched out his long, thickly muscled arms, flexing hands that looked more like the paws of a raccoon or opossum than human. His face was the worst part. Grossly distorted, and his eyes bulged with blood lust. Fangs like railroad spikes deformed his mouth as they pushed his human teeth every which way.

Lizzie wailed a penetrating cry that shattered my eardrums. Even knowing it was coming, it was still a terrifying display to see.

I tried to go for my gun, but she had my right arm in a death grip as she screamed in terror, and I couldn't shake her loose. I was forced to reach behind my back with my left, grabbing the butt of the gun from under my shirt as I drew it out of my waistband.

I pointed it directly at the monstrous face as I flicked off the safety, thumbed back the hammer, and pulled the trigger.

There was a dry raspy snap, but no gunshot. No boom. No smell of burning powder or a muzzle flash.

Shit! I'd been so paranoid of accidentally having it go off in my pants that I hadn't chambered a round when putting it in the waistband of my jeans.

Before I could even attempt to fumble the slide back with one hand, the transforming beast that had been a high schooler moments ago lashed out with one arm, knocking the gun from my hand and sending it flying off into the darkness.

My arm went numb up to my elbow and I was sure something in my wrist must've snapped. The creature had done it with the casual motion of swatting a fly. That strength was more than enough to tear me limb from limb, and I would be as helpless as a child against it.

Lizzie let out another head-splitting shriek directly into my ear.

I turned to see what she was screaming at.

What had been a pretty young blonde girl in a pink cardigan was now a prehistoric wolf wearing a torn sweater, its long ears sticking up from what looked like a wig. The image was so absurd, I hadn't realized the creature was now no more than a foot away.

Snarling as they closed in, we both froze in place like the helpless rabbits we were. Prey to be torn apart and overpowered.

Just as the she-wolf pounced, there came a mechanical coughing of rapid gunfire. Bullets struck it in the thigh, chest, and side of the head, blowing its brains out. The massive animal slumped to the floor as if it were a puppet with its strings cut, lifeless, and bleeding.

The attention of the entire room turned to the source of the shots.

Joey Ackerman stood at the edge of the stage. The basement door behind him swung shut. He had come up just in time to save our butts. He held the AK-47, smoke still curling from its barrel as he turned it on the crowd. The gun let out another of those lethal burps as it sprayed the creatures on stage, forcing them back.

For a moment, it was as if the world was holding its breath as silence and shock overtook, then everything went to hell as chaos rushed in to fill the void. An earth-shaking roar rent from the crowd, every voice as one in outrage that shook the very building itself. My ears all but bled as my shorts turned from white to brown. A chorus of angry howls rose from the throng as they began shedding their sheep's clothing, showing their true, evil nature.

My terror reached new levels as I watched the demonic crowd emerge. My knees knocked as my legs shook.

They ripped clothing from their bodies, becoming less and less human with each passing second. The scene was terrifyingly, horrifyingly mesmerizing.

Lizzie let out the most helpless, shuddering gasp I'd ever heard.

A woman's skull reshaped itself into a triangular canine form as her jaws pushed out into a snout.

Another man hunched as his spine elongated, forcing him to all fours, tips of claws sprouting from under his fingernails.

Each visage and form was more grotesque than the last. The townsfolk of Midnight Falls let their masks fall away, and the Adlets—dark, wolf-like creatures from the darkest nightmares of humanity—arose in all their horrific glory.

Friends.

Neighbors.

Teachers.

Students.

Small business owners.

Little old ladies.

People I'd passed on the street.

No more. They were all gone.

Within seconds that felt like years, we were now facing a pack of hungry enraged monsters, willing and wanting to tear apart the transgressors who had killed several of their numbers. Revenge would be slow, and they would enjoy it.

But they were not stupid. They did not rush us with sheer numbers. It would be easy for them to overrun us. Joey's assault rifle would cut down the first to bombard, and none seemed eager to be the first.

"We have to get out of here now!" Joey yelled.

"How long before your bombs go off?" I pushed the still hysterical Lizzie behind me as we backed away from the horde. She trembled against me.

"It doesn't matter now. We messed up."

Shit. How? "What do you mean?"

His face was ashen with a grim set to his pudgy jaw. His expression was not that of an elementary school science teacher trying to shed a few pounds, but of a hardened war vet facing a jungle full of Viet Cong.

He shook his head, barely perceivable. "The basement was empty. Well, not empty, just full of junk. It was being used for storage." He paused to eye the beasts, lying in wait to make their move. "There was nothing down there that would've indicated it was their den. No blood, no bodies, no dead animals, and no altars or shrines. Just holiday decorations and the furnace. I set the bombs, but their lair has to be somewhere else. We have to get out and help Brad with the backup plan. We have to burn this place down with all these things in here."

My gut bottomed out. God damn it! I knew this wasn't going to work, but I'd allowed myself to hope that good would triumph.

Nope. Now, we had to try to just escape with our lives.

We kept slowly backing away from the beasts around the stage toward the back door, only to find our way blocked. Several of the Adlets had circled behind the other side to cut us off. The ones on all fours were the size of large ponies, while those that walked on two legs were easily seven feet tall.

There was no way through them. To focus the gun on the small group blocking the door, Joey would have to turn his back on the larger throng. They would rush us, and we'd be buried under an avalanche of fur, fangs, and claws. Their bodies would muffle our screams as they tore us apart.

More wolves were slinking around the far end of the stage to join those at the back door. We would have to make a move soon. They had us trapped, and it was only a matter of time before one thing or another would force us to make a choice.

"Quick, over here!"

Lizzie. I hadn't realized she was no longer behind me.

I didn't want to take my eyes off the monsters, but I forced myself to glance over. A few feet away, Lizzie yanked on a black metal grate. It was a cage used to block the ladder leading up to the catwalk that ran around the walls of the auditorium.

I followed it with my frantic gaze, breath caught in my throat. In addition to housing the lighting rigs, it also gave access to the windows placed high around the room to allow in natural sunlight during the day. The walkway was twenty or so feet off the ground, well above the reach of the tallest Adlets.

"If we can get to the windows, maybe we can get out." She rattled the cage again.

Joey kept the gun trained on the beasts slowly edging closer to us. "There's a latch on the side. It should be unlocked. They had to open it to set up the stage lighting. Just push it up, and it should swing open."

"It's stuck!" Lizzie cried, her voice tinged with panic, back on the edge of hysterics.

With all my willpower, I shoved down the part of me that was screaming in terror, nearly in hysterics myself. I forced myself to turn my back on the monsters to help her.

The latch was stiff and in dire need of oiling. By adding my strength to hers, it popped free with a sudden *snap*, and I wrenched the grate open.

Lizzie didn't have to be told. Before the grate had struck the wall and started to bounce back, she was already up the first three rungs.

I didn't wait. I was right behind her, one hand on her butt to propel her upwards.

My panic was at the boiling point, and I was seconds from throwing her off the ladder to save myself before she was up and onto the catwalk.

Grabbing a handful of my shirt, she helped me haul myself up the last few rungs. I took a second to collect myself, panting, before looking down, expecting to see Joey, but instead, I saw the problem.

The little guy couldn't keep the gun on the monsters and climb at the same time. He needed both hands to hold the rifle. To make things worse, the pack in front of the back door had grown enough to begin slinking towards his back. When he turned to point the AK at them, the other group would start closing in. The nearest beast was close enough that, if it lunged, it might take Joey down, rifle or no rifle.

I threw myself facedown on the walkway. Rough metal digging into my chest and stomach, I stuck my head and shoulders through the hole and reached out my arms. If he could get up even just halfway, I might be able to grab him.

"Joey, hurry up. Take my hands."

He glanced up, then back at the creatures. "It won't work. You're too high. I'm going to toss you the rifle, and then try to climb as fast as I can. The second you catch it, start shooting."

"What if I miss the catch?"

"Don't miss," he shouted. "Now, catch!"

He tossed the rifle, and it sailed straight up and into my hands perfectly. In a million tries, I could never have made that catch again. I aimed and, praying I wouldn't hit Joey, pulled the trigger.

The AK belched a short chattering of bullets, then clicked empty.

Well, shit.

Although Joey had jumped on the ladder, the second he'd tossed the gun, he'd barely gotten halfway before the creatures recovered and lunged. The closest Adlet had crossed the distance like a flash of light, faster than any animal had the right to be, and sunk its fangs into the science teacher's leg.

I was close enough to watch his face twist in agony. His hand clenched, gripping the ladder so hard, his knuckles turned white.

Tossing away the rifle since it would do me no good without ammo, I reached for Joey's hands.

He saw me and reached back. Holding onto my jeans and legs, Lizzie allowed me to stretch a few more inches until I was able to clamp my hand around his wrist. Locking his around mine, I tried hauling him up, but the Adlet kept him anchored. It was like trying to lift the building itself. We locked eyes, and I could see him begging me not to let go, not to let them eat him.

The beast that had once been Debbie Holmes, an enormous thing with thick kinky black fur, launched itself into the air, and its jaws snapped shut like a steel trap on Joey's left buttock. The weight of the animal jerked him out of my grasp, dragging him off the ladder.

"No!" I yelled.

The rest of the pack fell on him, and he was buried beneath a writhing mass of dark fur. His blood-curdling screams lasted only a second before they were cut off by a wet gurgling, drowned out by tearing flesh and snapping bones as they ate him alive.

I stared in horror as my brain quit operating from the shock. He was gone, and my mind couldn't comprehend it.

One of the creatures looked up from their meal directly at me, and I knew instantly what was coming next. I tried to shimmy my ass back through the opening. It wriggled its haunches beneath it, and with a strength I didn't think possible, it launched itself straight at my face.

Long bloody fangs snapped on empty air, mere inches from my face, and seconds before Lizzie managed to help me pull myself back onto the catwalk.

My heart thundered a mile a minute. I could have sworn I was having a heart attack as black spots danced across my vision. Panting, I grabbed my chest.

Lizzie slammed the trapdoor shut and bolted it. I didn't know if they could climb, but that would slow them down if they tried to follow us.

"Joey's dead." Her wide watery gaze met mine.

"I know. I couldn't save him." I gasped, trying to steady my breathing, my heartbeat slowly returning to a semblance of normal.

"Now what?"

I shook my head. "We have to get to the windows over the back door to and try to get Brad's attention. Maybe he can help us get out of here, and I hope those things can't get up here."

We made our way along the catwalk to the back of the Community Center. The windows were long rectangles, maybe two feet high, big enough for us to get out, but it would be a long drop to the ground. I wasn't sure how high it was since I had never really been behind the Center much, but it couldn't have been more than two or three stories. It was too dark to see out with the stage lighting behind us turning the glass into mirrors. All we could see were our startled reflections. Our eyes hollow and haunted, we looked like a couple of escaped POWs.

Below us, the Adlets prowled, most of them following us around the gym, some still tore at the mangled corpse that had once been our friend.

To make matters worse, the windows were locked. We needed a key to open the latch, then it had to be cranked open with a tool.

We had neither.

I took off my shirt, leaving me in a tank top, and wrapped it around my good hand. The windows were heavy stormproof glass, and it took half a dozen shots, putting as much of my strength into it as I could, to crack the glass. It spider-webbed, but didn't shatter. It took a few more hits at the center of the impact to get a hole going, and then I was able to pry out enough shards to get a sizable hole for us to squeeze out. Even with my shirt for protection, my forearms and wrists were covered in gashes by the time I was done, and my knuckles were badly bruised.

Lizzie stuck her head through the hole and looked down. "Holy shit, yes!" she whooped.

I stuck my head out, too.

Brad was supposed to have chained the doors shut, only undoing them to let us out, but he had done one better. Not only had he chained the doors shut, but he had also parked the stolen gas truck a few feet from the back door so that it could be pulled forward and used as a barricade.

The man himself was leaning on the bumper, smoking a cigarette, staring up at us in puzzled amazement.

We waved to him to signal for help.

He was already reading our minds and hustled around to the truck's driver side.

From the window, the ground was a good twenty-five-foot drop, but if he pulled the truck closer, we could land on top and lessen that to only ten or so.

A loud commotion brought our attention back to the monsters trapped below. They had stopped milling about and were now dedicating their efforts to getting up to us. A couple were trying to navigate the ladder, but either due to their size or the way their true forms were made, they were having difficulty. Despite that, one was nearly two-thirds of the way up.

The group below us was trying a different tactic. Several had attempted, like the others, to simply jump, but they couldn't reach the height. To overcome this, several had made stepping platforms of their bodies, allowing others to stand on them. They were jumping high enough that their claws were dangerously close to finding purchase on the lip of the catwalk.

We had to get out now. It wasn't going to be too long before one of them got lucky, and it would only take one to kill us, trapped as we were.

There was a loud *bang* as the front bumper of the fuel truck struck the backdoor.

Brad had pulled it as close as he could. It was still a treacherous jump. One wrong move, and we could easily fall off.

I went first. Lowering my legs and hanging onto the window ledge, my feet were only inches from the roof of the cab. I let go and landed hard on the truck. I didn't touch down securely, and lurched to one side, nearly toppling off the truck. I managed to right myself seconds before going over.

Once I had regained my balance, I stood below the window to help Lizzie. As she was climbing out, there was some sort of racket. She screamed and lost her grip as she tried to lower herself, but I caught her.

We both nearly toppled off the truck as she thrashed about wildly in my arms. I had to crush her to my body to hold her still and keep her from falling. She fought me tooth and nail until I was finally forced to release her, and she bounded from the roof to the hood, down to the rocker panels, and then the ground like a rabbit.

I looked up and let out a startled yell of my own.

A large furry head with a mouth full of razor-sharp teeth was sticking out of the hole in the window. One of the creatures had found its way up to the walkway, but its bulk was too large to squeeze through the hole. Not that it seemed to stop it from trying. The creature was doing its best to force its way through. The laminated glass bulged, and the cracks grew.

Shit. It wouldn't hold for long.

There was an ear-deafening *bang*, and the Adlet slumped in the window, half its head blown away.

I turned, looking over the edge of the truck, and there was Brad, standing with his feet apart, both hands gripping the handle of the .44 Magnum he'd acquired from Joey. Gray-blue smoke coiled from the barrel, just like in one of those old westerns.

It had been one hell of a shot. But if one of them could get up there, then more would follow.

We had to do this now.

I climbed down from the truck with Brad's help. Once at ground level, I realized, at some point, I must've rolled my ankle. It hurt like hell and forced me to limp to the back of the truck with Lizzie supporting me.

"Where's Joey?" Brad eyed us. His stern face set in an expression that showed he already knew the answer.

"He didn't make it." I lowered my gaze, refusing to meet his eyes.

"Did he set the bombs? Did you guys manage to burn their nest of whatever?"

I shook my head. "It wasn't in the basement. Their den must be someplace else."

"Well, shit. What do we do now?"

"We need to burn this place down while all those things are still in there. Then we have to get the hell out of here."

"Do you have the backup dynamite?" Lizzie asked Brad.

He pulled it out of a fanny pack he had slung on one hip. "But I got nothing to set it off with. I think Joey had a trigger or something, but fuck if I know where it is." He held the stick of TNT in his hand, and it looked comically small.

"Does dynamite explode if you shoot it?"

We both looked at Lizzie in disbelief.

"What? They do it in the movies all the time and it works."

It made as much sense as anything else tonight. We had just barely escaped a pack of wolf monsters that had once been townspeople. Fuck, why the hell not end the night with a little John Wayne action?

Brad gestured to the gun he had stuck back in his pants. "That could work, but the problem is, whoever shoots is gonna have to be pretty close. When it goes off, the blast might kill them. This thing isn't a very big target, and this gun has a mean kick to it."

"Give me the gun. I'll do it," I said.

He frowned at me. "No offense, Josh, you're a good kid, but you are shaking like a leaf, and I doubt those stick arms of yours could handle this canon. It's ok to ask the black man to do it." He smirked at his own joke.

"You don't have to do this."

"I know, but this is bigger than any of us, even if no one ever knows what we did here. We'll know, and that's all that matters. Just do me one favor, okay?"

"Sure, anything, man."

"Make sure my funeral is better than Joey's. I mean it. I want the full package. Expensive casket, a twenty-one-gun salute, and pretty women crying 'cause they can no longer sleep with my beautiful black ass."

It made me laugh.

Damn, I thought, he was one hell of a guy to crack jokes at a time like this. My grandfather had a theory about people. He used to say that they were either potatoes or eggs. Potatoes were tough until you put them in boiling water, then they went soft, while eggs were fragile, but boil them, and they become nearly indestructible. Brad was definitely an egg. Under pressure, he didn't crack.

And he might potentially be volunteering for a suicide mission. "Thanks for doing this, Brad."

"Pssh, racist." He laughed, shaking his head. "Expecting the black man to blow himself up." He grinned, and brilliant white teeth shone in the moonlight. "You two get to a safe distance and keep going. Don't worry about me."

Lizzie grabbed the man for one last hug. Too tough and manly for hugs, Brad and I gave one another the customary chin nod.

Lizzie helped me hobble down the alley behind the buildings while Brad placed the explosive. We stopped when we reached the street nearly a block away, and looked back to watch.

He'd duct-taped the stick of dynamite to the truck's fuel tank and had walked halfway down the alley before pulling out the Magnum to take aim.

As he fired, we held our breath, and after a few seconds of nothing happening, he fired off two more shots. When that didn't produce results, he moved a few paces closer and fired. Again, nothing happened.

He moved closer still, fired, and...everything went to hell.

CHAPTER 19

The world erupted into pure chaos. The explosion ripped through the air, deafening in its intensity. At our distance, the blast was too loud to hear. It was all just a confusing mass of sensation.

The shockwave slammed into us, a monstrous hand swatting us like flies. The force flung us most of the way across the street, and we were thrown facedown on the sidewalk. My face bounced off the ground with a sickening crunch of bone reverberating through my skull, and blood gushed from my re-broken nose.

Shaking my head in an attempt to clear the static in my brain, it took me a couple of minutes to realize someone was shaking me. Squinting, I looked at Lizzie, her face a mask of blood and fury. She had a cut across her forehead, and it was streaming blood. Black soot covered her cheeks and her blonde locks, making it look like she'd stuck her finger in a light socket.

She was alive, thank God, but the sight of her injuries made my stomach do a slow flip.

Her lips moved, but the words didn't come out. The volume knob on the world had been cranked to zero and replaced with a piercing, high-pitched whine. My brain was a yo-yo, bouncing around inside my skull.

A glance in the direction of the Community Center proved the fuel truck had exploded, ripping through the building with the force of a bomb. A mushroom cloud rose, staining the night sky with a sickly glow. Fire and brimstone. Chaos, everything had become pure chaos. What was left of the street was crumbling to dust. There was nothing left. Buildings had suffered massive damage, and there were fires everywhere. Light poles and electrical lines had toppled. The few cars unlucky to be close enough were twisted burned out shells.

It looked like a post-apocalyptic hellscape.

God, I hoped Nimrod was okay.

Lizzie grasped my wrists, yanking me upright, and we lurched down the street like a couple of drunkards. Every step seemed to jostle my brain inside my skull, rendering me dizzy and nauseous.

I tried to get my bearings, to steady myself with slow breathing, but it was like trying to stand on a ship in a storm, threatening to capsize, to hurl me overboard.

Finally, my stomach could take no more, and I pushed Lizzie away, heaving into a nearby bush. The retching brought some small relief, but it wasn't enough. My skull still felt loose, and my stomach twisted in knots. Lizzie stood over me, a worried look on her face. I tried to tell her I was okay, that I just needed a moment, but the words wouldn't come. They were lost in the maelstrom of noise and pain inside my head.

Muted sounds started to return. Sirens and car alarms blared in the distance, mingling with the screams of panicked people in a symphony of fear and confusion. A few stragglers ran around in the distance, not paying us any mind.

Lost and disoriented, we stumbled through the darkness until we found ourselves in someone's postage stamp backyard. The house was silent, with no lights and no sign of life. It was as if this half of Midnight Falls had pushed the pause button.

We made our way to a tool shed, hoping to find some refuge. The door was locked with a thick padlock, but the chain was our salvation. With a desperate tug, we managed to pry the door open just enough to slip inside. The darkness was suffocating, and we could barely make out the junk and tools stored along back wall. Shelves were crowded to overflowing with leftover containers of oil or boxes of nails. It was a tight fit for the two of us, but it was better than the madness outside.

Time slipped away from us, lost in the fog of confusion and terror, as we attempted to catch our breath. It felt like we'd just escaped the Community Center moments ago, but now it was gone.

We'd been so preoccupied with our own survival that we hadn't even thought of Brad. Was he still alive? Was he badly hurt? Had he made it out before the blast? I didn't think so. There had been too much damage, the blast too large. He'd risked his life for us, had sacrificed so we could escape. A lump formed in my throat, my stomach a hollow pit.

Both Joey and Brad were dead.

Questions swirled in my mind, adding to the mounting dread.

Exhaustion descended on me, a lead weight around my neck, dragging me down to the cool, hard floor of the shed. Adrenaline and pain had kept me going for so long, finally taking its toll. I wanted nothing more than to curl up in a ball and slip into a coma.

Lizzie had torn off parts of her shirt and wrapped her forehead in a haphazard bandana approach. Her cut, upon closer examination, had been little more than a scrape, but head wounds bled like crazy. My nose was a mess, the blood caking around my nostrils. She stuffed bits of cloth inside to stem the flow, but it was like trying to plug a leaking dam. She wrapped my wrists, too, where glass had cut me. I hadn't noticed until she fussed. Some of the gashes looked deep and might require stitches. By the time she was done, her shirt was little more than a rag, barely covering her breasts.

We both looked like we'd been through a war, escapees from a sci-fi action plot gone wrong.

But we were alive. For now. And that was all that mattered.

I suppose it *was* an apocalypse, but not the kind with zombies or robots. No, this was an Armageddon of sanity and reason.

We had blown up a building full of monsters. Shape-shifters that had been walking among us all this time, hiding in plain sight. Joey had been right. They weren't human, and they never had been. They were dark vile creatures, pretending to be human, wearing their skins like some twisted costume. I couldn't stop thinking about Lizzie's research books. All those sightings from Maine to Michigan, from New Mexico to Oregon.

They could be anywhere.

They could be anyone.

How many more were out there, hiding in plain sight? If they could live here so openly, in a small town, then they could be anywhere. Behind any smiling face could be a snarling mouth full of fangs, waiting to tear us apart. The monsters were among us, and we were just starting to realize how deep their influence ran.

I couldn't tell how long we'd been holed up in the shed. The concussion I got from the explosion made my concept of time fray around the edges, but there was some comfort in the coolness of the concrete floor with Lizzie's head slumped on my shoulder as she slowly lost our fight with exhaustion.

At some point, I must've dozed off, too, because I was jolted awake by the sound of movement as something moved stealthily outside. A shush of footsteps in the grass or rustle, I couldn't tell.

My heart thundered in my chest as I nudged Lizzie, urging her to stay quiet. I clamped my hand over her mouth before she could make a sound, signaling for her to listen. Her eyes widened with panic when she heard it.

I grabbed a heavy hammer from a toolbox and handed Lizzie some wicked-looking fork-shaped gardening tool.

Silently, we waited, listening to the thing outside, waiting for it to find us. It shuffled around the perimeter, making snuffling sounds. Not human. It was scenting us out, looking for us, and it was only a matter of time before it found our hiding spot. The shed door shuddered as the thing outside nudged it. Whatever it was, was big and strong, and once it got inside, we were dead. In the cramped confines of the shed, we had no chance. We froze like rabbits, holding our breath as every nerve and muscle in our bodies tensed.

The door slowly creaked open as far as the chain would allow, moonlight spilling inside, and the thing shoved its big furry head through the slot.

We both screamed in terror before we realized the canine head sticking through the door wasn't one of the Adlets, but the goofy blond head of my idiot husky.

Nimrod blinked at us in surprise before giving us his dumb doggy grin and shouldering his bulk the rest of the way through the door. The lead I had used to tie him up in the backyard dragged on the ground behind him.

In all the confusion from the explosion, it must've scared him enough to tear himself free, and after wandering the neighborhood, he'd come looking for us. The big goofball had found us, and I'd never been happier to see him. Tears stung my eyes, relieved that he'd survived. In the commotion, I'd forgotten all about him. I'd never seen him in a fight, and I didn't think he could take one of those beasts on, but I felt a little better with him around. He would be able to warn us if the creatures were nearby like he had that first night one of them had been creeping around the house.

He bathed Lizzie and I in kisses while she cooed to him.

I pulled myself up, using Nimrod's collar to steady myself. Making my way to the door, I peeked out to see what was going on. It looked like the entire sky was ablaze. The red glow came not just from the direction of the Community Center, but from several surrounding areas. The fire must've been bigger and spread faster than I'd thought. Firefighters would have their work cut out for them if they had to run all over the Falls putting out flames. The local brigade was mostly just a handful of volunteers since budget cutbacks a few years ago, according to what I'd heard from other people who worked for the Gazette.

"What are you doing?" Lizzie asked in a hushed tone as she stroked Nimrod's fur for comfort. She looked like a scared child holding onto her teddy to protect her from the monster under the bed.

The monsters weren't under the bed, though. No. They were out there somewhere, and they would be pissed off after what we'd done.

"We have to get out of here," I whispered back. "If he can find us, so can those things."

"Where do we go?"

"We should try to make it to my car, then we get the hell out of town and don't stop until the wheels fall off."

"But what about the lair?"

"What about it?"

Jesus Christ, I didn't give a shit about their lair. We had tried, and we'd failed. Now, it was time to get out of Dodge, and Lizzie's inability to see that was starting to piss me off a little. Two of the four of us hadn't survived the night, yet.

"If it wasn't in the Community Center, then where is it? They would've needed a place big enough that they all had easy access to, but where no outsider would think to go. Somewhere hidden, yet out in the open. If not the Community Center, then where?"

Was she kidding?

"Who cares? What are we supposed to do about it? We don't even have any idea where it could be."

But that wasn't true. I suddenly had a revelation. A place they all could meet where no outsiders would go. The Community Center had only been built in the last decade or so. I remembered seeing something in the paper about it opening when I was a kid. So, where had they met before then?

My mind went back to the old photographs, the ones older than just the last ten or twenty years. Every single one of them had been taken outside, in a staged picnic area, in an open field, and in the background was an old church. Because those Harvest Festivals had taken place in the field behind the First Church of Midnight Falls at the end of Church Street. The building had stood on that spot since the 1700s and had been rebuilt in the 1800s after being struck by lightning.

"Hey, Lizzie, do you know if your grandmother's church has a basement?"

"What? Why?" she asked, puzzled, Nimrod's massive head filling her lap as she stroked it.

"I think that's where their den is. It's the oldest building in town, and it's in all those pictures from before the Community Center was built. I don't think they ever moved their den."

She looked at me. It was hard to see her brow furrow underneath its make-shift bandage, but the motion made her look like a confused Rambo.

"I think it does. There are two doors at the back, behind the pulpit. You can't really see them because of the way it's designed, but one of them leads to the pastor's office. I don't know where the other one goes, but it could lead to a basement. Or maybe it's just a closet. I don't know."

She'd been right before. We had to stop them. "Well, let's do it."

"What, are you insane? You wanted to leave town. Why would you want to stick around and do something so crazy?" She shot wide glares at me, her tone that of a petulant child.

I could tell she was scared. This had suddenly become all too real for her now that the proverbial dust had settled. She'd been all gung-ho until the shit had hit the fan. It had stopped being a fun B-movie for her, and now she'd gotten a close-up with the things that go bump in the night. Our stances had reversed, and she was the one who wanted to flee.

"Think about it. Most of those things were probably killed in the blast, or at least horribly injured. Everyone else is busy trying to put out fires and find out what happened. The church is in the opposite direction. We sneak over and check it out. If no one's there, we find a way into the basement to see if I'm right, and I bet I am. We set the place on fire, and then we haul ass out of town. We'll be long gone before anyone figures out what happened, plus the fire will be blamed on debris from the explosion." God, it sounded so simple and easy. "You don't even have to go in. You can wait outside."

"No, you're right." She sounded weary and beaten down. "We need to finish this. It was my stupid idea, after all. I mean, you said we should just go, and I should've gone with you. We should've left this awful place and never looked back."

"And *you* said we shouldn't run from our problems, that they always catch up to you. Not to mention, your research said these things mark people and follow them. You heard what that asshole said at the festival. They would've come after us sooner or later. At least, this way, we showed them not to fuck with us, and any of them left will think twice before coming after us."

That seemed to cheer her up a little. She smiled, and that beautiful smile lit up her face, showing the innocent little girl next door she must've once been.

We snuck out of the shed and tried to stay as quiet as we could. As we made our way through the dark, deserted streets, I couldn't help but feel a sense of foreboding. The silence that hung over the town was thick and oppressive, broken only by the occasional distant shout or siren, vastly different from a couple short hours ago.

Lizzie was keeping pace with me, but I could tell she was scared. Who wouldn't be in a situation like this? The monsters we'd encountered were unlike anything we'd ever seen before. They were twisted, unnatural things that defied explanation. And yet, here we were, creeping through the shadows like thieves in the night, trying to get to the church before they found us.

We crossed the playground of the abandoned school, and sadness flooded me as I looked at the empty swing sets and jungle gyms. It was as if the very life had been sucked out of the place, leaving it a shell of its former self where kids would never play again.

We trudged along School Street, our footsteps echoing through the stillness of the night. The desolate road seemed to stretch on forever, each block feeling longer than the last. As we made our way towards the church, the darkness seemed to swallow us whole. Every step we took was a gamble, a roll of the dice in a game where the stakes were life and death. We couldn't afford to let our guard down, not even for a moment.

To our surprise, we managed to make it there unmolested.

The church loomed before us, its windows black and lifeless. Even in the darkness, I could make out the chipped white paint peeling off its clapboard. Its ancient frame loomed large against the night sky. There was a soulless emptiness to the place. The steeple was a tall, sinister finger pointing towards the heavens, but there was no God here.

The parking lot was empty as if it had been vacant for years. Cracked uneven asphalt with fading white lines. It was clear that no one was here, not a soul in sight. Completely silent. Everyone was across town, either helping with the rescue efforts or rubbernecking. The nearest house was at least a block away, and it, too, was completely dark and quiet.

Something was off. In any other town, there would've been dogs barking or crickets chirping, but here, there was only deafening silence. It was as if the entire town had been engulfed in a vacuum of perpetual dark stillness.

I secured Nimrod to a nearby bush, making sure he was hidden from anyone who wandered by. The lovable mutt gazed up at us, oblivious to the dangers that lurked in the shadows. I prayed he wouldn't start barking and give us away. The plan was that, hopefully, he'd start barking if someone stopped at the church, and it would give us some warning. We were going in blind, and when coming out, we would be in a hurry. We didn't want to go running into some curious bystander, or worse, some of those things slinking back to their den to lick their wounds, only to find some tasty snacks waiting.

We crept up to the heavy wooden doors. I tried the handle, and the latch slid bonelessly. I was able to shoulder the door open with little resistance. It was odd, really, that the church was left unlocked. Even in a town as small as this, where everyone knew each other's business, I would expect some level of caution. Maybe it was a testament to the naivety of small town life, that fundamental trust in the goodness of people. The hinges gave a long, protesting whine as it swung open. If there was anyone inside, they would've heard it.

I tried to shut the door behind us as silently as possible, but it still slammed with a resounding thud, shattering the stillness like glass. I winced, afraid it had alerted whatever creatures prowled inside.

We were now trapped, and the slightest noise could spell our doom.

Crossing the sanctuary wasn't especially difficult. The giant stained glass windows still let in plenty of streetlight through their multicolored panes. Moonlight filtered through the panes, casting an eerie glow on the rows of pews and the pulpit. It was as if the very air was alive with the whispers of an unseen ghostly congregation.

Lizzie and I moved with caution, but even then, every creak, every rustle made us jump and our hearts race. More than once, we almost scared the crap out of each other when we thought we saw something move.

We made our way to the back of the sanctuary, our eyes peeled for any sign of movement, and there it was, just as Lizzie had said. Two doors. One labeled "office" and the other "boiler room." I jerked my chin toward the boiler room, and Lizzie nodded, showing she agreed.

The knob refused to budge, locked tight against my efforts. The door was a different story. Old and worn, it yielded under the pressure of my hands. I could have kicked it down like they did in 'Miami Vice,' but my ankle was still throbbing from the earlier fall.

So, I took a step back and threw my weight into it, my shoulder making contact with a thud. I stumbled back in comical fashion, but the door gave way, popping out of its frame. Behind it, I expected a dark pit of endless blackness. Instead were a set of stone steps, seemingly leading down into the depths of the Earth. The soft flickering of candlelight beckoned from below, casting an eerie glow on the walls around me.

The smell that came roiling out was anything but pleasant. It hit me like a punch in the face, causing my eyes to water and my stomach to heave.

Lizzie recoiled, tears streaming down her face, leaving tracks in the soot on her face.

Even with my nose packed with blood-soaked bits of shirt, I could make out the stench of death. The sickly sweet smell of spoiled meat and decaying earth. How no one smelt it during the day with the heat was baffling to me.

Descending into the basement was like stepping into the abyss. The flickering candles barely illuminated the darkness, casting ghostly shadows on the rough-hewn walls of cyclopean stone. Thick support beams loomed overhead, holding up the weight of the building above us.

But it was what lay in the shadows that made my blood run cold.

Blood and bone and raw, torn flesh covered every inch of the basement. The stench of death was so overpowering, I had to cover my nose with my shirt just to breathe. Flies buzzed around the bloated corpses, their wings creating a sickening drone that filled my ears. Primitive art hung from the walls and ceiling, made from bone and wood and gut string. Bizarre dream catchers and wind chimes swayed in the stagnant air, their macabre designs sending chills down my spine. Standing candelabras made from spinal cords and antlered deer skulls added to the morbid atmosphere. Skins stretched drum-tight over frames made of long bones completed the surreal scene.

However, it was the strange symbol from the book we'd found that tied it all together. It was etched into every surface, a twisted reminder of the horrors that lay within this pit of darkness.

That crooked Y shape was carved or painted everywhere. Scratched into stone, carved on bone, and painted in blood on hide. At the opposite end, the centerpiece of this cadaverous tableau was an altar. This one was far grander than the one in Mrs. Sexton's coal bin. This was the granddaddy of that tiny thing. A massive stone slab, blackened from ages of dried blood, was lit with a number of candles. A book, like the altar, was the original that our find had tried to facsimile.

It was larger and bound in some kind of rough material that, no doubt in my mind, was human skin. Blazoned on its cover was that symbol. There was something wrong with it. The air felt full of some sort of greasy electrical charge as if it were radiating a malicious aura, and the symbol etched into its cover glowed with an unholy light. It was as if the book was alive, pulsating with dark, malevolent energy.

As we cautiously approached, I felt a strange sensation in the pit of my stomach. Just looking at the book became difficult, as if fingers were rummaging around the edges of my mind. Intrusive alien thoughts that were not my own began to creep in.

My brain tried to tell me not to look at it, but I couldn't help it. I *wanted* to look. I *needed* to look. I *had* to touch it, to feel it on my skin.

Yes, it would be lovely. Lizzie would feel how amazing it would be on her skin, too, as I took her naked on the altar. We'd rut like savage animals with the book between us. And as we fucked, we would tear out each other's throats and bathe in one another's blood, anointing the book and the stone with hot crimson in a tumultuous whirlpool of glorious depravity, life and death endlessly intertwined in an utterly primal bestial act. We would call to Her in our pain, and Mother would...

Would what?

Panting, my skin tight, I stared, tried to grasp logical thought.

I shook my head, trying to clear the perverse thoughts invading my mind. Yet, they were tempting. Hypnotic. I could feel the book's pull, its seductive power, but I knew, deep down, it was wrong. Right? I think it was wrong. Depraved. It was like a siren's call, drawing me closer to the rocks.

I had to resist despite not wanting to.

Lizzie had the same temptation in her eyes. Her pupils dilated and her breathing grew shallow. Her head was tossed back as if in the throes, her cheeks flushed. The erection in my pants was harder than any I'd had in my life.

We were both under the book's spell, and it promised only destruction.

I snapped out of the dream-like state, crashing back to reality. Every part of my body ached. Fatigue and pain clawed at every raw nerve. I could feel every cut and bruise. The smell of blood clotting in my nose forced me to rip out the bits of shirt, and I gagged on the rancid stench filling the room.

Looking for Lizzie, I found her standing near where I'd been slowly moving toward the altar as if sleepwalking. Her face was dreamlike and blank. One hand cupped her breast, pinching the nipple between her fingers, while her other dug feverishly between her legs.

I raced to her, shook her as hard as I could, trying to snap her out of it. Her body had been taken over by some otherworldly force. Something malevolent that was manipulating her like a puppet on a string. The fear in her eyes was the same fear deep in my gut.

And yet, despite the terror that coursed through us, there was an undeniable urge to give in to the darkness.

I pulled her close, relishing the heat of her body against mine. It was as if we were the only two people left in the world, and the only thing that mattered was the desperate need to hold onto each other. As if the warmth of another human seemingly broke the hold the eldritch thing had on her, her eyes slowly came back into focus. She jerked the way people do when they doze off while sitting and then wake when their head falls, now fully conscious and aware.

"Josh? What happened? I remember us coming in here, the n...feeling so hungry and aroused."

"It's this thing." I gestured to the altar and its contents. "It's putting thoughts into our head, playing with the darkest, most primal parts of our consciousness."

Again, I felt the sensation of fingers in my mind as if rummaging through files in a cabinet, searching, looking for something it could latch on to. I shook my head and pushed it away, gritting my teeth, sweat beading on my brow.

"You have to fight it, Lizzie. Concentrate. Push any and all thoughts out of your mind, and remember why we're here."

She stared at me with her innocent green doe eyes, trust emblazed in her depths, and I loved her more at that moment than I think I ever loved anything or anyone. I don't know if it was the trauma bonding us or what was doing the thinking and feeling for me, but it still resonated with me. Strong. Powerful.

She took a deep breath and squeezed my hand in hers. "Okay, I am fine now. I think I have a hold on it."

I opened my mouth to speak, but a dark, harsh voice spoke from behind us.

"You have nothing. You have no idea what powers fester in these hallowed halls."

Spinning, we realized we were no longer alone.

Minister Halworthy stood near the base of the stairs in his long dark robes and his high stiff collar. With his black garments and waxy insipid skin, he looked more like a vampire come to life than a preacher.

In the candlelight, he reminded me of Count Orlok in that old black-and-white film, 'Nosferatu.' He seemed to glide rather than walk as he moved toward us. The shadows hollowed his high cheekbones and deepened the dark circles around his sunken eyes, giving them a more skull-like appearance than normal.

"You stand on the holiest of ground, outsiders, dirty un-wanted sinners, blasphemers. You behold the presence of the Sleeping Mother, here at the heart of the place of power. We are Her children, and though She slumbers, She hears the cries of Her children's pain. It rouses Her from the depths of sleep, and so She turns dreams into nightmares. Those nightmares She sets loose on the world, for we honor Her with the blood of those traitors who spilled the blood of Her children."

His insane proselytizing opened my eyes to a terrifying real-ization. His sermons, the speech at the festival, and even Lizzie's grandmother's words had all seemed like typical religious crap

I'd grown up listening to and learned to tune out, but underneath it hid something darker. More visceral.

The thing that had crept into my mind was what the altar had been fashioned for. Its books were etched with its arcane symbol. The Sleeping Mother? They'd been cavorting with some ancient and malevolent deity all along.

I recoiled as I dared to delve into that unfathomable abyss. It was incomprehensibly ancient, older than the very fabric of time itself. It was shapeless, yet held a form beyond the grasp of mortal minds. It was as feminine as the notion of motherhood itself. It slumbered beneath a bottomless ocean of dreams, all real, but as fragile as fleeting bubbles of soap. Below that endless surface, it slumbered, but its slumber was not peaceful. It was restless as this great Mother listened for the cries of its offspring. For, at any moment, it could be stirred from its torpor and rip reality asunder. Pain and anguish seasoned the soul and tore it apart, feeding its flickering flame of existence to stave off oblivion for a few more precious moments while entropy decayed the very edges of its universe.

The truth of life and being was merely a cruel jest with an even more brutal punchline.

In an instant, the connection was severed, and the ground rushed up to meet me.

I found myself lying on the cold unyielding stone floor. The putrid odor of death permeated my nostrils, and the tendrils of those unspeakable things that had writhed within my mind slithered away, fading like watercolors seeping into the paper, leaving behind only a vague impression of what had been there.

Lizzie's frantic cries and violent shaking jolted me back to reality, and I struggled to reassemble my fragmented thoughts, arranging them into some semblance of coherence.

I gingerly sat up, my mind feeling greasy and sullied. I feared I would never be clean again.

Suddenly, I couldn't stand to be in this basement anymore. I wanted out. I needed to get out and as far away as I could. Fuck this place, fuck our mission, and God help the poor bastard who stood in my way.

"You have seen, and the Mother has opened your eyes. You have been touched by the truth and you have been found less than wanting. Those of us who are The Chosen shed our mortal disguise at Her caress and take on the form. Our Mother birthed us to feast on the flesh of the outsiders. I will show you Her mercy and offer up your flesh on the sacred altar to the Sleeping Mother, as the new blood was to do this very evening."

With that, he began to change. His bones started to shift, and fangs sprouted from his gums, his human teeth falling to the floor and clattering into the shadows.

Without a moment's hesitation, my body moved with a primal instinct as I seized the nearest candle stand and plunged the antlers into the Reverend's throat.

His face twisted in shock as the sharp bone punctured his flesh. A torrent of blood gushed from the wound. I had driven the candelabrum with such force that the tip jutted out from the other side of his scrawny neck. The other antler had caught him in the shoulder, plowing deep furrows through his vestments and into the meat.

To mine and Halworthy's surprise, Lizzie had done the same thing. She'd grabbed a stand and stabbed the preacher almost simultaneously. Her antlers had pierced his chest and abdomen, respectively.

We watched as the light faded from the eyes of the half-formed creature that had once been Minister Halworthy as it crumpled lifelessly to the ground.

Without a moment's pause, we sprinted through the cellar, overturning lit candles and igniting anything that would fuel the flames. The stretched hides caught quickly and spread like wildfire to the surrounding clutter. The acrid stench of burning flesh and singed hair mingled with the noxious fumes as the room filled with a thick cloud of smoke.

As a final act, I upended several candles into the blasphemous tome, careful not to let it touch me. The flames that consumed it emitted an oily flat light and a smell like bad eggs and burning rubber.

We fled the basement before the fumes and smoke could overcome us. Rushing up the steps, we took them two or even three at a time.

But, as we got to the top of the stairs, we realized we'd just jumped out of the frying pan and into the fire.

CHAPTER 20

Coughing on thick acrid smoke, we emerged into the sanctuary of the church.

The door across from the basement stood open to the pastor's office. It appeared Halworthy also lived in the small church office. A ramshackle desk, a battered chair, and a cot barely big enough for a grown man were crammed in the room. He must've woken up when I'd broken the door to the basement and had rushed to see what was going on.

We hadn't noticed or even considered the man could've been in the building. Had he not been a monster, I might've felt a pang of pity for his pitiful existence. Now, he was burning in a literal hell where he belonged. We had vanquished him and destroyed their lair. With most of their pack broken and unable to pursue, they wouldn't be able to chase us on our way out of town.

It was too soon to celebrate, though. We weren't quite out of the woods yet.

The basement was on fire, causing the floor to give off an almost ethereal glow and heat. Thick black smoke billowed out of the open basement stairwell like a chimney, funneling it up to the high church ceiling. Soon, the flames would spread and hopefully burn this whole thing to the ground, burying that profane thing in the basement forever. There would be nothing left but salted, scorched earth. Any Adlets left would be forced to find a new home elsewhere after picking through the remains.

Lizzie and I quickly made our way down the center aisle to the front doors when they slammed shut. We skidded to a halt at the worst thing possible and the last person we wanted to see.

Sheriff Earlywine stood before us like a malevolent giant, his massive frame filling the entryway like a blockade. Soot and sweat covered his face and uniform, making it appear black. His eyes burned with that black hatred I'd witnessed several times before. The big man trembled with rage as he stepped forward. Each footfall sounded like thunder as he slowly moved towards us.

We stumbled backward, my heart racing with fear and adrenaline. The man before us was a behemoth, a towering hulk of muscle and sinew that could crush us like insects with a flick of his wrist. But it wasn't just his size that made him terrifying. It was the madness glinting in his eyes, the malevolent intent that dripped from his every pore.

As he emerged from the shadows of the condemned balcony and into the moonlight filtering through the stained glass windows, a sickly yellow glow suffused his features. His eyes burned like twin suns, his face twisted into a snarl that revealed his tobacco-stained teeth.

"You thought you could get away from me?" he growled, his voice a low rumble that shook the very foundations of the abandoned church. "You thought you could just walk away from everything you've done?"

His heavy boots thudding in time with the scared beating of my heart.

"Of course, it would be you. I'm actually glad I caught you here. You've been nothing but trouble since the day you arrived. I told the council members you would be a problem. You were too tempting, too easy. A weak sissy faggot like you, a prey no true child could resist. You killed my boy, and now I'm going to kill you. *Slowly*. I'm going to make you suffer. I'm going to make you beg me to kill you. I'll break your legs and make you watch as I rape your bitch, over and over, until she bursts and I tear her apart with my cock. Then, I'm going to bleed you bit-by-bit. Do you know how long a man can live while having his guts eaten? Hours, and every second is agony. I might even rape you first just for the hell of it, show you who the big dog really is."

A pathetic helpless whine escaped from Lizzie's throat.

More afraid than confused, I needed to try to stall for time until we could find a way out of this. "What the fuck are you talking about? Jarred died in a drunk driving accident."

My heart was pounding in my chest as we backed away, my mind racing as I tried to come up with a plan. We'd come too far to be killed now, too far to let this madman take us down without a fight.

I shoved Lizzie behind me, shielding her with my own body as we retreated back up the center aisle. The deranged Sheriff stalked us like a wild animal, his eyes gleaming with a mad light that made my blood run cold.

"No, he fucking didn't!" The reply came out more as an animalistic growl than human speech. "No, you humiliated him at that damn party. I told him to wait just a couple of months, and he could tear you apart at the Harvest Feast, but he was too stubborn, too new to his blessing, impatient for his first kill and taste of flesh." Earlywine paused, resting a hand the size of a ham hock on the back of a pew as though he needed to emotionally prepare himself for what he would say next. "He followed you and that whore back to your house, probably planning to break in and rip you both apart. It got him shot and killed."

The realization hit me like a bolt of lightning, illuminating everything that had happened since I'd arrived in town. The pieces of the puzzle finally fit together, revealing a horrifying picture. The creature that had been watching me and Lizzie from outside my bedroom window was none other than Jarrod Earlywine. Joey had taken him out with a well-aimed bullet, and now the vengeful father was after us.

"I didn't shoot him, that was Joey Ackerman. I had nothing to do with it." They couldn't hurt Joey now, and it was the truth.

It made complete sense why Earlywine had stalked and harassed me. He believed I'd been the cause of his son's death. In a way, I couldn't help but agree with his sordid logic. What parent wouldn't do everything in their power to avenge their child? But, at the same time, I knew his actions had been twisted and misguided, driven by a grief which had turned into blinding fury.

There came an echo from the back of my mind, the ghost of a memory stirring. I saw a mother sleeping soundly, her child suffering as it cried out. The memory vanished as soon as it appeared before I could grasp it.

"*No,*" he roared. "No, it was *your* fault. Because of you, he died."

Earlywine's massive hands gripped the wooden pew with a force that made it groan and splinter. He shook his head as if trying to dispel a swarm of gnats buzzing around his thoughts. The struggle was etched on his face as he refused to come to terms with the truth. His eyes flickered with a mixture of rage and despair, and I knew he was on the brink of losing control.

"I wanted you dead. I wanted to kill you myself, but they said no. We have to honor tradition. Let the new blood take revenge for their fallen kin." He straightened with a deadpan expression of fury. "But there isn't a council anymore. There is no one here to stop me. I will have my pound of flesh, and bone, and blood. We should never have left old ways behind."

Lizzie trembled behind me, emitting noises of choked terror from her throat.

I tightened my arm around her from behind, trying to rationalize a plan that wouldn't form.

With each hitching breath the Sheriff took, it seemed as if his barrel of a chest swelled larger and larger. His uniform shirt, already struggling to contain his considerable bulk, became stretched to its limits. Seams strained and buttons held on by lessening degrees. Gaps formed in the spaces between as they pulled beyond their limits and fought to hold. When they finally popped off, they did so with such force, they made audible sounds upon impact wherever they struck, pinging the floor, pews, and even as far as the stained glass.

The ripped shirt revealed a massive chest buried in thick muscle and dark hair that began spreading, covering every inch of skin. Even under the fur, I could make out every ripple of muscle. Shoulders broadened, shredding the remainder of his shirt as his torso elongated and thickened. His leather gun belt, which still held a revolver in its holster, a twin of the .44 magnum Joey had used to kill his son, snapped like a rubber band and fell to the floor with a loud thud and a jingle of keys.

Oh-shit pummeled my brain.

He dropped to his knees as he let out a colossal roar that shouldn't have been possible. His neck was now as thick as my waist and dark fur crawled up it. His face twisted and bulged outwards as his jaw elongated and stretched to form a blunted muzzle. As the snout pushed its way from his face, he spit out a handful of human teeth, no longer needed, as they were replaced with rows of fangs like hunting knives. They gleamed white in the moonlight, filtering through the smoke. His eyes had changed, had gone from glowing yellow moons to blazing red furnaces of hatred.

There now stood before us a true monster. The other Adlets had been nothing compared to this nightmare. They'd been tall, gangly, but this thing stood easily over eight feet, and its new size absolutely dwarfed the man it had been. It appeared more bear-like than wolf from its bat-shaped ears to its large paws the size of hubcaps, tipped with nasty claws resembling scythes. This thing was in another league. The king of Adlets, their alpha, their pack leader. A creature made for one sole purpose—the slaughter of any and all that stood before it. It was a prehistoric hunter from a long ago age when men still hid in caves, huddled around their campfires in terror. Afraid of the things that lurked in the night.

And *this* was what they feared, for it was the devourer of men.

The apex predator and undisputed top of the food chain.

Shit. We had to move.

"Go!" I yelled at Lizzie and shoved her to the right of me as I took off to the left.

Earlywine had backed us all the way to the front of the pews. Standing and blocking the center aisle, there was no way to slip past. The side aisles were clear, and if we split up, one of us would have a chance to escape while the beast went for the other. It bought time in a game where our chances were zilch. As much as I hated to admit it, a small, dark part of me hoped the beast would choose Lizzie, a circumstance of sheer unadulterated panic with no chance to think of anything but survival. Deep down, I knew the truth. Behind those wolfish eyes was the twisted mind of the man who'd been stalking me for weeks. It wasn't a mystery who he would go for first.

It wanted me dead.

I took off, sprinting to the end of the row and pivoting down the aisle, my heart pounding in my chest like a demented sledgehammer. I didn't dare look back. If I saw it charging, I knew I'd freeze and be torn to pieces before I could blink.

No, I focused only on running, pushing myself to the limit, my injured ankle nearly forgotten in the white-hot fear driving my body. I had to get to the end of the aisle, had to get to the front door. Nothing else mattered. Time ceased to exist beyond that moment. It felt as though I were running in slow motion, my legs encased in thick molasses. My lungs burned as I sucked in gulps of air and smoke.

The thing that had been Earlywine struggled to free itself from the remnants of the Sheriff's uniform. Its snarling jaws snapped hungrily as it eyed us, but it seemed to be having trouble regaining its footing after bursting forth from the sheriff's body. It gave us enough time to sprint the length of the church before it could give chase.

Lizzie was ahead of me, her hand grasping the door handle as if her life depended on it. And for a moment, it seemed like we might actually make it out of here alive.

But then, without warning, a sudden chill ran down my spine. A deep sense of dread washed over me, and I knew something terrible was about to happen.

I threw myself to the left with all the strength I could muster, but it was too late. Some kind of massive missile hurtled past me, clipping my shoulder, and sent a bolt of fiery pain through my body. It crashed into the vestibule, knocking me off balance, and blocked the front doors with the sheer force of the impact. The force propelled me sideways, launching me through the side door that led to the balcony. It flew off its hinges, slamming into the stairs with a deafening crash.

For a moment, I lay there in a daze, winded, my head spinning with pain and confusion.

My face had slammed into the rough surface of the hand-lettered sign to 'Keep Out: Dangerously Unstable,' smearing it with my fresh blood. I managed to roll over with a groan, and while leaning against the door, to my horror, I saw what had hit me.

The thing had torn a pew from its moorings and hurled it through the air like a deadly javelin, aiming to crush us both as we reached the door. I stared in stunned silence at the twisted metal and shattered wood that had nearly crushed me.

Oh God. *Lizzie*. Was she okay?

A groan, and I twisted to look where I'd last seen her.

No. *No, no, no.*

She hadn't been so lucky. The air punched from my lungs and my eyes watered.

Her body was contorted in unnatural angles, her once beautiful frame now mangled beyond recognition. The pew had crushed her spine like a twig, leaving her, no doubt, paralyzed and helpless against the unyielding doors. Blood poured from her lips, and each breath was an obvious struggle. Her green eyes, once full of humor and light and life, pleaded with me to help her, but not only was I was frozen in horror and shock, I couldn't fathom how to process the extent of her injuries. I violently shook, staring at her, bone-deep cold in a way I'd never experienced. My breath hitched as tears splashed my cheeks. Her legs were twisted in grotesque ways, and bone fragments protruded from her flesh like jagged teeth.

A sickening wet gurgle emanated from her throat as her lungs filled with blood. It was a hopeless sound, one that pierced my heart like a thousand knives. I knew she was beyond saving, and it ripped the beat from my heart. She'd been a goner the moment the pew had struck her.

A large black paw with long claws reached out, grabbing a fistful of her blonde hair. It snapped her neck like she was some child's Barbie doll.

I let out a strangled cry, crawling out of my skin, the sound echoing in my head.

It appeared to be the only mercy granted tonight. Her pain had ended quickly and before she'd even truly known it had happened. Her limp, mangled body hung, pinned to the wall, an obscene insect in a grotesque diorama.

The beast stuck its head around the door frame, leveling its gaze at me and fixing me with its glare.

I inhaled hard, barely a second to react.

Snarling, it lunged. Titanic jaws snapped inches from my face, its copious mass preventing it from entering the narrow staircase, keeping it just out of reach. The chomp of its fangs was like the closing of a steel trap, each one with enough strength to turn my bones to dust.

Panic and adrenaline flooded my system. I scooted back, a panicked rat. My hands grabbed the railings, propelling me up the stairs. My heart felt like it was about to burst through my chest, and my legs were jelly, but I kept moving, driven by a desperate need to survive. I could hear it behind me, closing the gap, snarling and stomping, and I knew I had to keep going.

Its enormous paws clacked against the wooden steps, sending vibrations through the stairs like a minor earthquake. I could hear the grinding of its teeth, the snuffling of its nose, the rumble of its growls, all amplified in the confined space. The creature's rage had blinded it and left it running on pure instinct. If it had used its rational mind, it could've bitten a limb and dragged me out or shoved one arm into the narrow space to grab me. This mistake had allowed me to escape its grasp and flee to the first landing where the stairs doubled back on themselves, leading to the open balcony.

Fueled by anger, the brute slowly began forcing itself inch-by-inch up the stairwell. The wooden walls around it groaned and bowed under its power as it slowly began closing the distance. I didn't hang around to find out if the creature would make it or not. I had the slimmest chance of escape now. While it was wedged in the stairwell, I could try letting myself off the edge of the balcony just as we did when jumping from the Community Center windows onto the truck. If I didn't break my neck jumping, getting unstuck from the stairs would slow the Adlet enough for me to break one of the stained glass windows and get outside. I didn't have a plan for after that, and there was a good chance it would just run me down in the street and kill me, but it was all I had.

Reaching the balcony, I drunkenly stumbled up the last few steps and gasped for breath. There were a couple of old chairs, caked in decades of dust, and with every step, the ancient wood groaned and creaked beneath my feet. More dust puffed into the air as the entire balcony creaked.

I had barely made it a couple of steps when my weight caused the entire balcony to shift violently. I froze in my tracks. I hadn't realized the balcony was held up by jackstraws. My plan would be laid to nines if the whole thing just denigrated under my feet, plummeting me into the waiting jaws below.

There was a great moaning sound as the entire platform shivered and shook as the Adlet finally managed to squeeze through the narrow stairs onto the landing. Its head and shoulders rose over the flight of stairs. Reaching out with its paws, it braced against the walls on either side, claws digging deep furrows as it pulled itself higher. Instead of shouldering its way through this bottleneck, it was trying to push through in one lunge. Even if it didn't make it through, it was doubtful that the balcony could withstand such an impact, not to mention the animal had to weigh half a ton, easily. There was no way the platform would hold when my buck fifty made it sway drunkenly.

As the beast launched itself, trying to tear itself free of the narrow stairs, I turned and leapt for the edge of the balcony. I extended my foot, intending to step on the rail and jump clear of the structure when it fell.

But I never found my footing. The rail gave beneath my foot. Behind me, it sounded like the world imploded as the enormous shaggy behemoth smashed through the barrier and onto the open deck of the balcony. The weight of its charge sent it smashing through the weakened structure, bringing the whole thing crashing down as it collapsed in on itself.

Together, we fell as more timbers rained down on us, burying the both of us alive.

CHAPTER 21

Dust and splintered wood filled the air from the destruction of the loft. I squinted, trying to make out anything through the thick cloud. What light there was came through the floorboards as the flames still raged below. The heat was unbearable, scorching my skin and filling my lungs with acrid smoke. Every breath was like swallowing hot coals. If I didn't get out soon, I would either suffocate or burn in the inferno. Pain, white-hot and blinding, seared through me like a branding iron. I tried to move, to drag myself to safety, but my body wouldn't cooperate. My limbs were lead, numb and useless.

A sharp agony tore through my side like a hot knife, twisting and burrowing deep. My hand trembled as it traveled down to investigate the source of the pain. I gasped as my fingers brushed against a jagged shard of wood, jutting out of my gut, pinning me to the floor. Blood filled my mouth, coppery and thick. I spat it out in disgust, my mind racing in panic. I had to move, had to get out before I burned to death. The floor was a massive glowing hotplate as the flames raged in the basement. Blisters erupted on my palms, red and raw.

I cursed, fighting the urge to scream as I tried to push myself up with my hands. It was like pressing down on a bed of hot coals. Sweat soaked my shirt, mingling with blood and grime. My body trembled, barely able to bear the agony. Blackness crept in on the edges of my vision, a hungry beast, the darkness threatening to swallow me. I refused to give up. With gritted teeth, I forced my body to move, to push through the pain. I managed to lift myself a few inches, only to fall back down again, defeated.

But I couldn't give up.

The shifting of debris brought me to a sudden halt before I could call out for help in vain. Even in the heat, my blood turned to ice as I witnessed the true force of nature that was the Sheriff's savage drive. Part of a building had collapsed on it, but that wasn't enough to keep it down. It roared and snarled, muscling its way out from under beams that should've crushed any other living thing to a pulp. Once free, the monster shook itself like a dog, dislodging a shower of dirt and splinters. Its eyes, glazed with rage, found me, sprawled and helpless on the ground.

Shit, shit. It had me in its sights, and there was nowhere to run. I was crippled, unable to flee, and at the mercy of the beast.

Lowering itself on all fours, it slowly stalked forward, an unstoppable engine of destruction. Lips peeled back from pink gums, it bared its fangs with a snarl.

This was the endgame, the final act in a deadly pursuit of cat and mouse. There were no more tricks, no more places to flee. Death was coming for me, and it was done playing with its food. It would be messy and violent, a brutal reminder of the Sheriff's power.

It was over, and I just hoped it would be quick. Too many had died already, and I was too tired and beaten to keep going.

So, I embraced it, accepting my failure instead of running. A strange sort of calm settled around me.

The front doors of the chapel had been shattered in the destruction, one of them hanging free from its hinges, propped up by a few fallen boards and a thrown pew. It was open enough for a person to slip through, to make a final desperate attempt at escape. But I had no strength left to flee, and to be honest, I no longer wanted to. The beast that was Sheriff Earlywine would kill me, and it would be done with. Over.

I closed my eyes a brief beat, waiting for the final blow to fall, and the darkness to claim me forever.

The floor groaned and protested with each thunderous foot-fall, every step sending deep gouges into the wooden boards. I could feel the vibration of each one as it stalked closer, a predator on the hunt.

Its eyes glowed red through the thickening smoke as the moonlight waned, the only visible feature of the dark figure.

It seemed to meld with the darkness, becoming one with the shadows so that all I could see were those burning pits. I was hypnotized, like a bird looking at a snake. My muscles wouldn't move, and even my pain was forgotten. I was frozen in terror as it drew closer, less than a foot away. I could smell its breath, reeking of rotten meat and stale blood. A stench that made my stomach churn.

The massive shoulders of the creature hunched as it prepared to lunge, its long nails digging into the boards. I closed my eyes again, waiting for the darkness to claim me forever.

A furry rocket streaked through the door's opening, colliding with the beast broadside and knocking it off balance.

Snarling, the Adlet turned and snapped its jaws at the intruder.

Nimrod. Holy shit.

My big dumb dog danced just out of reach of the creature's deadly fangs. He bared his own teeth back at it, his ears flat against his head.

The two circled each other, their eyes locked in a fierce stare down, daring their opponent to make the first move. Though the monster was bigger and stronger, the husky was faster and more agile. His fluffy mane-like ruff seemed to give the bigger animal trouble, as it struggled to judge its bites properly. Each time it tried to lunge for my dog's throat, it got nothing but a mouthful of fur. Nimrod had no problem scoring hits on his opponent, but he lacked the power to do much more than bleeding the brute.

As the two fought furiously, I took the chance to try to move. My body was a broken mess. Every movement sent jolts of agony through me, and my neck felt like it was on fire. I needed to find a way to shift, but my muscles were uncooperative, wet noodles flailing uselessly.

Gritting my teeth, I scanned my surroundings, searching for anything that could help me escape this nightmare. The moonlight filtering through the trees illuminated the chaos around me—broken branches, fallen leaves, and the snarling forms of the fighting animals.

That's when I spotted a miracle. Lying just a few feet from where I had fallen was the Sheriff's discarded gun belt. It lay just out of my grasp. Its metal gleamed in the moonlight, a glint of hope in a dark and desperate moment.

I strained against the agony in my gut, stretching out my arm inch by excruciating inch, willing my fingers to close around the grip of the gun. It was a heavyweight, loaded with deadly intent. A weapon fit for slaying a monster.

As my fingertips brushed against the leather, a jolt of pain ripped through my side. The wood shard shifted, a savage reminder of my mortality. Blood seeped out of the wound, hot and sticky, my very life force ebbing away. With a growl of determination, I lunged forward, fingers curling around the handle. I felt something in my side tear, and there was a new warm trickle of blood.

It would be ironic to bleed out before all else did me in.

Obviously frustrated with the fight, Earlywine was done dealing with the dog making a fool of him. It pushed itself up on two legs and caught the husky when it tried to go for its exposed belly. The beast lifted my dog above its head and slammed it onto the floor like a ragdoll before pitching him against the far wall. My dog hit the wall with a bone-rattling crash and a loud yelp, then slid to the floor in a shaggy lump, motionless.

Shaking my head repeatedly, I fought angry tears. My buddy. My companion. He'd tried to save me. He looked more like a lifeless roll of carpet than a dog. I couldn't tell if he was breathing, but he made no sound at all.

The creature, its final obstacle overcome, turned to finish the job it had started, and the floor shook as it lumbered toward me.

Hot tears flooded my eyes at the thought of my dog dead, and I mustered enough strength to roll over. The superheated floor burned my chest through my shirt. My flesh singed, but the motion had been enough to allow me to grab the butt of the revolver. Rolling back over, I thrust the heavy Magnum in front of me with both hands and thumbed back the hammer.

These things had slaughtered Joey, Brad, and Lizzie. Not to mention...

"You killed my dog!" I screamed at the nightmare standing over me.

At this distance, it was roughly the size of a billboard. There was no way I could've missed it, and I pulled the trigger.

Muzzle flash blossomed from the barrel as the gun bucked in my hand. Again and again, I pulled the trigger, until the .44 clicked empty.

Smoke and dust shifted for a moment, bathing the chapel in moonlight.

In my state, I was afraid I'd missed. The gun had been heavy, and the recoil had nearly knocked it from my hand, but no, all six shots had taken it in the chest. A hole the size of my fist had been blown out where its heart should've been.

The beast's eyes were wide with shock in the moments it had realized what just happened. They rolled into its head as the immense body crashed backward to the floor, lifeless.

I choked back a hysterical laugh and propped myself up on one elbow. Against all odds, I had survived. I'd outlasted that bastard and his idiot son, escaped the deathly Community Center ritual, and braved the lair of mythical beasts who shouldn't exist.

I wasn't exactly unscathed, but I was still breathing. Metaphorically standing. It was understandable to lose it, cackling like a lunatic, right? Frankly, it was the only thing keeping me from curling into a ball, screaming in terror, and weeping.

As I laid there, I realized the heat from below had dialed back several notches. The basement was largely made of stone and not well oxygenated. Not to mention, old iron wood, dense as it was, didn't burn as well. Chances were, the fire had ravaged what it could, items and whatnot, then petered. The floorboards were still warm, smoke wafting, but it had waned.

Exhaustion overtook me, and I plunged in and out of waves of unconsciousness. Moonlight faded as night gave way to the duskiness of dawn. The moon retreated behind plumes of smoke that choked out the sky above the town as it all burned.

Fire cleanses the soul. A poetic ending for this cursed place.

Something dragged me back from the edges of oblivion. A low thunderous growl I could feel more in my chest rather than hear.

The dead hulk of Earlywine across the floor didn't move, but something in the shadows did. The darkness shifted. Faint and subtle, but there.

The growl grew until the blackness trembled with it. Before me, a pair of eyes glowed with a yellowish hue.

My breath caught in my throat as the fine hairs on my nape rose.

It was joined by another, and another. Over a dozen pairs in all. They peered at me from the retaliative safety of the shadows as they circled.

Summoning the last of my strength, I lifted the empty gun. It felt like it weighed a million pounds. There was no way I could hold it for long, and there were no more bullets. It was a bluff, but it was the only card I had to play.

The eyes squinted as if pausing, seemingly cautious as it seemed their prey was not as helpless as it had appeared. I thumbed back the hammer, and to my own surprise, my hand was steady.

"Go ahead, let's do this," I called to them. "Yeah, you'll kill me, but I can guarantee I will take at least one or two of you fucks with me. So, who is it going to be?" My voice was pained, yet as steady as my hand.

The eyes milled about for a few more tense seconds before blinking out one-by-one. They were retreating to fight another day. They had more pressing issues to deal with besides a half-dead man who would probably soon perish from his injuries. If not, they had marked me. They would settle up our business in their own time.

When the world was silent and I was sure I was alone again, my arm finally gave out and the gun clattered uselessly to the floor. My arm was limp, and I couldn't raise it anymore. I was weak from blood loss and exhaustion. Still, I somehow managed to find my feet and, with the support from whatever I could lean on, I made my way over to where I'd last seen Nimrod. I couldn't bear to look in Lizzie's direction. It would be like watching her die all over again. But I had to hold my boy one last time, thank him for saving me.

He was lying in a heap, his shaggy coat matted with blood and dirt.

I fell to my knees beside him, my hands shaking as I reached out to touch him. His chest rose and fell with a shallow, ragged breath. Holy crap. To my relief, the big dope was still alive.

Tears streamed down my face as I gathered him into my arms, cradling him like a baby and ignoring the pain in my side.

"We made it, boy," I whispered, my voice barely audible. "We made it."

He must've just been stunned from hitting the wall. That wasn't to say he'd escaped unharmed. His breathing was labored, and he had a serious limp once he'd gotten up, keeping one leg off the ground as he walked.

Together, after gearing our courage, we managed to hobble out of the wrecked church and plopped on the steps of the stoop. I don't know how long we sat there, just a man and his dog, but we watched as the sun rose over the horizon.

The nightmare was over. Resting one hand in Nimrod's fur, I closed my eyes and finally allowed myself to slip away into oblivion.

EPILOGUE

I woke up in the hospital a few days later, aching everywhere, confused, and sunlight streaming from a window smacking me in the face.

My parents visited me the first couple days, hovering, and no wiser for what had actually happened, then they went home, assured I was okay.

The doctors told me I'd been found badly injured. I'd suffered several fractures and second-degree burns. The worst injury had been the wood shiv they'd had to remove from my side. It had pierced my diaphragm, causing one lung to collapse. I'd have diminished breathing capacity for the rest of my life.

They weren't wrong. In the weeks that followed, I learned anything more than a leisurely jog winded me.

Nimrod had been hurt worse than I'd known. The big mutt must've hung on long enough to see I was safe. Dogs are known to do that. Protect us, live longer than they should to keep their master's company. He stayed with me until the paramedics got us into the ambulance, then he lay down on the floor of the vehicle and quietly passed away. I buried him in the backyard of my childhood home under a nice shady maple. I knew he would like that.

Emergency services from neighboring towns and Midnight Falls had been called after the fuel truck had detonated, taking half the Community Center with it. Last I heard, they'd pulled somewhere around a hundred and twelve bodies from the destroyed building. Many were burned so far beyond recognition that they didn't even look human, according to the medical examiner.

I wonder what he would've said if he'd known they weren't human bodies, but the charred corpses of monsters pretending to be human.

A memorial service was held for those lost in the "tragedy." Yeah, tragedy.

The fire had spread to nearby buildings. The Post Office was a complete loss, as were a handful of businesses along the main street. Flaming debris had rained over the small town, setting fire to numerous other homes and buildings. This included Lizzie's grandmother's house, as well as Brad's, Joey's, and mine. Not so sure those were exactly accidents. The filling station behind our homes had gone up in flames, causing underground tanks to blow. There was almost nothing untouched.

People evacuated in droves. I'm not sure how many Adlets escaped in that exodus, but I knew they were out there. That was a fact I couldn't ignore.

Brad Jefferson, it turned out, survived the blast despite being that close to ground zero. He was in a coma for nine months. Somehow, the police connected him to the bombing. I'm not certain if that one can be chalked up to racism, or if one of the survivors had tipped off the police. As soon as he woke up, they had him on trial for over a hundred counts of murder. The trial took less than six months, and the jury found him guilty after only five minutes. He was sentenced to life in federal prison. I don't know where he is or even if he's still alive. I hope so.

Lizzie and Joey were included among the 'lost.' That's what the town called them. Lost. As though they weren't dead, just merely missing.

I didn't attend the funerals. I thought it would make me too easy to find. I did meet with Lizzie's parents, though. It was a short and not particularly pleasant visit. I don't know if they blamed me, were in shock, or what, but they acted as if they didn't care. Like they were relieved to be rid of a particular burden.

I visited her grave alone to say my goodbye, but it didn't provide closure or alleviate my grief. It haunts me still.

I never saw my folks again, nor did I ever return to Midnight Falls.

As I said at the start, once I was out of the hospital, I fled to my cousin's place to lie low before the Adlets found me. Since then, I've kept moving, running as far as I could, but I'm tired.

I can't run anymore.

You need to know this—monsters are real. They don't hide under the bed or in the closet, and they don't go bump only in the night. They're everywhere. Standing next to you in line at the bank. Sitting next to you on the bus. Having coffee at the next table. They smile at you and laugh at your jokes.

It's time to put this to bed. When I've finished writing this, I'm going to put it in a box and hide it under a loose floorboard in the bedroom. Not sure what I'm going to do after that. I haven't decided yet. I have my .38, but I don't know if I'm going to use it on them or myself. I guess we'll just have to find out.

But if you're reading this, then you already know how my story ends.

Yeah. Monsters are real.

Afterword by the Author

Dear Reader,

If you've stuck around to this point that means, like me, you are the kind of person who cares about the how and why of a story. As a reader, I love seeing behind the curtain and getting some insight into how the sausage is made, so to speak. Writing is one of the few industries where that isn't a completely disgusting aspect which ruins it. Usually. It's fun to see how some writers' minds work in the hopes of learning a tidbit of trivia that will enhance our own enjoyment of the work while making us feel like we're part of a special fan club.

I feel the story of how "Midnight Falls" came to be is just as interesting as the story itself, and after nearly fifteen years, deserves to be told.

It started with an image that just popped into my head. That image was the ending to the climax of the book. I saw a man trapped in a burning building holding a large revolver in the darkness where there were glowing eyes. The gun was the only thing keeping them from ripping the man apart, but he was bluffing and the gun was empty.

This is how most of the ideas for my stories come about. A fun little image or thought will pop into my head. I will examine, and then discard it. Then, if it comes back and won't go away, I consider why it keeps returning like a boomerang. Eventually, the only way to get it out of my head is to either write it down or crack my skull open and carve it out with a sharp implement.

One of my favorite Stephen King quotes, and one I think often about as a writer, is from the introduction to "Skeleton Crew." King talks about how writing for money makes you a monkey. He ends it with saying that writers don't even write for the love of it, but simply because to not do it is suicide. Fuck if that's not a bone deep truth. That the only way get these ideas out of my head is either to write them down, or put a loaded gun in my mouth. Writing at least saves money on having to repaint the walls.

So, I kept having that image pop into my head, to the point where my curiosity took over and I started asking questions. Who was this guy? How did he end up in this situation? What are those things in the dark? How does he get out of this, or does he even get out at all?

Possibilities, endless possibilities.

That's the great thing about writing, and I'm one of those free form writers. I hate the term panser, it sounds like a fraternity prank only the terminally dimwitted find funny. Like King, I don't outline, I just write the book the same way you read it. From start to finish. While I may know how the story ends, it's the journey, Dear Reader, that you come here for. The twists and turns of the literary snake are as much a mystery to me when I write as they are to you when you read it for the first time.

Those writers who rely too heavily on outlines and desperately cling to them as if they are some magical formula to write the perfect book tend to end up creating works that I find too stiff and formulaic. Ever read a book or see a TV show or movie and you can guess the twist about five minutes in? That's a writer with no confidence in their own ability. But that's not all writers. There are those who use the outline as more of a suggestion than a road map until the story goes off the rails and they're forced to improvise. Or the terminal outliners—the people who talk and talk about their books and have twenty-four page outlines, but never write a single word of the manuscripts.

The thing I love about free form is that there are no constraints, no limits, no rules, just adventure. Some writers find too much freedom paralyzing, they need constraints and prompts to work within. I'm not disparaging these other writers. They're just as much a part of our clan as we are theirs. We just bang our drums a little differently. Free form gives birth to more organic story-telling, I find. It's more surprising and enjoyable. When you let the characters tell you the story as it writes itself, things change for better or worse, but that's what makes them exciting.

When I first had the idea and saw that image of the man fending off unknown beasts with a bluff, I thought, you had to be a pretty stone cold mother-fucker with some massive brass balls to do something like that. That man was very different from the character who Josh became—a scared, dumb kid who was only brave because he was backed into a corner. He became a richer, better character than the simple two dimensional trope he started out as. I had fun exploring the town of Midnight Falls, not just because of the fantastical supernatural elements, but because it was built on the familiar bedrock of my own memories and places I grew up.

I never do anything intentionally, so when it comes to themes and subtext, I'm not that deep or clever. I just wrote a fun book about werewolves. I didn't set out to write a commentary or alle-gory about how creepy and messed up small towns can be. I had to have my readers explain the themes of the book to me.

The original draft was first written around 2010 or 2011. I'm a terrible record keeper and my memory isn't the best, but tragically, the laptop I was using at the time had a hard drive failure resulting in the complete loss of everything I had on it. I was unable to recover any files, and so I thought I'd lost roughly four manuscripts and many short stories. Cloud storage was not a thing at the time, or at least not something I had then, so everything was on my computer.

Over time, I was able to recover my first novel, which, like herpes, was horrible and seemingly impossible to get rid of. Written back in college, you will never see that abortion in publication. The first Tobias Halson book I was working on, and a novella at the time titled 'I Ran', were also discovered on a thumb drive, in more or less the condition they were in when I'd lost them, barring maybe a few chapters.

In 2013, I stumbled upon the first chapter of the original Midnight Falls manuscript. Depressed, completely crushed at having lost so much work and facing the daunting prospect of having to rewrite the entire thing from basically scratch, and suffering impostor syndrome, I was on the verge of just hanging the whole writer thing up and considering the Hemingway option. The issue was, I genuinely loved the story. However, if you're a creative tasked with the burden of having to remake something you created, you find yourself in a special kind of hell not many people can understand.

When rewriting something you've lost, the lost material takes on a sort of quasi-nostalgia effect, where your memory tricks you into believing that nothing you write is nearly as good as that original draft. It doesn't matter if it is or not because you're trapped, looking at it through tinted lenses. Your expectations are set too high through Memorex. And now I have to wonder how many people will understand that reference.

I decided to post the chapter online, which was the prologue of the book you just read, with the stipulation that, if people seemed interested in the story, I would go ahead and do the hard work of recreating it. I posted it in late November to early December of 2016.

Apparently, I have too much writer in me because, in the following months after posting, I went ahead and rewrote it. Like everything buried in the "Pet Semetary," it came back a little off. It's still very much the same story, though some names and small details changed. Joey, for example, was a mailman in the original instead of a science teacher.

It was a good thing I did rewrite it. Having completely forgotten about posting the prologue, I was confused when, several months later, in March or April of 2017, I don't remember which, I received an email notification that one of my stories had gone viral with over fifty thousand readers that month alone. I felt this had to be some sort of scam or mistake. It wasn't possible that something I, a mediocre writer at best, could've received such a reception. So, I found it hard to believe.

To be fair, I was wrong. I didn't have fifty thousand readers. I had almost one hundred and fifty thousand readers in just the first three months. The most readers I'd had in a single month for just the prologue chapter was a little over eighty-one thousand, in the month of July, I believe. By September, I had nearly half a million readers. Unfortunately, there was a change made to the Google algorithm that month which buried my work, and other people's, I'm sure, so my reader numbers dropped to just under ten thousand a month, which continued for the next several years. As of writing this, that sample still gets roughly two hundred new readers a month, and sits at a 4.2/5 rating.

For those who aren't in the literary or publishing spaces, it's hard to impress upon you how insane this is. The average New York Times bestseller sells roughly only ten thousand to one hundred thousand within their first year, and that's with PR and marketing behind them from publishers with incentives to get their books to as many people as possible. A rough draft sample of "Midnight Falls" did that in only two months with zero marketing. For a debut author, just a few thousand copies is considered a resounding success, and opens them up to big multi-book deals. This shit was bananas, and I still cannot believe it to this day. Not only that, but on one outlet, the sample had over 3k in glowing reviews.

So, with those numbers, which I had proof of, I thought I should seriously give the book a shot at being published. Especially given that the reviews of the book had been overwhelmingly positive, there was no doubt in my mind it would do well.

Boy, was I wrong.

Not about the book, but the process of getting published.

In 2019, I started querying agents with the same sample that had garnered so much attention and love from readers. When most debut authors start their journey and think they have a good book, most of them really don't know if what they have is gold or just a turd wrapped in gold crepe paper. I like to think I was ahead of the curve on this one with thousands of readers and positive reviews. I was armed with a little more knowledge than most going in.

The query process sucks. It just does. It's hell. Its like going to war. Like WWI where you slowly march straight into German machine gun fire and try to catch as many bullets as you can with your face. I spent months lobbing query letters like mortar shells over the berm, hoping to hit something, anything. Querying is maddening. It's a Sisyphean task.

After a couple of years and a hundred or so rejections, I started to doubt if my reader base was a fluke. That my book wasn't any good and I was fooling myself. I went full blown impostor syndrome, but I'd managed to make friends in that time with editors, agents, and former agents. It was from those editors and former agents I learned what the problem was. Why people who read my book loved it, but agents didn't. The answer was sim-ple—agents were not reading it. That made no sense to me.

The whole time, agents would keep saying things like "horror is dead," or "no one wants werewolf books," despite this clearly not being the case. Watching other authors successfully publishing horror and werewolf books, readers clamber for more and their number one request? More werewolves.

Anyway, after five years, doing everything I could from pitch events to submission events, and of course, querying every agent who looked like a fit for my book, in 2023 I started getting agents and publishers coming to me asking to read my work. One of them eventually offered me publication, and now you are reading the book. I should also note that many of the conversations between Brad and Josh or Joey and Josh in the book were actual conversa-tions I'd had with others.

Okay, this has gone on too long and even I'm tired of hearing myself whine. The point I'm trying to make is that the road to publication is a long one to hoe...straight up the side of a sheer cliff with people stomping on your fingers the whole time.

I'm sorry, but this is when I get on my soapbox. Yeah, you thought I was on it this whole time, but nope.

I'm a straight, white, college-educated cis male in the U.S. Barring being born with a silver spoon in my ass, I couldn't be more privileged if I tried, and yet this journey has been frustratingly far harder than it had to be due to how broken the industry is. And I'll say this loudly for the people in the back. It's even harder for marginalized voices. For BIPOC, Neurodivergent, LGBTQ+, etc., those groups in this industry, it's nearly impossible with hurtles at nearly every turn.

This isn't one of those 'so-and-so was rejected X amount of times, so keep trying' bullshit feel-good stories about perseverance that the industry keeps trying to fool people with. No. The industry is fucking broken, and now works harder to keep people out than it does actually publishing quality books. Not saying mine is quality, just calling out an injustice.

I...don't know how to end this rant. You know what, let me just thank you again for reading this book. Seriously, if you made it this far, you're a trooper. Or maybe you're listening to the audiobook to fall sleep and just left it running...

In which case, sweet dreams, Reader.

John Evans, Midnight Falls, 2024

CHECK OUT THESE OTHER GREAT READS FROM ROWAN PROSE PUBLISHING!

John Evans is the debut author of *Midnight Falls*. He also writes the *Tobias Halson Vampire Hunter* series and various short stories. Inspired by greats like Stephen King and Gary Brandner, he loves all things "old school" horror, and often claims his purpose is to give readers a little bit of fun Lovecraftian escapism from the scarier real world.